DISSONANCE

Volume I: Reality

AARON RYAN

Never forget the Number One Rule:
One look, and it's all over.

Published in 2024, Edition 1.

Amazon ISBN # 9798872707004. All other Paperback ISBN # 9781965372128. Amazon Hardcover ISBN # 9798873631063. eBook ISBN # 9798990326699.

Cover creature art by Rodrigo Vivedes (https://www.artstation.com/rocoviart)

Edited by SSJ Services. Published independently.

This is a work of fiction. Any similarities to persons living or dead, or actual events is purely coincidental.

For Sweeps, Bren & AJ:
my true loves.

You've helped me to survive.

| CHAPTERS

I NOTE ON AI

We live in an age of AI. Every day, more and more services spring up promising revolutionary and innovative results using artificial intelligence. The authoring industry is not immune to this.

I want every one of my readers to know that not once did I employ, nor will I *ever* employ, the use of AI to sculpt any part of any of my stories. Those who know me know that I am staunchly and adamantly opposed to such cheats.

I'm very proud to be a verified human. The ability to create is a gift that I was endowed by my Creator, and I will never forfeit that nor set it aside to propagate something synthetic and imitative.

Everything you've read by me in this saga, and in my other works, is 100% entirely created by me, the genuine article. I'm a verified human, and always will be.

To my fellow authors, I urge you to preserve the sacred gift of human creation and never stoop to such lows. Always cherish this gift you've been given. If you encounter writer's block, take a break. Don't cop out. Don't take the road more traveled by. Don't cheat. Toe the line for all of us, and keep creation – *true* unadulterated creation – alive.

Long live humanity.

Sincerely,

Aaron Ryan,
Verified Human

I NOTE ON FAITH

I am a Christian author. What does that mean exactly? It means I worship Jesus, and I serve my God in Heaven. That implies certain standards should be upheld, and that my life should be lived in certain ways, with certain morals, by certain convictions, and with a sense of honoring God in all I do and in all I write. I seek to tell **true** and inspiring stories.

One thing I've always strived for is verisimilitude. I've wanted my books to be on par with what we read out there in the world: to be adventurous escapism, to provide a gritty sense of reality, and to provide a real glimpse into the ebbs and flows of the struggles that humanity faces. That means that life isn't always glimpsed through rose-colored stained-glass windows. It means that with the good comes the gory. With the sheer valor comes the shock value. With the awe comes the awful. Does that then mean that I will ever drop an F-Bomb or take my Lord's name in vain in my works? **Never**. But does it mean that I will bury my head in the sand

and pretend that we humans down here don't talk a certain way, walk a certain way, act a certain way? **Never**.

I want my works to reflect the real, genuine authentic struggles that humans face, and as such I want the real, genuine, authentic reactions that come with being human. If an alien is going to eat you, you might not say "Oh, shucks." You might say something, hmm, *a bit more colorful.* But I want my readers to know that I've always struggled with this, and do not mean to offend anyone with material some might find objectionable. I'm a Christian, but I'm also an artist, and artists seek to stretch themselves and strive for truth and reality in their works. That does **not** mean that I need to go overboard and pepper you with revolting material or words that Christians have no business engaging or indulging in. As such, I want all of my faith-based readers to know that I am highly conscious of what I put out there into the world, and am constantly checking it against my spirit before I do so. Nothing you'll read in my novels is much different from what we experience on this ball in space, and I trust you'll see that I've walked a fine line here, and I ask for your forgiveness if I've offended you in any way.

I pray this work of mine provides you with an awesome and incredible odyssey of escapism and adventure. I pray you are moved at times by the Holy Spirit as you read. I pray that you understand God better, and that you know that God knows my heart, and I tried my best to tell a **real** story, understanding that we're all down here, **all** of us, just trying to do our very best in creating what we feel led to create. I thank you **so** much for reading my novel.

In Jesus' Name,

Aaron Ryan

1 | REALITY

There was no way I was going to make it. That was my reality.

I've had this dang thing in my pocket for six days now, and we had successfully evaded becoming anyone's dinner so far, but for how much longer? I had no idea. It was getting hot, whatever it was, and it wanted out of my pocket. Markus didn't even tell me what it could do or why it was so important. Just gave half to me and half to Rutty, and then bolted. I only got a few brief looks at it, but it was some kind of stone or gem, about the size of a silver dollar, flat, and encased in some kind of silver circlet with strange glyphs on it. Now I kept it wrapped in a rag.

The back of my throat scratched as I muscled down a swallow, and I feverishly swiped away whatever bug it was that I suddenly felt on the back of my neck, hiding there behind that dumpster. I was pretty sure they had passed by already, but with gorgons, you could never be sure. The way they would glide noiselessly across the ground was just plain creepy as hell.

I remember when my little brother Wyatt Rutledge, aka "Rutty," and I would skip rocks across the alleyway during the heat of the summer when it was safer, and Jackson would come looking for us to whisk us back into school. It was all fun and games until he forgot to keep it down and yelled at us. Then that berserker gorgon got him. We called those ones berserkers because they were just weirder than the rest: flailing and twitching, but also faster, and much, much meaner. It was weird; they came a few years after the original gorgons. But no one ever saw where they came from, apparently.

I never understood how any gorgon could hear a rock ricocheting across dirt up to 100 meters away, but it got there fast and then did its thing. Jackson never saw it coming. That trippy Medusa-esque stare they give you: I don't know what it is that comes out of them, but it's some kind of paralyzing telepathy…something psychological…and it got him fair and square. Slap a few snakes on their heads and it would have completed the ensemble, straight out of Greek mythology. But these things didn't slither…they sliced through the air at you. There was of course nothing we could do once it had zeroed him.

We tried to look away as it came in, and then just ate him slowly. I'll never forget that. The sound of it. That was seven, no, eight and a half years ago now. I can still remember his stinky coffee breath when he'd catch us playing. Kinda wished we could wake up and find him skulking around the alleyway trying to catch us again. But that'll never happen.

Rutty had scouted up ahead, and I could see the occasional green pings of his laser-pointer: a priceless treasure we had ransacked from a home on a previous recon.

Last name *Ramsey*, I think. They had the good sense to clear out before all hell broke loose. I envy them, but I thank them more that they left some goods behind. Where they were now was anyone's guess, if they were even still alive.

I took one last look back and mustered up the courage to raise myself up over the lip of the dumpster, hardly daring to breathe. The night air betrayed me and revealed my slow steady fog breath in short wisps. *No fair.* I pulled back. It just didn't feel like it was time yet. Good thing too. I checked myself and started. Just as I did, another gorgon came floating down from above, not twenty feet from where I was.

I was trying to remain calm, but it just stayed right there, hovering. I glanced at my watch. I only had six more minutes and the Blockade would close for good for the night. I'd never make it out of this zinc plant and back in time. I looked back and Rutty glared at me open-eyed, silently mouthing "Come on!" I shook my head and looked back.

For whatever reason that gorgon just wouldn't move. It was like it had gone to sleep or something. It wasn't looking my way, at least not yet. I looked down at my watch again. Five minutes. The Blockade had to be, what, fifteen hundred feet away, out past the alley of the zinc plant, up the hill, through the forest, and over the yawning field? Fifteen hundred feet divided by three hundred seconds. Five feet per second. I could do that like nobody's business, sprinting. My stomach growled. I needed to get there. It was getting colder. I shivered.

I looked back at Rutty. He was watching it too. No one in their right mind would mess with a gorgon. We looked up at them when they came, admiringly somehow, trusting naively that this would be the dawn of a new era of intergalactic growth and some kind of evolution. What hubris. I'll never trust again.

Rutty looked at me and back at the gorgon. It had started to slowly shift somewhat to the left, like it had detected something. I scanned the ground over where it seemed to be looking. Was it a rat? A mole? No way to be sure. Gorgons always had *such* good hearing; but they could only track something if it moved. All I could do was stay still.

I looked down at my watch again. It had fogged over a bit. Stupid mist. Wherever a group of them gathered you could always count on misting. That's what we called it when that translucent fog came rolling in. It clung to the gorgons and swirled around silently as if to mask their approach and presence. It was theatrical, for sure, but super freaking cold. And we had all learned to control our breathing and our heartbeats, like we were taught, in the name of zero volume.

I wiped the moisture off of my watch face. Four minutes. Six point two five feet per second. My strides would have to be longer and loping. It would be close.

I reached slowly into my pocket. My mouth creased into an open o as I monitored the gorgon. My fatigues were damp from the fog, and I couldn't get my fingers around the rock. It was even hotter than before. What the heck was this thing anyway? Markus never said what exactly it was before he handed it to me and ran off. He just screamed to get it back to the Blockade. I have no idea if he even got away, as I've been living in the shadows to keep it safe.

But that's what he wanted us to do.

Was now the time though? He never said.

My fingers touched it and as they did, my right boot lost its grip on the pavement and skidded out past the dumpster with a God-awful cement scratch. I stiffened.

The gorgon whirled around and hissed. I hate that. It's the most spine-chilling sound they make. My heart stopped as I kept my leg bone-still on the pavement. I slowly moved my eyes and shifted my head ever so slightly to where I could see Rutty: his eyes were ringed with fear. We both knew that if they were going to get me, then that meant that he had to leave me and take off, so that at least one of us could make it. After all, he had the other half of it. They would be preoccupied with me. That was the whole plan. If we got separated, maybe our Blockade's luck would hold and at least one half of it would make it back.

I could feel the gorgon staring down the alley. Good thing they couldn't see worth a darn in the day *or* night. But their smelling and hissing, I'd had just about enough.

Rutty shook his head at me as if he guessed my thoughts and knew what I wanted to do. I could tell he was flashing his eyes back and forth between where I was and where it was at, hovering silently there yet moving closer, every hiss making its freaky neck bob down and up as it tried to zero me.

I didn't really have any other option. My ammo was spent, I'd lost my Beretta, and Rutty had the RPG launcher. It was too dark to see if he was even loading it, and now that the gorgon was practically staring us down, it might get him before he even had a chance to cock it.

The menacing shadow drew nearer. I couldn't see it, but the sniffing grew louder and louder. I tried to keep my leg perfectly still as I slowly extracted the amulet from my pocket, willing my bones to stay in a state of suspended animation. A single bead of sweat fell from my lanky hair onto my neck. I knew then that I was in deep fear. I looked at my watch. Two minutes and ten seconds. Eleven point five four feet per second. This was going to be close.

I could dimly make out Rutty lifting the launcher up over his shoulder from under that tarp.

Without warning, the object of the gorgon's previous fascination across the street revealed itself again, causing the creature to whip around and sneer at it with that spine-chilling hiss. It was that little tabby cat that I had seen many years ago, hunting a mouse or some other poor morsel. The gorgon's back arced reflexively as it moved away from me and back toward the cat. Gorgons aren't picky, and a cat is a dainty morsel for sure. I didn't waste any time, and neither did Rutty. Everything appeared to slow drastically, and more sweat beads cascaded from my hair onto my neck. My left boot pushed me up with the speed of a gazelle, and I lifted my right leg, which had just started to tingle.

The gorgon, fixated on the cat, heard all of our commotion of course, and whirled right back around. I was still holding my breath, but the rest of my body screamed to *run*. That's when it saw me and let out that bone-freezing shriek that they do.

And that's when Rutty launched. The torpedo sailed right past me at a hundred and twenty meters per second, and my face was baked in the heat of its exhaust. I could feel my hair thrown back and the sweat get hot on my neck. We called them torpedoes because they just did so much more damage than your typical RPG. Our guys had souped them up. They were incredibly incendiary when they met their mark.

Ain't no way I was gonna get eaten today.

Rutty launched that sucker, and then immediately tore away up the alley in front of me. I wasn't gonna look back.

Then, the explosion.

The gorgon was vaporized instantly of course. Pretty much anything can be vaporized. *Sorry, Cat.* But where there's one, there's more. And now they were on to us. And they could move like the wind. They don't like heat, and their power is in thin air where they can move quickly.

But so could we. I was never quite as fast as Rutty, and every single race we had relegated me to second place once more. But I nearly caught up with him this time, and the sweat was dripping down into my eyes as I bolted. I clutched the amulet hard, and the heat of it burnt my hand.

The hisses grew louder.

They taught us to run fast, and they taught us not to look back. "Always listen," they said. "Just… listen." I had seen what happened when you looked. *You just… don't… look.* Jackson taught me that.

So, amidst the stamping thumps of my Army-issued boots on that cold alleyway with nothing but thin, decreasing night between me and my assailants, I listened. If the hisses grew louder, you just ran faster. I had already seen enough to know what was happening behind me. Their arms would be outstretched right about now, and their lower jaws would be descending, straining at the thin dead skin under their hollow eye sockets. If you thought they were getting closer you were supposed to drop, then get up and change course like greased lightning. Hopefully they would skid past you.

Maybe two hundred and twenty-five feet now?

My watch buzzed softly against my frantic arms. I could feel it amidst the pounding rhythm of my desperate feet. The one-minute alarm, and then the Blockade would close. I could see the trees racing by above me, framed against the night sky, yawning up as I drew closer.

And there it was, ahead…that great and glorious wall. Rutty was almost there. The gorgons knew not to come too close, or they'd get hammered by the guns. They were flesh and bone creatures like most other lifeforms, and they could be blown apart, sure. But their most powerful weapon was fear.

I wasn't going to look at my watch, and I wasn't going to look back.

The Blockade drew nearer. My best guess was it was still some hundred feet away. It was a wide gaping hole in a berm, and underneath was our sanctuary.

Gritting my teeth, I began to hear them behind me, slinking closer and closer. I could practically feel one of their arms wafting behind me. That hiss…oh that freaking hiss. They also have this unnerving hum when they can sense they're going to eat soon. It was almost like singing. A horrible song.

In my peripheral I was sure that was the blueish-green mist overtaking me as they drew closer and closer.

Thirty seconds. I had never run so fast in my life. Each little sound behind me was like a death knell to my courage and stamina. I could feel the tears coming, mixing with my sweat, and my heart labored. *God, please don't let me trip.*

Twenty. Eighteen.

I kept running.

Fifteen. Twelve. Nine.

I kept running.

I felt the hair stand up on my neck as one reached for me and scratched my shoulder through my shirt.

And all of a sudden, like a mist driven away by the wind, they sailed upwards and departed. Whether it was the sound of the Blockade blaring its horns, or the Captain screaming for men to lock and load, I don't know.

Four. Three.

I kept running.

I jumped across the threshold as a shaft of warm air blew over me: my own exhaust as I bellowed across the last few feet of open field and hurled myself past the door, slamming into Rutty who had landed just ahead of me with his gun drawn, pointing at the door. He grunted as I knocked the wind out of him.

Two. One.

Clang.

The Blockade had closed. I was in. I heard the momentary muted thunder of gunfire above me, and guessed that at least one of those things bought it, but they collect and eat their own, so of course we'd never know.

For now, I was in.

Sorry, Cat.

•　　　•　　　•　　　•　　　•

"I wasn't going to use it; I wouldn't even know how."

My defense rang hollow, as they could see it all on the security cameras, and they knew what I was going for in my pocket. Many years ago, they were able to tap into the zinc plant cameras, so now that worked against me.

"You *were!* You were going to try to use it! You were given one charge: keep it safe and bring it back here. *Not* to use it. You don't even know what it is or what it does. You were going for it in your pocket, and Rutty saw the whole thing!"

I sighed and rubbed my aching shoulder. Medical had patched it up after the gorgon scratch, and I now sported a nice white rectangle. But arguing was pointless. So, I argued. "*So?* Doesn't mean anything."

I looked at Rutty. His face sank, and he sighed. He was a brave brother, but he did see it, and he knew what I was going for. And Rutty always told the truth. The truth was one of the very last things we all had. Besides, I didn't even know what to do with it once I pulled it out. There was no denying it. Especially when Halcyon Crew takes you to task. They know better than all, because they're glued to those monitors 24-7, and they can spot a pixel flinch in a drunken stupor.

"The zinc plant was crawling with gorgs, and you knew that. You and Rutty were supposed to get your asses back here and *not* engage them. If that meant you had to stay in the cold and stick it out one more night until they floated off to God knows where then *that* was what you should have done! I don't care if that required you to stay out seventeen *more* days, Jet!"

"Captain, I don't even know what it does. Markus didn't say a word. He just bolted."

"I don't care, Sergeant! The point is that you're still a loose cannon, even at twenty-three, and you think you know better than all the rest of us what to do in a pinch."

I sighed. Whatever. I could see the amulet in the next room, and Harrison and DuPre poring over it like some newfound treasure, their greedy grubby little hands pawing at it. They were practically salivating. The two of them had literally snatched both pieces right out of our hands a few seconds after we had crossed the threshold, without even asking if we were okay. I sighed.

"Yep, you got it. You're right. I'm just a loose cannon. You're absolutely right."

Captain Stone – 'Stoney' to close friends and compatriots – bristled and sighed out of his nose. He crossed his arms. I gave him a few seconds. But then I could see the smile creep into the corner of his mouth, and his crossed arms betrayed his true sentiments. He couldn't hide that he was glad to see I'd made it after all.

"Cameron," he began, using my real name instead of my callsign, and shaking his head. *Jerk. No one calls me that.* They called me "Jet" ever since I outran a senior officer at age 15. But Rutty was faster than me; they should have called him that. He just never got the chance, I guess. "You never cease to amaze me." He took a few steps closer, until I could feel the hot breath coming out of his nose as he laughed. "Glad you're back home, son."

"You too, dad. Don't call me Cameron." I smiled.

My 'dad' was a respectable Captain, almost a Major, and he maintained order, but he did love his 'kids.' I knew he loved me, even though I wasn't really his: he had adopted me after, well, after everything went down. And I also knew that he wanted to keep whatever this thing was safe, and figure out how we can use it against the gorgons. Letting him down was the last thing I would want to do. And deep down, he knew I was a fighter.

The Captain looked me up and down. "Welcome back, Jet."

"Thanks, dad."

"Get outta here."

"Sir, yes sir."

Captain Stone play-slugged me in the shoulder, and I turned to Rutty and winked. All clear. We walked out together and snickered. The Captain turned back to face Harrison and DuPre in the next room. His smile faded as he watched whatever it was in there, pinning his hopes onto it, and sighing once more.

After all, it was that or nothing.

•　　•　　•　　•　　•

"Man, you're so lucky dad is a softie."

"Dude, he ain't no softie. There's just too few of us left to be mad at. And he isn't our dad."

"Yeah, I guess." Rutty took a huge messy bite out of the candy bar that he had stowed away. Can't remember where he had found it, but it was on the way home. Completely unopened too, and that's a rare surprise. Said "100 Grand" on it, and that one was a new one for me.

"What kind is that anyway?" I asked, pawing at the wrapper. "100 Grand? What is that?"

"Oh man, you've never had one of these? They're *gooood*. Too good to share, if that's what you're thinking." Rutty pulled his hand away, resource guarding like a mutt. But just as swiftly his expression changed. "Nah, just jokin.' Have a bite."

I wiped away his disgusting spittle from the edge of where he'd gnawed off a chunk, sniffed at it suspiciously, and then exacted a meek portion of it for inspection. *Wow* that's good, I thought. I could taste the crisped rice, and a flood of memories came back to me from when I had had my last *Whatchamacallit*: a bit stale but still sweet and somewhat crunchy. "Whoa, that is really good." Before he could intervene, I stole an actual bite-sized bite.

"Hey! Get your own, butthead."

We snorted. I loved Rutty: he was half compatriot, half punk, and that's a good balance. He was nearly four years my junior, so I always felt like I had to take care of him. He didn't need it. Rutty was awfully good at getting himself out of (and into) trouble. And he was great company. Of all the partners I've cycled through – had to, as the gorgons picked off so many – he was the best, and not just because he was my brother. I never thought I'd consider him as an upgrade from the ones before, God rest their souls. I loved him crazily. He had this incomparable swagger to him, and this overly mature confidence that made you love him or revile him. I picked the first one. After all, I had been told more than once that I was quite swaggerly myself… so Rutty and I were more or less two peas in a pod. And no matter how you sliced it, he was the last surviving part of my family with me, and that made for an inseparable bond.

We had been through a lot together in the last six months, and we had had some close shaves. Rutty had kind of a paint-by-numbers approach, which is why him grabbing that candy bar utterly surprised me…he didn't even wipe it down. But hunger does that to you, and we were *hungry* on that patrol.

We walked down the corridor and rounded the corner past the giant hum of the data room with its warm drafts baking us as we approached. A small gust made my hair flick back as I turned to look in.

There it was. The Beast. It was always running, computing possible scenarios, number-crunching, analyzing, trying to find a way past the ones at the ocean shore. Whatever it was they were guarding out there, we just could never seem to get a clean look. Whatever drone we launched, no matter how high up, the enemy flew higher. After all, they came from up there. Satellites over the ocean were disabled, so aerial recon was impossible. Whatever mission we launched, no matter how clandestine, to figure out why it was they wanted us to stay here so far inland, was lost on us. But the Beast would figure it out. It had to figure it out. This thing was powerful, and it had been fed so many AI computational algorithms, it might just figure it out and then decide to destroy us all. We'll see.

Whatever web archives it could salvage and rummage through, it would do so, day and night. The satellite data they fed into that thing, the loads of wiki garbage, presumably meaningless to us, needles in haystacks, were fodder for investigation. Previous aerial reconnaissance before they came, geothermal scans, activity history, maritime routes, deep dives, offshore drilling, transportation, commerce, coastal patrols, incidents, accidents, sunken vessels, tide patterns, underwater venting, cable routes, trade zones, international borders, all of it: constantly pumping through those cores, a trillion bits of minutiae crossing over and under each other in its highways and byways, and us, silently waiting…and hoping. It was long since we really had any tangible hope.

It was warm in the data room, and it was warm outside the Blockade. It was warm everywhere from the heat of battle and loss.

Rutty hit his bunk, flashed me a peace sign with one hand, and playfully slugged me in the shoulder with the other. "See ya, bro," I winked, and kept on walking.

I hit my own bunk forty feet down the hall and around the bend. Block 237. In the Blockade, it was easy to get lost, but as we were part of patrol, they liked to move us around and keep the fittest runners closest to the front doors, so that we didn't have far to go to rest – or perhaps it was so that we didn't have to go far to report. The numbers started on the right side and ran counterclockwise around to the left, climbing higher. Mine was 237. Rutty's was 218. It was well on half a mile from the front door to The Mound at the opposite end. All that garbage out there made the mound one heckuva stink, so no complaints from me about being positioned far from it. And when runners came in, you'd always get a whiff of fresh air once again through the front gate…if it were a strong enough gust to make it past the heat of The Beast, that is.

We'd been in here a while.

I unslung my pack and hoisted it on the hanger on the wall, and then peeled off my boots with a grunt of relief and comfort. "Hey Mom," I pensively greeted as I did so. "Hey Dad. Hey sis. I'm back." I stared at their empty bunks.

I don't know why I always do that. Their bunks would never be inhabited again. At least not by them – nor me. Didn't matter if I really needed to stretch out or if I had Rutty over. Sleeping in their bunks meant that they weren't coming back, and I wasn't ready to acknowledge that to anyone, much less myself. When Rutty slept over, he stayed in my bunk and I slept on the floor, inhaling my reeking boots… but preserving their memories in honor. I'll take the stench over forgetting *any* day. Plus, having him over was like having a little bit of a home again. I can't remember much of that time anymore. I wish that I could. War and tension do that to you.

I gave their bunks one last reverent look and then turned over on my side, facing away. I needed sleep. But my eyes wouldn't close.

•   •   •   •   •

I remember when the gorgons first arrived in 2026. Admittedly, we were all enthralled. I was too. Sis was especially enthralled. Somebody in Guatemala spotted the first one, if I remember correctly. It just came drifting down, straight out of the sky, near sunset: so humanoid, and yet enshrouded in mist. They had angelic qualities to them. Some of us wondered if they were messengers from God. Their bodies were cloaked in that blueish-green vapor. It was really creepy, but for whatever reason it's the creepy things that draw us in the most. We just can't look away, like a moth to a flame.

Then there was another. And another. And five more. And then more. And then twenty more. Fifty. Four hundred. More kept coming, just slowing down to a geostationary orbit fifty feet above the ground all over the earth.

The dogs were perpetually screaming and howling; some of their ears were reportedly even bleeding. They were running mad, whining and cowering in terror, fleeing to dark corners with their tails between their legs.

I was almost seven then. Rutty was three. Sissy was five. But I remember it all.

In the sixteen years since then, they laid waste to pretty much everything, except the Blockades of course. Oh, they knew where we all were, and they didn't like it when we ventured out, for any reason. They got especially hot if they saw any of us heading in any direction that even *remotely* resembled going toward a coastline. No matter the continent, they wanted us pigeonholed far inland. We could never figure out why. Some straggled around by day still, but all we knew concretely was that they mostly reappeared every evening, near dusk. Where they all largely disappeared to during the day no one ever really knew. Apparently, they didn't like sunlight, and they would almost entirely vanish for a month on end during the summertime when it got into the high eighties and nineties. Those were our reprieves. It was times like that that we actually praised all the ozoners that went before us: inconsiderate humans with their carbon emissions, fossil fuels, aerosols and CFCs; they didn't know it, but they were actually *helping* us. Warming up the planet. Making the atmosphere hotter and hotter: more inhospitable to not just us, but them as well. I heard recently that a team of guys actually wrangled a gorgon in the heat of summer, while wearing some kind of protective eye shields, and they stripped it down: it just flailed, writhed, and screamed as it baked in the hot summer sun. Sizzled and smoked even. Apparently, they had some vampiric traits too. Never found out any more about it because you can't trust all stories, and I for one don't plan to wrangle any gorgon to see if it tries to suck blood too.

I remember the first time I saw one for myself. Back then they weren't really evil to behold; they just had this sort of ethereal quality to them, angelic almost, and they just sat there and hummed. Floated. We tried to make contact with them, of course; but they never moved. For three months they just stayed there, as more and more of them slowly floated down, taking up positions. We were all so uneasy. What the hell were they? Why were they here? Where did they come from? What did they want? All those questions piling up stunk more than The Mound, frankly.

But then, we got our answers, sure enough. Whether through some kind of telepathy, or some primitive form of timing, they all began to move. One by one, they clicked on, like a countdown had finished or a switch had been flipped.

And that's when they started hunting us down. Nothing we did mattered. Hiding was of little use. Shooting at them only made them move angrier, and they'd get faster. And that high-pitched shriek and dropped jaw thing. Lord. I remember a man kept shooting and shooting at one perched on the corner of a pretty tall building – I think he had a sniper rifle – but with each shot the gorgon hurtled downward faster and faster, until both it and the man disappeared in a thunderous cataclysm of concrete and dust. The gorgon was the only one that came out of that pit, a little fatter than it had been before it smashed down.

There were thousands of them in the air, swooping in all directions. Airplanes were overwhelmed and thrown out of the sky. It was pandemonium to the power of frenzy, to the power of chaos. The earth was upended on that day, and in the days following. The military had no time to scramble, though they had mobilized…but these things were everywhere. And those poor souls who had to man helicopter gunships: they didn't stand a chance. And then the news once reported that a swarm of them passed – *passed, mind you* – an F-35 jet on patrol. Frozen pilots plunged into the sea…the ground…the history books. All our hopes went up in blazes of glory. There were *so* many jets and commercial airliners at the bottom of the ocean now.

Each nation responded in whatever way they felt they should. There was no consensus in the United Nations, because there was never time or safety in order to mobilize a gathering: and many world leaders were already filling the bellies of the gorgons anyway. North Korea shot missiles in vain; thankfully, their nukes were intercepted before they killed us all while trying to mount a meager but impotent counterattack. Iran was the same.

The saddest part of it was the Gaza war just a few years prior. The Israelis and Palestinians had never quite afforded each other full truce; they would throw one another at a gorgon if it meant they would escape with their lives. Traps were set by one side or the other to lure in gorgons and devour whole households of their enemies. Despicable. Same with Ukraine and Russia. People desperate to sabotage their fellow humans just to get a few paces ahead. But the gorgons were faster than all of us.

The subject of nukes was never off the table… there was just no one who could get them mobilized, and where were they even supposed to detonate one? The chances of the entire human race getting wiped out by friendly fire were all too high.

Everyone everywhere was impacted. Every nation had thousands of them flying around. Those that could shelter in place could find out a little bit here and there on the news, but eventually there was no central news, and nothing to find out what was happening at other outposts. No CNN, no MSNBC, no news sites…I mean, they were there, but none of them were updated. VPN's hosted phantom sites that were frozen in time years back with no updated content. Their content and IT departments had been eaten.

The gorgons just caught, froze, and ate us, one by one. Rinse and repeat, in a grisly shower of cataclysm.

In a few years, eighty-five percent of the world's population was gone. The survivors lingered where they could, flitting from place to place, eking out a life of survival amidst the shadows. Since that time, the earth became a ghost town, abandoned, with overgrown ivy and out of control moss. Mildew and weeds. Vehicles everywhere, abandoned in mid-transit. Crashed airplanes. Trains off their tracks.

Animals roamed the streets freely after a while, escaping their enclosures. Most were picked off right there in their zoos. Even the king of the jungle was eviscerated by a single gorgon. Cheetahs couldn't outrun them.

Sure, automated systems still ran: sprinklers, night lights, A/C systems, etc. We still had power and utilities; just no humans to routinely man them, so, eventually, several systems failed. Fuel rods in some nuclear reactors, unattended to by human intervention, heated out of control; in some countries they failed, and the prevailing winds from radiation killed off many of the survivors over time as well. At least the radiation got some gorgons with that too, though.

Electricity went out over whole swaths of the earth for some survivors; then hypothermia and disease did the rest. We figured the gorgons killed off eighty percent of us almost straightaway; then, the ensuing natural calamities got another roughly five percent after that.

Someone was still creeping around and running things where and when they could. Independent heroes or troops ventured bravely into dangerous territory to keep things running, or to jumpstart failed hydroelectric, solar systems or power plants. Clandestine operations were springing up all the time all over the globe, desperate to keep us running.

Those with nursing or doctoral backgrounds stemmed the tide somewhat, but they had to learn fast. We weren't lacking in medical supplies, as long as we could conduct a raid on a hospital or clinic; it was just ramping up quick education to those who could actually wield them.

But for the most part, it was like trying to pour a cup of cold water on a raging inferno. Eventually, we would lose. Earth became unoccupied and barren, a desolate wasteland of lifeless quiet and a graveyard of ominous vacancy – except for *them.*

Once a gorgon had you in their sights…you just froze. Initially, it seemed it was just out of primal fear or terror. But no: there was actually something emanating from them that paralyzed the viewer: we thought it might be some kind of chemical agent, energy transference or something like that that seemed to be taking place. We had scientists working on it. That's why we called them gorgons: the power they had to literally stick you to the ground right where you were, and you couldn't move, and then they could float over and have their way with you, all the while whispering with that spine-chilling hiss: the sound of countless breaths of voices mingled together in wordless agony. I don't know which is worse: knowing that you can't run, or being eaten alive while you can't even scream. I remember the little girl though: she was about my age, and I could tell she was crying while that gorgon ate her. She definitely felt it. All of it.

Sometimes they wouldn't even need to paralyze you; they'd simply catch up with you, whisking behind you as you fled for your life: like me today just before the Blockade. They were just *fast.* Some people closed their eyes as they fought back, once we learned of their paralysis method. But that was pretty futile; you were just shadowboxing, swinging at nothing. One way or another, they would get you, and the best you could do was just to hide and ride it out and for God's sake, be quiet. One of them was just as bad as a swarm of them.

The most unnerving thing? You just don't think of humans as a food source. We have memories, souls, history, purpose. We aren't just some wild gazelle or antelope out on the Serengeti: we aren't just some prey. When you eat a human, you destroy purpose, memories, sanctity, and life. It was an abominable act. But of course, gorgons don't know any of that. They're just predators like any other shark or cheetah or hyena.

A gorgon was no respecter of persons.

I shivered and turned over, pulling a thin, ratty blanket up over me. It felt like a scratchy Brillo pad, but it was something, at least.

You know that point where your body craves sleep, and you know that you need it, but your eyes just won't stay closed? Yeah. That's where I was. For sixteen long years we had lived under the shadow of these things: wishing to high heaven that they'd just go, and hoping to hell that they wouldn't find us out in the wild out there. Our world had been forever changed. My life had been forever changed.

I was one of the "lucky" ones who happened to be born at the right time in history so as to witness all of this, to live it out, and to have to accept it as just how life was. The ones who came after me – and there weren't many, because why would you? – would never know what it was like to see them all drift down out of the sky. To hear them all suddenly start to move into action as if a switch had flipped: it was the switch that was labeled "annihilation of man." To actually watch one of them eating one of us whole. To hear that bone-chilling slimy hiss. You don't ever forget that sound. These babies were lucky enough to be born inside the Blockade, and to be kept far in, near the center, away from the threat that for them lingered only on the edge of legends and myth. But if they could sleep in peace because of our tireless labor? Fine with me. Ignorance is truly bliss.

However, it wasn't a myth for me.

Losing my family wasn't a myth.

That cat today wasn't a myth.

The amulet wasn't a myth.

The amulet – even now I wondered what they were doing with it…but more so I wondered what it would do for us. What would Stoney do with it? Where were the rest of them? What would the Beast reveal? It was unearthly, to be sure, and they had found a few of them before, but only recently had scientists discovered that they arrived at the same time the gorgons did. There had to be some kind of tie-in. At least, that's what we all seemed to now be pinning our hopes to.

With these and a million more questions pouring through my mind, somehow, I was able to fall asleep, though I don't know when, as it was pretty fitful. The room hummed with an unearthly rigor, the sound of countless engines throbbing throughout the Blockade. I was uneasy.

There was no way we were going to make it. That was our reality.

2 | NEWCOMERS

It was too early.

My door rushed open.

"Jet. 0600. Chow time."

I woke up with a start and flicked my head at the all-too-blinding light coming from the corridor. Rutty was there. Dangit. Why did I give him my lock combo? Can't he just leave me alone? I hated early risers. There was no point.

I looked at the clock. "It's 5:53, man! What are you *doing?* Go back to your candy bar." I clumsily hurled a pillow loosely in the direction of the door. I was a cranky wake-up.

"Come on, man. Time to go shoot bad guys."

I groaned. Bad guys. For one, we didn't even know what gender they were. Two, "bad" is an understatement when you factor in the impending eradication of the entire human race. Our fuel cells, hydroelectric batteries and solar-generated power wouldn't last forever. Three, you don't shoot; you hide. *Bad?* Come on. I groped around for another pillow to throw.

"Come on buddy. Don't make me call you *Cameron*, Cameron."

"Oh man, I'm gonna beat your ass."

Rutty snorted and let the door close. Blessed relief! He was gone. Thank you, God.

And in what seemed like the blink of an eye, since life is just that kind to you, the 0600 alarm went off.

I sighed, drug myself out of bed and angrily poured myself into my boots like a thick drink.

•　　•　　•　　•　　•

Breakfast wasn't much better than waking. These weren't eggs, and that isn't bacon, and no one was fooling anyone. I don't know where we got the coffee from, but it definitely wasn't beans from 2042. They were staling somewhere, and they were the best we could get. But we did have milk, and we did have agriculture within this dump, so for that, I was grateful. The thin shave of lettuce, and the sliced tomatoes on my plate were at least something. But hydroponics only went so far, and over time, the nutrient density of foods became less and less, so we were relegated to crap like this.

I popped a sugar cube in my coffee, and mixed it around in a few loops.

Rutty sat next to me, reading. Rutty loved books. He was always reading something, hungrily consuming it whenever he could get his hands on one. He always had a book in his backpack. I looked over. Right now, he was reading some obscure book called "Deception in Siena" by an author named Frank Curtiss. He didn't tell me what it was about.

I don't like to think while I'm eating, so I was noisily muscling down the "food" and playing some mindless game on an available iPad. They kept a few of these around for entertainment and education. Oh, there was still Wi-Fi, and there was still Internet, thankfully. These things still worked, if you powered them down to save battery and charged them sparingly of course. Lithium-ion batteries have a shelf life too. Each time I would play on it, I couldn't help but imagine that someday, inevitably, it would come down to the planet being saved by tablets such as these, we'd be in some Armageddon scenario relying on one, and it would finally kick the can just as we were about to disarm whatever doomsday weapon was set to kill us, because I used it for stupid games like these, and killed the battery. But I didn't care. It kept my mind fresh. It was some kids' game about fishing and numbers. One of the few things that was installed on it. Seemed so elementary, but to each their own, right? Like I said, I don't like to think while eating. I couldn't shake the thought, however, that fish sounded *way* better than the crap I was spooning into my mouth.

Thank God we still had satellites and 6G, though for how much longer we didn't know. Without those, we never would be able to communicate with anyone on the outs. NASA was kaput. SpaceX didn't make it and Blue Origin exploded on impact on the last one. There would be no more space missions anyway, because out there is where *they* came from. We were safest underground, where sporadic communications could still reach us, and we could still get enough signal to communicate with other Blockades. At last count there were a little over six hundred Blockades remaining throughout the world. Some of them just weren't well-equipped enough to make it. Some were too near the water, so the gorgons concentrated their attacks on them. And others, well, they didn't close their doors fast enough. Like I mentioned, the gorgons can move fast. I don't even want to think about what they did once they got into a Blockade and into bunkers filled with families… children.

President Jean Graham, "Madame President" as we still had to call her, was rarely on there to console or instruct; they were always shuttling her around to, *ahem,* "safer" locations to keep her on the move. She had definitely outstayed her welcome, being a four-term president after the suspension of Congress, but we were used to her now. And she was good, actually. She spoke with a somewhat debutant determination, like she'd just been voted in minutes ago. She was convincing and inspiring, even though she was now seventy-four. Thank God she got elected while she was still fairly young, or she'd be a slow-rotting geezer by now.

We had about ten more minutes before we could get back and shower; and then twenty before we'd have to report to weapons. Various personnel bustled throughout our makeshift cafeteria, if you can call it that. More like an AM/PM help yourself slop-shop. Pans of this and trolleys of that. I tried not to think about what I just ate. That helped.

"Well, I stink."

"You do," I heartily agreed.

"Yeah. Gonna shower. See you in Weps."

"K." I needed to get back too. Sitting in my boxers here with imitation eggs, polyester bacon and stale coffee wasn't exactly my idea of gourmet dining. If only we all tasted like these eggs, perhaps the gorgons would gag, leave us alone, and go find a different planet to ravage.

I drained my mug and trudged off. Just before I passed out into the corridor, I stuck my finger in my eye to pry out the sleep gunk, and that's when I noticed the new guy. He was a bit older, salt-and-pepper hair, and he had on our crappy jumpers, sure enough, but I'd never seen him around before, and I didn't care for the way he was staring at me over the lip of his mug: cocky and presumptuous.

"Can I help you?" I asked. I didn't want to and wasn't going to help.

"Nah, all good here," he smirked, not losing the cockiness. Pretty thick southern drawl though, betraying his origins.

"You new here?"

"Bassett. Trudy and me got here early this morning." Just then I noticed Trudy standing behind me with her tray of food. *Good luck with those eggs, Trudy.* She winked and sneered at me as she passed, clicking her tongue.

"Oh? Where'd you guys pull in from?" I asked curiously.

"Alpharetta," he said, scratching his graying five o'clock shadow.

I paused, and my brow furrowed seemingly on its own. "I thought Alpharetta was wiped out years ago." That's what I had heard. It was right by Atlanta of course, and all the major cities had a higher concentration of gorgons. That's why most of us who survived were in the rurals. Montgomery, Atlanta, Charlotte, all the way up to Richmond, they were wiped out. It wasn't even a fight. It was more what you would call a trouncing.

"It was. We're pinballing and using the tunnels too." So, it was true. They were digging corridors *between* all the major cities to allow movement underground too. Gorgons didn't seem to like it underground. Whether it was too hot and stuffy, or they couldn't see, or they wouldn't be able to move as fast, or all of the above, we had no idea. You don't sit down to a nice cup of coffee with a gorgon and ask them questions. That's why all the Blockades were underground.

And here in Clarksville, Tennessee, there was a lot of green around us past the old zinc plant, and a lot of mounds to build them in, at least during the daytime when we could catch a break. But the end result? The human race had essentially been reduced to moles. The first few years were excruciatingly quiet, burrowing, tunneling and hollowing out the hills since they had thought we were all primarily in the cities. We'd get as much done as we could in a day and then hide by night. There were hordes of us working those holes and sweating like pigs. And the gorgons would simply venture out during the day anyway, if they were hungry enough.

Trudy was applying some lip balm. Mint, I think.

"We all know the gorgs are out in force at night, and that during the day, for the most part they thin out. So, we've been working by day mostly, and some at night, using infrared. Took us a while to get here," Bassett said, sitting back against the railing behind him.

"Wait - you're the Beta company sent to replace Candee's team?" I asked him. The Captain had mentioned it to us, but I had forgotten.

"That's right. We're here to offer some assistance."

Trudy looked down. Suddenly I was very aware that I was still in my boxers. "Yeah, well, we've got things going pretty well up here. Current events would tell you that we just made a pretty acquisition that might help us out." I didn't know if Bassett knew about the amulet, but the way his lip curved up on one side told me he was on to me.

"Time'll tell," he paused. "Nice to meet you, Jet."

I hadn't said my name, so that made me flinch, but I think I hid it well. I didn't smile and certainly didn't say it was nice to meet him back, but gave him my best *aware of your presence* nod, and went out.

I stopped halfway down the corridor and knew I shouldn't, but I decided to look back. Bassett and Trudy were both watching me. I had half a mind to moon them both, but shrugged and went on my way. *You never get a second chance to make a first impression,* I thought.

Trudy was pretty though. Maybe I'll moon her later.

•　　•　　•　　•　　•

"Get a load of the new guys?" I asked Rutty. We were both showered and ready to go, and strapping on our, if you can call it "armor" (it was really just padding and a few prayers), we were gearing up for another patrol. No idea what would happen with the amulet today, but no rest for the weary: we were needed.

"What new guys?" Rutty asked, eyebrows up. He looked around feebly, but all we saw in the locker room were familiars. Rutty had taken longer than usual to shower, and so we hadn't met up in weapons like we said…but hey, any excuse to take a prolonged break under actual running hot water and soap. I remember when our generators went out a few years ago, and they were out for a freaking *month.* No hot water after a patrol meant a lot of pissed-off and stinky people. Thank God they placed a high priority on fixing them post-haste.

"I didn't notice anybody new?" Rutty asked.

Just then the lights dimmed and flickered briefly, and we all looked up. We waited for a second. It was not out of the ordinary, and we still had power.

"Yeah, came from Alpharetta-" I went on.

"Alpharetta?" Rutty asked incredulously.

I exhaled. "That's what I said too. Those were his words though. Took them a while to get here, he said. I have my doubts."

Rutty chuckled. "You always have your doubts. That's why I like ya, ya cynic."

"You're a cynic," I hammered back.

We slapped on our scarves over all. It was gonna be cold out there. Twenty-nine days until January, but who's counting. Not hot or bright enough to keep the gorgons away, unfortunately, and this was always the worst and gloomiest time of the year, because there were more of them to contend with. November through February was the scary season. So much for mirth and holiday spirit.

"Better grab an extra water bottle, bro," I cautioned. We had run out after two weeks on the last patrol. Recons usually only lasted a few days, and we could make a bottle last, but this last one was two and a half weeks of hell.

"Oh yeah, good call. You too."

"I got mine, I'm good. Anyway, yeah, Bassett and Trudy. I didn't like 'em, because, ya know, I'm a cynic and all. He's a cocky punk. She's….I don't know what she is. Pretty though," I breathed airily.

Rutty intimated a cheesy 70's porn beat back to me with his trademark grunts. Slimeball. I would call him immature, but I admittedly found it funny, so, whatever. "Get movin,' geek."

"You first, Loverboy."

"Hey, I never said I was in love with her, I just said she was pretty." In the fleeting glance I had at her, she definitely had a desirable charm, but I was too suspicious of Bassett to care, really; and I think I wondered more what she was doing with him. Which sounds like jealousy, really. Which meant that I was actually interested in her. Which of course meant that Rutty was right. Which meant that I would have to beat his butt here in a minute. Which I would relish.

We grabbed our packs and headed down the hall to weapons. I hated losing my Beretta before that last run through the alleyway, but such is life. One man's trash is another man's treasure, and I could only hope that some other patrol would find it and return it. I don't know. I liked the feel of it, and I had gone through a lot of guns. That one was a Beretta 92. You had to pull the trigger a bit longer, but oh that wonderful recoil when you shot it. I don't know what Rutty's heater of choice was, but he loved to also heave that RPG shooter over his back too. So glad he had that thing. Poor cat. I don't like rocket launchers. You only get a single shot, and it takes forever to mount, insert, and you have to focus on something that you *can* hit, like something near to the threat, to get maximum explosive damage. Just give me my Beretta (I got a new one) that I can point and click over and over like a mouse, and I'm good. Until then, we all had our standard issue XM5s.

The only problem with guns and rocket launchers? They were loud. *Anything* loud out there was not good. You had to have already scoped out where you were going to hide right after you fired, or that bullet would be your swan song.

We arrived at weapons, and others were there before us. Pettijohn, Wilkes and Ferro. We didn't see Jentzen or Hickey, and that worried me. But there was Captain Stone, lowering his communicator. He was ashen. Stopped us in our tracks. "Cap?" I asked. He paused.

He didn't look up, but sighed heavily. "Dupre."

Took me a second, but then I remembered Dupre was working on the amulet.

"Got too close to it while it was conducting. And we're pretty sure he damaged it. Harrison is checking it with Anderson."

Dupre was a good guy. He was kind of a social moron, and thus you could never really engage him unless in stunted conversation, but he was well-mannered and quiet. A real science nerd. Too bad. The amulets had to go through a process of conduction to see what they could do. It was already hot, I remembered. Where I had had it in my pocket throbbed in memory. Heat was a weapon we could use against the gorgons, and this thing could generate heat, so they had to test the limits. Maybe that's what they were trying to turn it into: some kind of heat weapon? Anyway, apparently there was a recommended safe distance in so doing. What I was even thinking fishing for it in my pocket yesterday was now beyond me.

"Harrison thinks he got fried taking it out of the clamp. His back was turned so he didn't see it. Halcyon looked at the footage and verified it."

And just then I remembered why the lights flickered just out of the shower this morning. That must have been when he got electrocuted.

"I'm sorry, sir. He was a good guy," Rutty consoled.

"Yes, he was," Stoney breathed angrily, and started for his info pack.

We had this thing, all of us did, really, that there was only one fate worse than death: and that was death by gorgon. Still, electrocution was no way for a man to die. I wondered what his thoughts were at that very moment as the current coursed through his body. But my musings were cut short as Dad started tapping his pen on his clipboard and quietly chanted names in a silent roll call.

"Ferro."

"Here."

"Pettijohn."

"Here."

"Wilkes."

"Here."

"OK, you guys are Alpha team; you take B Range. Southwest. Bring back whatever usable intel you get, and whatever food and water you can find, blah blah blah, but you know the drill: salvage any and all ammo and explosives you can. You know the usual sources. And keep on the lookout for survivors."

They nodded. I stowed a brief misgiving that they were still a team of three. It didn't seem fair. But then, it wasn't fair that our planet got invaded, and it wasn't fair that Rutty and I lost Santella. Life just wasn't fair.

"Private Shipley."

"Here."

"Sergeant Shipley."

"Here," I echoed.

"Lieutenant Trudy."

"Here," I heard a voice breathe behind me. My heart stopped. How she had slithered up so quietly behind us, I didn't know. I whirled around. There she was, the new girl, in all her mystery and shapely perfection. No sign of Bassett. Good.

"Hello again, Trudy," I said. I looked over at Rutty. So, she was a lieutenant, a senior officer. I liked that. Made her more desirable.

"*Hiiiii,* Trudy…" Rutty teased to her, waving seductively. Trudy clicked her gum at him. I didn't even know we still had gum, unless they had brought it with them. Man, I missed gum.

"Team, this is Lieutenant Allison Trudy. She and Sergeant Bassctt arrived last night from Alpharetta."

Again, murmured astonishment that Alpharetta even existed. For myself, I was astonished that her name was actually Allison.

"They're your new Beta team additions, picking up where Candee left off. They'll be joining the Shipley boys in C Range to the northeast. Head that way: there has been some scattered thermal and infrared movement reported up there, so be careful. Same drill, but as they're new, Jet and Rutty are going to play nice and escort them. Show 'em around. Make 'em feel there's no place like home."

Trudy clicked her heels three times as her eyebrows went up in mock glee. I chortled and turned back around, but the smile faded from my face. I liked her gum, I liked her personality, but I didn't like her Bassett. And where the heck was he anyway? Probably a *rules-don't-apply-to-me* guy like any other cocky truant or renegade.

"Bassett is with Halcyon now, getting the lay of the land. It's been quiet this morning, and it's supposed to get up to fifty-five in the heat of the day. You all know what that means. Low and slow, quiet as a mouse, and use your communicators only when necessary. I want close proximity low-volume exchanges as usual. Clear?" Dad lifted his head, awaiting acknowledgment.

"Clear," we answered.

"Report to Launch at 0900. Sentry will get you to the outs." He paused. "One last thing…you may bump into our Charlie Team night patrol on the way back. That'll be Myrtle and Frye."

I couldn't wait any longer. I had to ask.

"Sir, what about Hickey? And no update on Jentzen?"

The Captain was stone-faced. "Just Myrtle and Frye now. Lost Hickey last night. So, show these guys your usual kindness."

Dang. Two gone in less than twenty-four hours. And Jentzen was MIA. We hadn't lost that many in a few months. I never knew Hickey, but I knew Myrtle and Frye. I think that left us with fifty-three souls all told in here. Fifty-five if you counted Bassett and Trudy, but I was willing to exclude Bassett and count Trudy twice. Once for Allison and once for Trudy, of course.

"Get back before sundown tomorrow if you can. There will be a memorial in the pavilion for Dupre and Hickey at 1900 then. That's it. Beat it."

I always liked that dad never said *dismissed*. "Beat it" showed so much more colloquial jocularity, like a dad would say to his kids. "Dismissed" was just so military. We couldn't afford to get cold. The gorgons didn't like heat; we had to keep ourselves warm. Dad looked over at me, managing a feeble attempt at an encouraging smile. He nodded. I nodded back.

I turned back to Rutty. He knew Hickey a bit better than I did. "You OK, bud?" I offered lamely.

"Yeah. Sucks."

"Yeah."

We were both glad Dad didn't say how Hickey bought it. The rule was you simply didn't talk about it. But we all understood that if we didn't say exactly how they bought it, it meant only one thing. That's why he stated clearly that Dupre was electrocuted. Hickey on the other hand? We all knew then that a gorgon got her. And maybe one got Markus Jentzen as well.

Rutty made the sign of the cross over his chest and we gathered our things. I never understood that…why hadn't God protected us from the gorgons in the first place? Why did I have to lose nearly all of my own family? Why were we stuck in this hellhole?

Trudy had already about-faced and headed back out to the Launch. My guess was everyone's favorite human Bassett would meet us there. I was right. Here he came down the hall. We followed closely behind Trudy.

"Well, well! We meet again," Bassett sounded, theatrically. "Looks like we're teaming up. I got a good look at what they're up to out there today, but I don't think it's gonna be too problematic for us."

"Great," I scoffed blandly.

"Captain Stone gave us C-Range: to the northeast," Trudy informed Bassett. "Back by sundown tomorrow. He wants us to head for the university for some potential signals, and there should be plenty of supplies to harvest there, with more on the way, little stores and such. We just gotta cross the river."

Rutty and I looked at her incredulously. Crossing the Cumberland River was pretty much out of the question. It was a major water thoroughfare, and that meant that theoretically it would be crawling with gorgons. Sometimes we'd find them all settled nicely on the banks of the river, inverted, their heads plunged into the water. Whether they were drinking, or keeping out of the hot sun and cooling off, we didn't ask them. Trudy was right: the university grounds would be ripe for the picking – *if* we could get there. But I hadn't heard the Captain say that. Rutty and I looked at each other, quizzically.

"Uh, excuse me Trudy, I know you're new here," he began. She flashed her head over at him. "It's just that…I mean, I don't know what the gorgs are like down in Alpharetta, but we already know we can't cross the Cumberland. We've already tried that. And the flats beforehand, that's just a lot of open ground for them to see us moving and see us coming. Is that what the Captain said?"

She said nothing, just snapped her gum at him again. That was getting a little old.

"You tried the Cunningham, right? Or was it the railroad trestle?" Bassett asked, feigning actual interest.

"The Cunningham bridge, yeah, we tried it," I said. "A platoon of us, a few years ago. No one goes near it anymore, because they know that's how we'd get across. That's the reason why we never crossed the railroad trestle either."

"Naturally," Bassett fired back. "But have you tried either since?"

"No," I answered defensively, looking over at Trudy, who was smiling and enjoying the irritating ping-pong between us. "We've never been ordered out that far. It'd be nothing short of suicide because of the water."

"Just short of it, I think. Anyway, I get it. But Candee and his team tried the trestle. That's where we'll go. That's why we're here, kid." *Kid.* Oh, that pissed me off.

Sure, he was my elder, but not by much. What was he, forty-five? Fifty? Where does he get off calling me "kid"?

"Is that so? Why weren't we told anything about it?"

"Sergeant, we can stand here and waste time shooting off our mouths about it, but we launch in a few minutes, and I can explain on the way. Is that acceptable?" He gave a world-weary sigh and hiked his pants up, shifting the pack on his back in the process.

"Just remember who's in charge. You follow my lead. You step outta line, I smear you with sheep's blood and feed you to a gorgon myself," I muttered toward Bassett.

Bassett smiled excitedly. "Sounds great. I like sheep."

"Great." I fake-smiled back. I was beginning to feel threatened by this newcomer, and I wanted him to know I was Alpha here. I'm not entirely sure I came across poised, but whatever. Just didn't want this to turn into a pissing match.

I looked at Rutty. He looked cunningly back and forth between me and Bassett. "Fine by me too," he said, "as long as you share some of that gum, Trudy."

"Sure," she said, smiling sweetly. Rutty put out his hand for a stick, and Trudy fumbled with her mouth and tongue, sending the chewed-up spearmint clump plummeting down into his hand, saliva and all. She tilted her head and smiled at him again, then zipped up to the Launch, her pig tails bobbing lightly.

Rutty nodded and smiled. "Nice."

I rolled my eyes, but I still liked her. I just didn't like him. I wished I had a sheep ready.

•   •   •   •   •

We ascended the Launch. Floodlights greeted us at the top. The Sentry hailed us silently and then stepped aside.

The Launch wasn't really a "launch" per se. That was just what we called the last platform before the doors. There wasn't anything to do from there *but* launch…because the inner lock would seal behind us, and there would be no re-entry. Too risky. Reminded me of that movie trilogy with the tributes who all had to go in and kill each other off in some form of sick games put on by a higher society. Once you were out there, you had to play the game.

Each time you went onto the Launch, you had to place your thumb on an ID scanner which would scan your thumb like a big red tongue, and then prick you, saving that "before" blood for when you got back. That's why we called it the "ol' lick-n-prick." It would scan you for a cold; if you had one, you were sent back. No one could be coughing out there. Every Blockade had one. The blood was automatically stored in a vial with your name and ID number on it, and then put in those spinners they have in medical right before you got back, in case you came back with a gaping flesh wound and needed a transfusion. It was the best, most current record of who you were *before* you went out.

Everyone who goes out comes back changed.

Like those movies, we also had a countdown. It was quiet, and then the doors would open silently, slowly, cautiously. And we would peer out silently, slowly, cautiously. So far, the enemy hadn't caught on to our daily routine, or they'd be ready to lock and load the minute that crack opened in the door. But they always remembered the gun towers. Retractable, able to do a full three hundred sixty degrees and swivel straight vertical, they were a halo of protection for us, all eight of them: our last defense. Each Blockade was ringed with them. Whoever drew up those plans was our savior. And of all the sources we always needed to procure, ammo was always top of the list. It kept us alive in ways that food couldn't, because it provided the one thing that food couldn't: hope. The only bad thing about ammo? You can't eat it.

We took up our positions, locked and loaded. You wouldn't have even known we were there but for the *snick-chick* of the cocking of our M5s. Bassett pulled out his motion detector and switched it on. M-decks were so helpful. They were capable of tracking movement from a thousand feet away, and that was some comfort, although gorgons could cover that span in a matter of seconds. So, once you detected movement at the far end of the display, you were usually supposed to drop the dang thing and either hightail it for the hills, or spray gunfire like your life depended on it…*because it did.*

The Sentry backed off as we inhaled deeply. Last breath of stuffy air for who knows how long. Bassett signaled to him that we were ready, which irritated me. The Sentry looked confused, and then moved to face me instead. He knew *me,* not this new guy. I nodded silently. The Sentry raised his hands, palm upwards. I did the same.

Palm upwards. That's what we were taught growing up. It meant that we were open to receiving whatever came our way. Willingness. Even if that meant death through fighting. It meant that we were willing to sacrifice our independent selves for a greater cause, a greater good. It's all I could muster myself to do. I wasn't a God-fearing man like Rutty was (I saw him signing the cross again to himself and praying) but it was close enough. If there was a God, I trusted that he knew that I was part of the team and just trying to do my best.

The Sentry gave me a thumbs up signal and stepped off the platform, down the stairs, and turned around. Without a word he reached over to a panel on the wall and pressed a button. I don't think I'll ever get used to the ritualistic nature of a launch: so mysterious, so silent, so sacred and solemn. Everyone, the Sentry perhaps best, knew that we might not make it back, and so they treated us with reverence and sent us off with their prayers and willing hands.

The hatch began to close as two slabs of cold iron simultaneously moved from the top and bottom of the corridor to meet in the middle. There was a slow rhythm to them that drew us in, knowing that everything we held dear was inside, and now we would be unwelcome until the appointed hour of our return.

The slabs met noiselessly in the middle. We were now outside. We couldn't see anything inside except for a tiny plexiglass window through which the Sentry was now monitoring us. I turned my head back to the outer hatch. Ten feet wide and seven feet high, it was a mirror of the inner hatch: rusty from the rain and elements, but still functional and inanimately committed to our survival.

We waited, silently.

As per usual custom, the gun towers gave the all clear and then the outer hatch began to slide apart. We could all see the morning daylight come springing in. A few inches, and we'd be-

A sudden grating shriek stopped our hearts. I could feel all of our eyes go wide as we tried to pinpoint the sound. With guns raised, all of us triangulated the source of the sound: the hatch was rusty and grating against the slides. I turned and held my hand up to the Sentry, still watching us. I heard Bassett reach for his communicator and snarl "Stop the freaking door!" as I barked the same thing. But there was no need: both gun towers nearest us heard it as well, so Command got three of the same requests at once. It came to a screeching stop.

For a moment, all was still. We listened, but couldn't see anything. We were exposed for a gut-wrenching minute.

"Positions," I breathed. We all slowly crouched down to hear *and* see. I could feel my heart pounding as my tendons flexed and my kneecaps shifted. All of us knew that narrow slice to be the only thing we could fire a last salvo through. Whoever was responsible for greasing the doors needed a thorough beating.

Nothing on the horizon. Gorgons could hear *really* well. If this had happened at night, we'd be covered in a feeding frenzy in a solid twenty seconds.

We waited for what seemed like an eternity, our hearts still pounding. I felt my head throbbing. Still nothing.

Rutty was closest to it. He silently fished out of his pack a small can of WD-40 and applied it to the door generously. He always had everything in there. *Good boy, Rutty.* Thankfully, it made no more than a murmur of its own. He finished and stood back up, looking at me angrily. Trudy hadn't stopped shaking her head the whole time.

I slowly turned back to the Sentry and cautiously waved to him to continue. Everyone was watching me; now we all turned our attention back to the door slides. One second passed… two seconds… three…

With the tiniest hint of screech that was over before it had begun, the slide wheels re-engaged, and the doors began to move again. We all breathed a collective sigh of relief. But it wasn't over yet. They finished their noiseless separation and we all slowly poured out into the field. Standard practice was to post up on the grass and lean into the Blockade and wait. Bassett and Trudy did the same; that was at least some comfort to me that they actually knew what they were doing.

No sign of gorgon mist. Bassett's m-deck wasn't sounding any motion blips. That was good news. Nothing above. We all figured the gunners would have seen something, but they had nothing to report either.

Nothing but a bright morning out here. I looked at my watch. 0912. Roughly thirty-one hours before we had to get back. That was gonna be a hike to the university and back…if we would even make it. Barring any more unexpected surprises like deafeningly loud Blockade gates or loud gum-smacking by Trudy, we should have enough time to get there and back by tomorrow evening.

We stepped down off the berm and were now crossing silently into the field, forward, weapons ready. I only trusted Rutty in this ragtag group. He's the only one I really knew out of all of us.

We had a long two days to go, and it was too early.

3 | ON PATROL

We always had high hopes that we'd find something out here. We just weren't exactly sure what might find us.

The sad part was that you could never do an endzone dance or shout for joy if you actually did find something good. Any new acquisition was just a fact, and we just put it in our pack and moved on. No celebrations out here; it was time to survive and get whatever-it-was back to the Blockade and see how it might benefit us.

We made it to the trees, and were more or less heading in a northeasterly direction. The trees were fairly naked at this time of the year, and they offered a marginal amount of distracting cover. Being under cover, we'd be at least somewhat harder to spot. But that was a double-edged sword: in the forest meant cooler temperatures, and that meant possible gorgon sightings. The crappy part of all of it was that once you ran into one, you just had to shoot and run.

You hoped you nailed it and it fell, but everything was so dang loud, which just summoned the rest. And you would just cower down under something and hope to God that they didn't have a berserker with them.

And then, even with that, I'd heard reports of teams that had gone out and had a gorgon spot them…you'd have to really go all palms up before that, all the way. By that, I mean, willingness: to let your partner die. Because, if a gorgon zeroed your partner, and you shot at the gorgon to keep your partner alive, that just meant that you'd summon a whole horde of them, and then you'd *both* be toast. It was kind of an unwritten rule that if you had any inkling that there were more of them close by, you had to let your partner go, or *nobody* would return to the Blockade. I suddenly recalled something out of an old movie: *"the needs of the many outweigh the needs of the few…or the one."* Sometimes it sucks to be a human. I sighed. Packing heat was a double-edged sword. Great in time of need; in time of need: not so great.

Another thing: every time I set foot out on the grass, I missed Jack dearly.

Jack was our Jack Russell Terrier. A Mother's Day present for my mom from I don't even remember when. Too long ago. Anyway, he was fun, he was smart, he was trained, he was playful, and he lit up our lives, and the lives of everyone else in this Blockade. He must have been the last Jack Russell alive. Unfortunately, however, he was loud, and the only thing you couldn't train him out of was his bark. I would trade that last yelp I heard for every playful bark he ever gave to our family. We got the gorgon that took him, but that was no consolation.

Gorgons are kind of like sharks, or goats. They eat just about anything, and as fast as Jack's little legs could carry him, they were no match for a gorgon on the wind. They had to close the doors, and I was just a little guy then.

I'll never forget it. Thank God Rutty didn't see it. I was up on the Launch calling for him, watching desperately, as if that would somehow usher him back on a tractor beam of my tears. He was getting geriatric, but he could still run. Our family had gotten Jack before we came to this Blockade, and he didn't bark much then…except at *them*. But being with humans again, and no longer a stray, *unfortunately* did wonders for his spirit; he was too carefree to know that his planet had been invaded with monsters that wouldn't think twice about making him a meal.

I can still see him running all out toward the gate. Last thing I saw was a gorgon scooping him up and flying overhead just beyond my line of sight through the hatch. He yelped as he was caught, and then I heard the guns. I hope to this day that the guns got him before the gorgon did. I don't remember what happened after that.

We never found him. Just like we never found any more birds, tigers, wolves, antelope, bears, goats, elephants, horses, monkeys, owls, bats, eagles…nothing. Cows were the only ones, and they were now kept in stables below ground with us, with handfed grass, so we could get milk. Small cats, like the one from the zinc mill the other day, are another story, because cats by nature are reclusive *and* elusive. They're super quiet, and super-fast. I once saw a cat outrun a gorgon through the zinc mill…that sucker could run. They were still around with however many of us remained. You can really learn a lot from a cat: they are the right creature to emulate in such a predicament.

There were snakes around, too, and of course, insects. Insects would always be. Wouldn't matter if the planet had been blown up; insects would still survive floating around in space because they just never go away. Snakes were too slow to track their movement, and some of them were highly venomous. They were finding mates and breeding in the shadows. We had to watch out for those.

These rumblings passed through my brain as silently as my feet passed through the grass. We were on a preset path that had been carved out by previous teams. But you still had to be careful not to crack a twig, and so we all crept carefully along, guns drawn. *It sure would be nice if there were soft grass everywhere,* I thought. Fanciful thinking.

We pressed on. Nothing yet. No one spoke. No one wanted to take the chance. Any communications that came from home base were on a dB-attenuated headset. To top it off, Command never spoke a word at natural volume: everything was whispered. You really had to concentrate to listen. They directed us onward.

On occasion, out on these patrols, you could still catch a whiff of rotting deer flesh from the processing business southeast of us. The gorgons got most of them. Other than that, it was fresh, clean air full of the scents of tulip poplars, red maples, sweetgum, and dogwoods.

After a solid half-hour's march, we had crossed a clearing and were knee deep in the woods again. We were coming up on a home when we ran into our first sign of trouble. Bassett's tracker blipped a signal dead ahead, about sixty yards to our north. Command radioed nearly at the same time, "Contact. 54 meters, bearing 352."

I was on point, and I froze, motioning to the others to do the same. Up ahead, there was movement beyond a small shed. We all stopped and slowly raised our weapons. Trudy was taking up the rear, and looking back I saw her turn around and glance behind her, as if she were trying to determine how far a sprint would be to get to cover, or back to the Blockade. In fact, that's what we were all doing, because that's what we were supposed to do. It's what we were trained to do. In unison, we all gently hunkered down and scanned the ground around us to our left and right, determining obstacles to avoid, plotting ideal escape routes should it turn out to be an unfriendly.

Just our luck. It was. We saw the mist first.

Slowly, out from the left side of the barn ahead, we saw it slink out, creeping as they did, swaying this way and that, trying to figure out what it had heard or where it should go. These things were sometimes mindless drones, just like a shark, and never really knew where to aim for until they picked up a blood trail. They couldn't smell very well either, and it seemed they really couldn't distinguish scent from scent: at least we thought they couldn't. But here we were at nearly 1015 hours, and the sun was riding proudly up the crest of the sky. Oh, he'd cow us if we moved, for sure.

However, our luck held: we crouched as stoic as statues, and we were low to the ground, our camo blending into the background of the forest and the trees. Rutty quickly scanned around for any more of them: the movements of his head imperceptible from afar. We all did, really, and happily no others were to be seen. This one was a rogue. We could see it skulking over there, drifting ever so slightly to our left. Bassett breathed "scram": I heard it, but only because I was right next to him.

The thing just floated there. You could never tell why, and you just had to wait. Waiting was the worst part, especially if you had to make the Blockade doors like last night. Without warning, it accelerated and disappeared up over the tree line, into the fading pines and sugar maples. The pulse on Bassett's m-deck slowly faded into silence, and then…nothing.

Standard ROE was to wait for a solid minute to ensure that we weren't being tailed, that it didn't return, and that it was in fact alone. That was a long minute. But finally, I breathed out "all clear" in my headpiece, and Command echoed back an ever so faint "copy."

Simultaneously, our joints creaking ever so quietly, we stood up and slowly continued our northward march. We made for the far tree line to the right, since that gorgon had evidently decided to head off westward. In any case, this was our set trajectory we had been assigned by Command. We were moving slower now, due to the sighting. At this pace, in another hour we would be to the flats.

Command had tried all sorts of tracking: infrared, thermal, etc. Infrared would sometimes pick them up using satellites, and that was helpful, but there was a terrible latency with relaying intel, and as they were cold-blooded, you couldn't really pick them up with thermal very well. Additionally, Command was stationary; we weren't. We were on the move, and had to rely on Bassett's m-deck to register air flow differentials and variations coupled with a silent radar ping. It did the job alright, but its batteries didn't last forever. Thank God it was solar-powered.

We trudged on.

We'd be at the river at 1200 hours, and I wasn't looking forward to it. Looking over at Rutty, I could tell he was thinking the same.

· · · · ·

We paused for a break about thirty minutes post-sighting. We had just passed a clearing: the last one before a wide-open space that shouldered up to the Cumberland on the northeast. We'd only done less than three miles at this clip, and that was typical because of the need to keep it quiet.

Trudy and Bassett took the first watch.

We'd been on the move for nearly three hours now, and not a single blessed one of us knew what we were in for once we reached the open expanse of the fields just before the Cumberland. There were only two crossings: the Cunningham bridge to the southeast, and the train trestle to the east, but nothing to the north. But we were drawing nearer to the river, and however you sliced it, that meant trouble.

Rutty inched silently over to me, leaning over for a whisper. "I dunno about you, but I don't wanna get any closer to the river, man. I'm gettin' freaked out already."

I nodded. "Me too, buddy. May be a one-way ticket. You got a new sippy, yeah?" I hated saying that word. So cavalier for a cyanide pill.

"Don't leave home without it," he sighed. *Cyanide.* No one wanted it to come to that. The easy way out would be a bullet through the brain. But just in case we got separated from our pieces, a cyanide pill – we thought – would probably take out both us *and* a gorgon while it ate us. Better to burn out than to fade away, I guess. They were standard issue in our packs, but the less we had to think about them the better. The only drawback with a cyanide pill is that it sure wasn't instantaneous. Ergo, the scientists tinkered with them and added other things like arsenic, barium…even mercury. It was supposed to speed things up, but I'm positive it made it far more painful. But if it meant taking out a gorgon with our own exit that was going to be painful anyway, *c'est la vie.*

"Remember last year at the plant when you, me and Markus were *that* close?" I asked Rutty under my breath. We had run into a pack of gorgons sleuthing around the zinc mill together, and we were pinned down.

"Don't remind me." He chewed his gum furiously at the memory. That was the most panicked I'd ever seen Rutty…I swear the gorgons located us from the sound of his sweat hitting the ground, he was that out of his gourd. "Thought that was it…'till you started screaming and running. I forgot how you got away?"

I had bravely – or insanely, can't remember which – tried to distract three gorgons that had us cornered, by jumping up, screaming and burning rubber back to the

Blockade. I think I did the fastest running I ever did then, as the wind sliced through my hair. Maybe yesterday was nearly as fast. Rutty would have beat me back of course, but I needed to get them off of his tail. Thankfully, they had already spotted us, so it was OK to shoot. So, I did, firing backwards as I ran. Took one down, though to this day I don't know how I did it, because I couldn't look directly at them of course. Surprised myself. I only made it back to the Blockade because the other two stopped to pick up their own dead. Seems like if they couldn't get us, they were content to feast on their own. All of that gave Rutty time to escape, I reminded him. He showed up back at the Blockade the next day. That was a nervous few hours for me.

"Yeah, that's right. Thanks again, man."

"You still owe me."

He chuckled. "Yeah I do. Wonder if we'll run into some more today."

"I dunno man…right now I'm more interested in the new folks. Maybe they'll enlighten us." We both glanced up at Bassett and Trudy. It was then that we noticed that Bassett had his binoculars out and was peering out through the trees, over the sad brown banks that led to the Cumberland. That's where we would be most exposed. Nothing to hide behind there. Trudy was faithfully monitoring the m-deck. No sign of movement. That was some relief.

It was getting hotter, and there were some midge flies buzzing under the trees as Bassett turned back to us and knelt down. Trudy's eyes followed him back to us silently.

"No movement, guys. All's quiet," he reassured us.

"Yeah, for *now*," Rutty fired back.

Bassett smiled grimly. "Have faith, kid." *Stop calling us kids*. "There's no reason to think that they're lining the entire bank. They may have moved on. These things don't just drink water; they've gotta feed too. Trudy used to be on the science team in Alpharetta, so she's got some insight to lend here too. Our best bet would be to hold this trajectory and make a beeline east straight to the other side. You know what that means though."

Now I did. "You mean over the trestle."

"Well, not exactly," he breathed.

I stared at him. He had to be kidding.

"*Under* the trestle? You want us to *swim?* You're kidding, right? That river's like a hundred feet deep, with a current to boot! And it's gotta be barely above zero."

He wasn't kidding. "Well, we can't fly, and they'd spot us up there if we make one bad sound against metal. That would be an echo nightmare, and a death sentence. Yeah, we gotta swim it." Bassett looked at us, waiting for emotional sign-off. I saw Trudy look back our way. She obviously didn't like it either.

Rutty grunted in disbelief. I joined him and shook my head. "There's no way we're going to do this," I countered. "We get spotted, and we won't be able to run, we'll be freakin' waterlogged and frozen over."

"Jet, I get it. I need you to trust me on this. I don't want to run into these things any more than you do. But the river will provide some natural sound cover. Ninety percent of our bodies will be below water."

"Yeah, but the other ten percent is us trying to swim while holding up our guns and praying that the current isn't gonna sweep us downstream. That's gotta be at least two hundred fifty feet across." Thankfully, at least our packs were waterproof.

"That's right. But the current isn't strong. Halcyon showed me footage. It'll be hard, but not impossible. We can do this," he tried to encourage us. "There's no other way to get across with more cover, and we have to have cover."

I did note that while on patrol, he had a different air about him. The cockiness was gone, and he was all business, but more of an encouraging coach. Something in the way he said these last words gave me an inexplicable measure of belief in him, although I didn't want it to.

I sighed. This was not good news. The trestle would provide some cover from being seen from above, despite the obvious drawback of having to get wet. And he was right – *dangit* – if one of us so much as bumped the stock of our rifles against a bridge beam, that would be a sonorous death sentence that would ring the gorgon dinner bell.

"Have you ever seen one move, Bassett? I mean *really* move?"

"I have."

"So you know how fast they are."

"I do. And so, I know how fast we've got to be. I promise you we can do this." We locked eyes.

Last night he seemed so cocky. Why was he acting all paternal now? Had something changed? And that stupid southern drawl. Annoying. Did he have some kind of heroic reputation to uphold, something we were all clueless about in Clarksville? Or should I still suspect him and keep my guard up? Still, something in me told me to relent. I was in command, and he knew that, but we were a team, and the only way we were going to get to the university grounds was by being a team.

I relented, and decided to trust him. I resolved to teach him proper diction someday, at least.

"Lead on, Bassett. But mark my words, no one has crossed the Cumberland in years. I'd like to live past today if that's alright with you." With each word I tried to communicate that I didn't like him yet.

"So would I, Jet," he said. "We'll see."

He patted me on the shoulder. Which, of course, I didn't like. This 'kid' business and shoulder-patting: seemed like he was trying too hard. I was willing to give him the benefit of the doubt, but only if he stopped acting like some overly affirming orphanage nun promising me a home.

Rutty looked over at me. I flicked my eyebrows upwards in futility, and turned to look at Trudy. She had a thoughtful smile on her face looking down at us. Bassett looked over at her and nodded. That wasn't reassuring either.

And suddenly I got the feeling that they knew something they weren't telling us.

The river was out there, and we were heading straight for it. I cocked my XM5 as quiet as could be. Sooner or later, we were going to run into a bunch of them.

I only hoped to keep up with Rutty while we fled. No, that wasn't true. I also hoped to outrun Bassett.

•   •   •   •   •

It was 1300 hours before we decided to set off again. We had all done a double-check of our rations and ammo, slung our packs on our backs and brandished our guns again. Rutty did the sign of the cross again in front of me. *Whatever.*

I was the rearguard. Bassett and Trudy went first. They were almost to the clearing. Bassett was fidgeting with something in his pack as we all looked out east.

We headed up Old City Ferry Road, and were almost to the trestle. Before we mounted up, we quietly discussed our approach. I proposed that if we were going to swim under the trestle, then we should stay under it for as long as we could, since it was elevated. We stay off the top, I said. They agreed. It was minimal aerial protection from unfriendly eyes, but it was something.

In two minutes, we'd be clear of the woods. We stopped and took a lay of the land. Bassett had powered back up his m-deck: thankfully, it said nothing. Trudy had spit out her gum so there wouldn't be any competing rhythmic noise with the low pulse of the m-deck. We watched and waited. I could hear my heart pounding again.

A staticky signal from Command broke through and relayed our coordinates and how far we had to go. Thankfully, our trajectory through the forest led us to the train tracks right where the hill sloped down, where it then became an elevated train out of the woods, and then over the water. We were able to get under cover pretty fast - once we summoned up the courage to move, that is.

The coast was clear. We moved. Slowly, cautiously, flanking each other. No movement reported from Command. All quiet on the m-deck.

We left the protection of the woods behind and issued from them like a slow-running brook, surreptitiously and timidly. Each step felt like a thousand pounds of sludge. My boots had never felt so heavy. The trestle drew near overhead, and we silently formed ranks underneath, walking along over lightly crunching gravel. Every step took muscular acumen and focused balance not to create too much of a soundwave. Single file, forward, we moved on, slowly, slowly. I looked down at my watch. 1323. I looked up at the sky: the noonday sun was riding high. Hopefully that water would be somewhat warm and not leave us like bedraggled rats.

As we slowly, deftly approached the river I had a horrible realization: we'd have to swim this thing not once but *twice*, unless we decided to make our return journey across the trestle itself, *gorgons be damned.* I just thanked God that I could actually swim.

North of us, in between where we were and the Cumberland, a commercial jetliner's burnt hull could still be seen halfway buried in the ground in the soft riverbank, blackened shrapnel all around it. The tail fin identified it as Alaska Airlines. I wondered how many of the passengers knew their crash was caused by a gorgon, or if they were paralyzed even before they hit the ground. There were gaping holes throughout the broken-up sections. A macabre scene of total destruction eshrined it in a blackened graveyard.

C-Range was coming up. We were still in the zone, a three-mile diameter around the Blockade that we called home. Eventually it would end, and our little island would butt up against the Cumberland, and we'd be isolated nomads: wanderers bereft of a safe haven, hoping against hope that our little patrol would yield something – *anything* – remotely useful. C-Range held both promise and dread. And we were heading straight for it. I'd never been so far. I'd mostly been assigned to our little spur of land, our inverted teardrop. Fitting, since all we could do was cry since our world got turned upside down.

But we were doomed to patrol it. And now we were heading southeast toward an unknown frontier of war: an expanse of water roughly two hundred fifty feet across that we'd have to swim to uncertain doom beyond. I looked around. No one looked optimistic, not even Bassett. *How's your trust level now, Bassett?* I wondered.

We were some fifty feet on our way under the trestle. It was a clear sky above, and that held both promise and threat, for we were uniquely visible under the tracks, coupled with our shadows, which made for vastly larger moving targets slowly creeping along the ground. We were never sure how good the gorgons could *actually* see; we just knew that their visual acuity and tracking were based on object motion, and that they had the ears of a bat. I looked down at my shadow, willing it to shrink smaller, when I suddenly noticed something out of the tail of my eye. There came the simultaneous threatening pulse on the m-deck, signaling movement to our north. I looked in that direction.

And then I saw what stopped my heart and took my breath away.

There, flying towards us along the river, suspended between earth and sky in glorious beauty, to our eternal satisfaction and in defiance of our ever-present danger, came one of the most lovely things I had ever seen, and something I will never forget: a sight of beautiful majesty, and a gracious gift of wonder that stopped my breath.

A Great Blue Heron: a glorious testament to nature, flying bold and free.

My heart was in my throat, but I managed to squeak out a whisper, "hold up!" and we all froze. Each of them ahead of me whipped their heads frantically around in all directions to determine my reason for the halt. But they all noticed it quick enough…a sight of splendor flying in our general direction. Where it came from, no one knew…and what arcane destination called him: that was also unclear. All we knew was, for that moment, time stood still: this beautiful avian creature was the purest non-human we'd seen in years. With its orangish-yellow beak and pinhole eyes set back from its long white crest, and that distinctive black spur off the back of its head flailing up against the wind, it quickly became apparent that it was fishing. What fish remained in the Cumberland was anyone's guess, but the heron appeared to be on to something, because its head twitched back and forth with every beat of its wings, gliding and thrusting back upwards, looking to and fro.

I heard Rutty breathe out a long, awestruck "whoa…" and I could just make out his cheeks thrust upwards in a smile ahead of me. I looked back at the heron: it was beautiful. It let out a gorgeous squawk.

For a moment, time and space entered a state of suspended animation as we beheld its glory; undimmed, untarnished, natural, earthly, raw, splitting the air with its perfect strokes, oblivious to war or famine or dread.

It let out another squawk, more like a honk.

That was too loud. My smile faded.

And then it was gone.

The gorgon came out of nowhere, from up ahead and to our left, summoned to action by the infernal noise of the intruder who dared to venture into its domain. We saw the mist first…it preceded the missile that shot up from the far bank to our northeast, and the heron disappeared in a plume of feathers and vapor. We heard a squawk and a splash as the gorgon brought it down. I could dimly make out the sound of frenetic splashing, but no muted sounds of bird calls or anything that might signify survival.

I swallowed hard, my eyes moistening; I heard Trudy choke back a cry.

The lull that followed belied the future, giving us a moment of despondent pause in reverence for the fallen heron.

And just then, in a flurry of pulse activity, the m-deck went wild. Bassett slowly looked down at the display, terrified of any sudden movement. The top of the display was lit up like a Christmas tree. Something was drifting down the display toward us. Something *big*.

Without a word, Rutty and Trudy put their backs to the train trestle frame, facing us. They couldn't see the river as their backs were turned; I don't think they wanted to look anyway.

And that's when we saw the rest of them. There, before us, about three hundred feet ahead past a last ridge of trees, a swarm of gorgons silently ascended, moving closer. Blue-green mist encircled them as a fog, and all of us felt a wave of fear wash over us, gripping our weapons tighter. As if on group sentry, the cavalcade of gorgons was looking around this way and that, a haunting sentry post full of their filthy kind. We had no doubt that we would be espied, there, leaning into the railings that supported the elevated train, as they bobbed their filthy necks, searching.

There was nothing we could do but remain absolutely still. Their visual acuity would have to see us breaking formation, and walking or running away. I had a cartoonish thought that hopefully my shadow wasn't flickering on the ground. *Why oh why did we come this way?*

The m-deck continued to pulse and vibrate. We didn't need the reminder of the approach of our enemy; Bassett and I could see it plainly for ourselves. A dense throng of pale gray silhouettes shrouded in vapor began to fan out, slowly, awakened to a new and deadly vigilance despite the noonday sun.

"Keep absolutely still," Bassett muttered.

Like we needed that reminder, I thought. I was confused: Command should have picked up the gorgon signals by satellite if they had been there for a while, at least if satellites were still flying over, surely they would have picked it up and relayed the intel of their location. Why didn't they tell us?

We could see all of them, clustered together and yet thinning out at various elevations and distances, looking around solemnly. We were too far away for them to lock onto with whatever it was that they did to freeze people where they stood, but they were still drawing ever nearer. Command came through dimly on my headset: "Stand by."

Stand by? What? What did that mean? Stand by for what? My brows furrowed, and I looked over at Bassett. He didn't turn towards me, but I could see his calm and collected eyes flicker over at me for a second as he watched the gorgons fan out. Why was he so composed?

Stand by for what?!? I didn't understand. Rutty threw a confused look my way and shut his eyes. I could see his mouth moving in silent prayer. I looked over at Trudy. She was cold and still, eyes glued to Bassett.

Bassett nonchalantly echoed the mysterious order: "Roger, standing by." I looked at him suspiciously. What was going on here? I kept still and turned my attention back toward the river.

That's when the flash hit. Due southwest, about three miles away. Like a nuke had gone off. Rutty and Trudy shut their eyes as the sky illuminated in the white light of a thousand stars, eating up the sun. I turned and had no idea what it was. That's when the sonic wave hit us. It began as a low hum, and then swelled into a dull thunder as it rolled over the hills. And gathering speed, it at last cascaded into a bellowing note-laden undulating boom that enveloped us and shook the dust from the stilts and beams of the trestle. We all looked up, fearing the structure would collapse.

We were steamrolled. A giant wave of elements swept over us like a rolling pin. Everyone else's screams blended into mine. There was no pain…only volume. Loud, cacophonous volume, but on notes undetectable by me. Hideous notes blended into screaming wind as the thunderous shockwave enveloped us.

I turned back to the Cumberland. The gorgons still gathered there had been watching intently, though unable to clearly see what happened. Then the blast hit them.

When one gorgon screams, it is cause for alarm. When fifty of them scream like that, you wet your pants. I nearly soiled mine. The dissonant shrieks and terrified cries of these alien beings *en masse* were absolutely horrifying and gut-wrenching to hear. They flitted about angrily. Some smashed down into the water. Nothing in my heart approached the realm of any semblance of pity, as I sat rooted in horror watching them convulse and tear madly at their own bodies in a vain attempt to stop the audio assault on their frail forms. Most didn't come back up. All of their eyes reflexively bulged, and poisonous cold mist swirled; their long bony arms went to their ears and covered them, as they wailed in pain and fled shrieking into the sky, racing away west in a dark throng against the clouds. We could hear the last of their howls trail off into an uncertain expanse before we felt it was okay to breathe again. Where they went, I don't know.

I looked back southwest. The noon sky had faded back to midday, and it seemed like a dream had passed. Or a nightmare. I wasn't sure which.

"What the hell was *that?*" I scratched at Bassett, not daring to raise my voice still. There was dust all over both of us. All over *all four of us*, really.

Bassett had held his breath as he watched it all unfold. Now he let it all out, and his head bowed. I swear a good minute passed before he turned to me and whispered two words.

"The beginning."

We looked out over the river. All was quiet. The heron was gone, but so were the gorgons. For now.

The mist thinned, and then finally vanished.

We always had high hopes that we'd find something out here. I just still wasn't sure what might find us.

4 | DISCOVERIES

The dust was everywhere. It was fortunate that all the gorgons had been driven off, because Trudy was retching noisily. And frankly, the rest of us were near it: constantly fighting the urge to cough and gag. Whatever it was that came rolling over those hills brought a torrent of detritus, silt and accumulation from years of abandonment. And it was now drifting down over all of us. We were coated in yellow. It got into our hair, our ears, our nostrils, our mouths, and it tasted tangy, bitter and stale all at once.

We looked incredulously at Bassett. When I say "all" of us, I mean Rutty and I. It was apparent that Trudy was in on it. I stared at her and noticed the look of joy that swept over her face, in between the retching. She knew. Now I remembered back in the forest having the distinct feeling that something was up. Son of a gun if this wasn't quite obviously it. And then she confirmed it: "It worked, Bassett."

"*What* worked?" I prodded, realizing the volume at which I was talking. "*What* worked?" I re-voiced, whispering. Their miserly and stingy hints thus far didn't explain what monstrosity of sound and noise just trundled over us like a rolling pin, and why it drove away the enemy. "It looked like a nuke. We should be dead!" I shot air out of my mouth to blow away some stray dust that was getting into my eyes from my hair.

"No, Sergeant, it wasn't a nuke," Bassett coughed and whispered in return. "If you were to call it an EMP, that would be closer to the mark," he said, standing back up and dusting himself off. He looked back toward the river and the coast was clear. "I asked you to trust me, remember?" He winked.

"Bassett," I growled, "I'm in charge of this deployment and this platoon. You knew about this all along. You were wrong to keep it from me; from *us*. The captain's going to hear about this," I threatened him acerbically.

"That's all fine, Sergeant!" Bassett barked back. "You may however be interested to note that Captain Stone had full knowledge of this operation, and green-lit it himself before we set out."

Well, that didn't make any sense. Now I was just even more pissed-off.

"There's no way. You're lying."

"Look, Sergeant…all of us are working together in our own little way. We all want to see those monsters gone. I don't know about you, but when I look east, that river's clear now. It won't stay that way for long. So, I suggest we all high-tail it to the other side of the Cumberland and find us a nice hole to settle in. I'm happy to regale you there. Sound good?"

"Sounds *great*," I nipped back, my eyes squinting.

Trudy giggled. Apparently, she was enjoying all this verbal jousting again. "Just relax, Sergeant Shipley, we can explain. And we will."

"You better."

Rutty watched both of us closely, unsure how it would all turn out. He coughed one last time and exhaled.

One unforeseen benefit of the gorgons clearing out? We could now walk over the trestle. It was dangerous, of course, but none of us fancied swimming in that water now. We didn't want to chance bumping into that beautiful heron's floating corpse…or something worse. We could quicken our pace a bit and yet still be cautious. By the looks of it, they had all cleared out anyway.

Our platoon doubled back to the ascension point of the trestle, and began our eastward march. We were twenty feet higher now, but that didn't give us any increased vantage. The skies were clear…for now.

We watched our steps, and kept an open eye on each track, slowly worming our way across it.

As we spanned the river, before we were even there, we were greeted by a ghastly sight below. We could all see for ourselves several sullen, scrambled shapes of rent and tattered gorgon bodies along the banks, all splayed and misshapen; all of them bleeding from the ears. Some of them were still twitching. But no real movement; thus, the m-deck was all quiet.

It was *awful:* a macabre scene of riling filth that made our stomachs churn. The ones that were still alive were all moaning silently, as if they couldn't muster up the strength to emit any further sound. They looked like slow-gasping fish. Briefly I wondered about putting some of them out of their misery. But no way. That collective stench: like a steaming pile of earwax mixed with rotten eggs. I wanted to vomit; I had to breathe, settle my stomach and just focus forward.

No one said a word about it. Yet we had all seen it. Conversation was unwilling; we knew that eventually they'd be collected and eaten by their very own anyway. They were all dead, and the ones that weren't dead were dead meat.

We powered through that gruesome scene, and eventually all four of us were off the trestle. We had now left home, and were officially on the other side of the Cumberland.

We were now legitimately in C-Range.

By the time we made it to the other side unmolested, it was now 1412. I had to take a leak, and so did the others. I restrained myself from trying to see where Trudy was going. Rutty did too. That gave me a chuckle.

There was a row of trees approaching, bordering a massive park yawning up on our right. But we kept everything quiet, slowly angling away from it, across the train car lot onto Sullivan. We could see the caboose of a train far up ahead, leaning on its side halfway off the trestle. Ahead of that was a jumbled mess of other tangled up cars that had jumped the track in some cataclysm from years past.

Bassett's m-deck remained quiet. Our guns were drawn, and we stuck to the shadows on each side of the street. We were less than a mile now from the outskirts of the university, and occasional relays of coordinates from Command verified that.

My eyes were wide. I looked over. So were Rutty's. We were in a land wholly unique to us, indeed, to many from our outpost. I think Candee and his team really were the last ones to try this way. There was a lot to see, a lot of places to rummage through, and a lot that we could possibly bring back. These patrols were so critical for the finding of staples like bottled water and canned food and snacks that hadn't gone bad yet. At the very least, we had to feed our own animals to produce milk. The hard part was getting it back if it consisted of noisy crinkly packs like potato chip bags.

Those were a no-no. We had to take the time to quietly open those and then move them into our own containers.

We also had to try and procure some ammo, so hopefully they had an armory or comparable supply. And we had to determine what those thermal images were that Stone had mentioned.

This time we were on point, and Bassett and Trudy were taking up the rear. We were close enough in front of them that the m-deck wouldn't pick us up, and they continued to scan.

It was hotter than anticipated. My watch was reading fifty-nine-point-five degrees…by the afternoon peak it would be over sixty. That was some comfort. A giant unexpected EMP, coupled with above average temperatures for this time of the year, probably meant that there would be less gorgons to worry about.

We slunk our way around onto Washington, zigzagging onto Union. In a little over half a mile we would be at Austin Peay State University. Trudy had reported that there would be dorms and more along the way. So far, nothing but abandoned office spaces and businesses in a good mix of commercial and residential, with various windows broken out, and cars littering the street with their doors open. Occasional dried blood streaked across windows. Whatever happened here was savage. Just like everywhere else.

Command would ask for updates every twenty minutes. Sometimes we'd beat them to the punch. We were still in their scanning range, silently threading our way into C-Range.

We were going at a bit faster clip now, perhaps with some suggested belief that the EMP had driven them off for good. Where they actually were was anyone's guess.

I couldn't shake the wish that the EMP had gone off well before that gorgeous bird had appeared. To see a Great

Blue Heron still in existence: that brought a music to our hearts that lifted us momentarily, only to see it tragically shot down seconds later. It was like watching a modern day Zapruder Film, only with fifty ghoulish Oswalds behind it.

Honestly, I found myself wishing I'd never beheld its beauty, and that was a tragic thought. I shook my head.

Looking up, I could see that at least Rutty and Trudy were showing a bit of sluggishness, and to be honest my feet were starting to drag a bit. It was time to take a break. I quietly signaled to our patrol that we would break in ten; we were approaching a large complex on the corner of First and Commerce: apparently the remains of what was once the county jail. *What better place to get imprisoned in, should they come back,* I thought morbidly. But they should have supplies in there, and perhaps communications and even ammo too. Seemed like an ideal first stop.

Bassett looked back a few times on approach, almost as if he expected another EMP to go off. I dare say he orchestrated it, if you asked me. Convenient timing with all those gorgons rising up in a huge throng, and sudden miraculous deliverance. No matter how you sliced it, something was up, and more people were in on it than just him, Trudy and the Captain.

In another five minutes we were there. Some of the buildings we had passed were either blackened from fire, or had collapsed from some calamity or tragedy.

As luck would have it, one of the back doors was unlocked, probably due to a gracious move on the part of the warden to give inmates their last chance at life rather than be sniffed, located, and then slaughtered in their own cells. But if you think about it, if it were me, those cells were hard to escape from; it stands to reason that they may actually have been safer staying put, and just not looking.

It was always eerie not discovering any bodies. Gorgons are disgusting scavengers: warm or cold, they'll take it away and eat it. No one had ever seen a juvenile or infant gorgon, and no one knew if they reproduced or fed their young or what. It was always the same size, always the same speed, always the same fear. Except the berserkers: they were bigger…and much worse.

 We crept down a back hall into what was arguably the foyer. Rutty closed the door silently behind us. We were in. Now it was time for food…and answers.

•　　•　　•　　•　　•

 After a preliminary sweep, we found neither weapons nor ammo; certainly neither an armory nor anything else we could ransack. Disappointing, but par for the course.

 "Alright, time to come clean," I said to Bassett, between bites. "What was that blast?"

 Bassett munched on dried fruit and thought for a bit. *Here it comes.* I watched him intently.

 "Yeah, I mean," started Rutty, putting down the book he had been reading while eating, "I'm grateful and all, that was super convenient timing, but *whoa* – did you know?"

 "I did," Bassett acknowledged casually, lightly wiping some yellow dust from his black boots.

 "Figures," I retorted, angry that I had not been informed. "Mind telling me why none of the rest of us did?"

 "Well, not all of us were clueless, kid. Trudy-"

 "Don't call me kid. Seriously."

 Bassett squinted. "OK, fine, Sergeant Shipley. Trudy knew. And yes, Stone knew." My face grimaced. "And yes, Halcyon knew. I didn't have clearance to let the cat out of the bag yet. I wanted to tell you beforehand. I'm sorry that couldn't be the case."

I sighed and shook my head. "Whatever, what's done is done," I said, not wanting to accept his half-hearted apology. "I don't appreciate the secrecy, but whatever it was…worked. All of this doesn't bring us any closer to the question at hand though. What was *it?*"

"Well, an EMP isn't far off from the description. But it's supercharged with explosives to, sort of, jumpstart and amplify the soundwaves on specific frequencies that it seems our little friends don't like too much. That's what they were doing in Nashville and along the coast. That's why we got hit so hard and got pushed so far inland. Had a team of guys experimenting with sounds above thirty-five thousand hertz. We all know that dogs get irked when they get hit by sound at certain frequencies. Seems the gorgs aren't too fond of it either. Trudy and I were on the team that worked on one of them."

"One of what?"

Bassett smiled and paused, looking at me. "One of *them.* We call it 'Subject Zero.'"

My eyes narrowed and I looked over at Rutty.

"You *caught* a gorgon?" Rutty asked.

He smiled again. That was getting old. "Yes, we did."

"How – what – how did it not get any of you guys cold?" I put to him. I remembered the story that I had heard of a gorgon getting wrangled. "Wait – were you *that* team?"

"The very one," he said. "The first ones to catch one of those monsters." And then his smile slowly faded. He looked past me, locked in a slow thousand-yard stare, and seemed to remember something sad. "But not without losses." He cleared his throat roughly and said no more.

"How did you guys do it?"

"It's the first step in the revolt, fellas," Trudy interrupted. "We just finally figured out how to neutralize whatever it is that makes them freeze us. It isn't calculus; it's simple reflection technology. We made a visor out of it. Went through a hundred prototypes. Same thing they use in borosilicate glass like the stuff that they make water bottles out of. We have two of them with us."

Yeah. 'Cuz we all talk about borosilicate glass and simple reflection technology all day.

I looked down at my water bottle. It always kept relatively cold no matter the temperature. I held it up, confused.

"Kinda like that. The visors aren't made out of glass of course, because they could just see our optics, lock on us, and freeze us."

"But you designed something that can shield us from what they do? Can we see it?"

"Well," she said, flipping an apple in the air and walking over. She dropped cross-legged on the floor by us without so much as a slow squat. "We're not all the way there yet. Right now, it's more of a "graduated resistance' sort of thing. Whatever they're doing is psychological, or telepathy, or something like that. These masks deflect the signal they put out that's meant to immobilize us." She unzipped her pack and extracted what looked like a whole-face 3M respirator, with a slim profile. The front glass – *er, borosilicate glass* – had a shimmery appearance that modulated when moved. I inspected it and looked closely. I could see a nearly imperceptible grid pattern interspersed throughout the face mask: tiny gossamer gridlines ran up and down through junction points in slim spidery threads. This fancy contraption was shielding their eyes from us, and our eyes from them. Or at least, was close to doing so. 'Graduated resistance' didn't reassure me much just yet.

"So, what happened to the gorg?" Rutty asked.

"Oh," she sighed, "it's in solitary. In restraints and with protective shielding between it and us. Got some blinders on it too, so it can't exactly see where we are and try to do that crazy Medusa crap." She giggled. Apparently, there was some entertainment value in it for her, beyond just studying.

Rutty was dumbfounded. "No way. You actually have one *alive* and in containment? That is *rich*. I *gotta* see this. When did you do it?"

Bassett looked at Rutty. "Four and a half months ago. Alpharetta. Still hot out, so we found one, a rogue, head down in a river, similar to where we were headed on the Cumberland. It was half asleep. We were almost on it, but it…woke…or whatever it is you call it when they start putting out that mist again."

"They stop misting when they're asleep. It's like they go dormant or something until they're in flight again," Trudy helped.

"Right. There were six of us. We just ganged up on it and threw ourselves on it. The screams," Bassett said. "We had another six that were standing watch, forming a perimeter around us, in case there were more of 'em. I don't know what we woulda done if there had been more. One did enough damage," he ended lamely.

Bassett's head drooped. If I didn't know any better, I'd say his face was laden with anguish.

Trudy could see that he was struggling, and picked up the slack again. "Four of us got severely injured in the commotion. The thing can really flail, and they just got thrown. Then the gorg just…did its thing while we were trying to restrain it. It got Joe's sister *bad*. Froze her part way, and then it started to…," she stopped herself. "We tried to save her, but she just lost too much blood. We lost another one due to internal injuries after we had gotten back to medical. A friend of mine, Raylin."

Joe. Joseph. One of those. So that was Bassett's name. And he had lost his sister. Well, that's something us Shipley boys and he had in common then. I registered an unwelcome pang of sympathy welling up inside of me, so I tried to shut it down quickly. I wasn't ready to like Bassett, Joseph or Joe just yet.

There was a lull. No one spoke. I figured it was proper that I was the first.

"Sorry, man," I offered in a bland monotone. "I never know what to say. Just…sorry."

Bassett choked back a swallow. "All good, ki-, uh, Shipley. *Jet.*" He managed a feeble smile at me. "All good. Her name was Steph. She was my kid sister. She and I were the only ones from my family to survive. She beat cancer, alcoholism and a car wreck. Only to be killed by a gorgon. Just doesn't seem fair, does it? But," he stammered, "that's the card we were dealt, so we just play it." He stared at the ground. "We just play it," he repeated.

I looked over at Rutty. Rutty shook his head. I guessed that he was thinking about Sissy. About dad. About the cards that we had been dealt as well.

"Well," Trudy continued, hand on Bassett's shoulder, "we all got pissed. Pig-piled on the dang thing, shutting our eyes. Those things have some serious claws, and they're like daggers."

Suddenly the welt on my shoulder flinched. I didn't need to be reminded. I knew their claws. I now knew them intimately.

"That's all we could do: bear-hug it and head-butt it. Took us well on five minutes to subdue it. There was a terrible mist all around us. The things actually breathe. It was starting to get hoarse, and it actually coughed. Robertson – he's a pretty big guy – just laid on it while the rest of us bashed it unconscious. Not that we needed to. Eventually it would have run out of breath with him lying on it, crushing it into the ground. But then, somehow, I knocked it out cold with the butt end of my rifle. Don't ask me how I did it, because I sure wasn't looking. I couldn't look. None of us could."

I looked down at her hand, and I could see the bite marks. That thing had bitten her while she was feeling blindly for its head.

This whole saga began to dredge up a newfound respect for these two. Trudy was pretty *and* tough. Bassett had shared losses and commanded the first team to hog-tie a gorgon and bring it back for studying. It wasn't everyday our little two-man team got blessed with such formidable additions.

"Another thing?" she added. "That mist is *deadly* cold. Like, *thick-of-night-floating-in-the-Arctic* cold. If they didn't freeze you, I think the mist itself would. It's hard to move when they're misting like that: you feel it in your *bones*. Your muscles just ache. Nature sure dealt them a good hand with all those pretty little mechanisms they get to use. Sure wish we had something like that."

"And they just play it," I remembered.

Trudy looked over at me. "Yep."

I wondered what it must have felt like to be right up next to one, enveloped in that cold, deadly vapor.

"Well, I'm sorry man. But," I had to prod, "why the secrecy on the EMP? How come the Captain never briefed us, if he knew? And how long has this been in the works?"

"Yeah," Rutty added, "and why was Halcyon in on it? Could they see infrared and knew where they were all along? Was it, like, an established nest or something?"

Bassett laughed. "Which question should I answer first? I think that was six of 'em in a row," he answered. "Well, you guys saw where the blast came from. Halcyon's main job was to make sure we had the all-clear. That's where it emanated from. We didn't want to clear out this gang of bandits on the river, only to drive a new batch of bandits their way in its wake. Thankfully, they're scattered mostly off west of us now. Why, I don't know. And to answer your questions, Jet," he turned to me, "for a while. We had to maintain radio silence on it because we didn't want to get anyone's hopes up. We also didn't want a false start of any kind."

"False start?"

"Yeah. Like in football. There are more of these out there. And there are some Colonels and Captains who really wanted to get that first strike in. We had to keep that at bay. But even more than that, this is a powder keg development, and potentially a colossal turn of events. We needed to get the word out and have everyone powered down for the extent of the blast radius, or we'd fry all the tech in our own Blockades. The repair time would set us all back months. This was only a test. It's the first…of many. And it all had to do with one of the amulets."

"The *amulets!* I knew they were the key to something big!" I exclaimed.

"Indeed, they are. When Markus made the handoff to you, he knew what they were, for sure. He was one of a number of operations similar to ours that all had to occur relatively simultaneously, otherwise these things might disappear. This op took some serious coordination. There's something in the amulets that tweaks the frequency of our sound waves *way* beyond anything we've seen on this planet before. It definitely isn't something that we've ever studied, and it's definitely something gorgons despise." Trudy nodded. "We couldn't play our hand too quickly."

"You sure talk cards a lot," Rutty joked. I was thinking back to Markus Jentzen; we'd still had no word on him.

Bassett turned to him. "Have to. I was a pretty dang good poker player before all of this. You never show your hand. Your keep your poker face and keep your cards close to your chest, otherwise, they're on to you. Couldn't take that chance. I had to manually trigger it with this." He pulled out an antenna switch he had been fingering in his pocket.

Rutty brought his face up to it and examined it closely.

"Hmm," I thought. "Well, there you have it. Where do you think they went, and how long do you think we have to regroup and prepare for another EMP?"

Bassett shook his head. "To that, I don't know, man. Trudy and I are special ops sent here to launch the first one, and thus give the movement some traction. But these things came when the gorgons did: the amulets, I mean. Right now, they're our best shot to send them packing. We're right on the perimeter of the blast radius that we set off, and that was another thing we had to test: the limits of effectiveness with the blast radius.

"You can see that some of them were driven off and *not* killed. The potency of the blast diminishes as the radius increases. Kind of like dropping a stone in a pond: colossal disruption at first; tiny ripples at the end. We had to test that too."

"And what about everyone on the perimeter of the EMP? Won't the gorgons just hang back there until it's safe to advance again? They're sure to be plenty pissed."

"Oh, I think not," he hissed happily. "I think we've given them fair warning that we're not gonna play by their rules. I think we just told them it's game time. We just told them we're serious about a war."

We all closed our mouths, lost in our own thoughts.

The mood had definitely turned cerebral and full of speculation. Could this actually be the beginning of the end of the war? I hoped so. Be that as it may, time was ever against us. I looked at my watch. 1638. We had lingered here long enough. "Well, we've got about half a mile to go.

It's almost 1700. I don't think any of us want to be out after sundown if we can help it, yeah?"

Everyone shook their heads.

"Let's get a move on. I figure we have another half an hour and we're there, provided we don't run into any company. You good, Rut?" Rutty nodded and yawned, arching his back and stretching his legs. "Trudy?" She nodded and took another swallow of water, and stood. I looked at Bassett. "You OK, Joe?"

Bassett lifted his head out of recognition and smiled grimly. "Sure, Cameron," he teased back.

I smiled faintly.

This Bassett I think I could grow to like. Maybe even play cards with one day.

•   •   •   •   •

Our packs slung across our backs once more, we issued out of the county lockup like snails, slowly willing blood back into our legs and feet. M5s at the ready, we moved again.

Going on thirty minutes in, as I thought, we reached Drane Street and Austin Peay University, filtered into the parking lot, hugging the side of Honor Commons, and checked the doors. They were still locked. *As if that would stop a gorgon.* Soon we were approaching the outskirts of Sevier Hall. Plenty to rummage through here. I just hoped against hope that we'd actually find something useful. Now that we had the amulets and I knew they actually did something, it didn't make losing Markus or Hickey – or *any* of the others, or even my Beretta – sting so bad. It didn't even make incinerating that cat feel so bad.

I moseyed up to Bassett as we crossed over the grass. His m-deck was on again and he was turning it this way and that, but all was quiet on the display. "That EMP really did the trick, huh?" I whispered.

"Yeah, at least for now," he agreed tentatively, looking around nervously as if to confirm that the device wasn't lying. The coast was clear; but that didn't mean they didn't simply relocate to a better hideout in order to sleep away the day. They liked to spring their trap with little warning. We'd seen it too many times before.

"We have to be careful…we're nearing where Command said they were picking up some thermals."

I noticed an old Subway off to the right, and motioned to the others. If there was frozen dough in there, that might still work. Might even have some bags of chips too, but again, we would have to be quiet with those. Trudy hesitated for some reason. I turned back to see her behind me, stopping for a moment, eyeing the abandoned restaurant nervously. She seemed to remember something, but continued on.

The cafeteria due south of it would be our next stop after that. We approached slowly. We could all see where the chip bags would be on the far counter: but they were all gone. Not one remained. The soft drink machine called to us through the panes. Our water wasn't filtered, but it did the trick. But soda? That would be a nice break – as long as it wasn't flat, which it probably was after all this time.

The glass front was shattered. Clearly some ravenous college student survivors had been here. I was just about to open the door when I saw it. Out of the side of my eye, there was movement about two hundred feet away. Something small was dodging in and out of cover on the far side of the dell beyond a hillock. "Target!" I whispered to the others.

All of us wheeled around with our backs to the glass, guns raised. Command hadn't said anything, and neither had the m-deck. I looked over at Trudy, farthest from me, who was bending over and trying to look through the shrubs on the far side. There was a courtyard clearing in front of us, red and white striped. Bassett's eyes widened as he looked up and down from the m-deck to the cafeteria beyond, scanning.

Then we heard some kind of faint bird call, but it was clearly human-manufactured.

And that's when the pulsing started.

I hate that sound. It's a light, flickering popping sound that grows in vibration intensity as the signal gets nearer and stronger on the m-deck display. You always hoped that whatever blip you saw on the monitor would be the only one. But you never knew what it was until it revealed itself.

All of us knew what to do. Without a word, we crouched down. Rutty and I aimed upwards toward the sky. God forbid a gorgon should float over the top and down toward us. Bassett and Trudy were to our left, and they aimed at the signal origin. I didn't envy Bassett for having to hold two heavy tools. I prefer a clean and steady shot myself. I'm sure he did too. But balancing the m-deck and his rifle took some patience and dexterity.

The blips stopped. We held our breath momentarily. More blips off to our left. We all threw our gaze over towards Harvill Hall, and saw something coming over the fields. Something small and brown. It didn't look like it was floating. It looked like it was running. And soon we would know for certain that it was more than one. The m-deck began registering multiple blips. Our hearts raced.

I made a quick, quiet whistle to the others, and motioned for Trudy and Bassett to take cover in the foliage to their left as Rutty and I backed into the bushes and under the tree cover to our right. Soon we would be lost to sight.

The team obliged and retreated into the foliage. We all waited.

The m-deck continued to register multiple signals approaching from our nine o'clock. As we continued to peek out through the brush, the twelve o'clock signal began to move again. And then suddenly there were signals at our four o'clock appearing on the display too. But how could that be? That would mean that they had been on our six relatively recently, tailing us, before we had turned around. Now we were turning our heads in all directions, scanning for potential assailants. Numerous bogeys were converging on our location from multiple angles.

"Command, we are being surrounded, I repeat, we are being surrounded. Henry St, old Subway restaurant, university grounds. Multiple unknowns." I relayed them our coordinates on my watch.

"Confirmed, use caution," came the reply.

Thanks. 'Cuz I was going to go in all haphazard-like.

I saw Rutty finger his sippy in his pocket, ensuring it was at the ready. I gritted my teeth. I hoped it wouldn't come to that.

The light was fading fast, but just over the horizon, in the dell, a hooded head with a masked face came into view. I saw it plop down on the grass and cow us with a sniper scope. A red dot appeared suddenly in my eye; I looked down and watched it travel down my face, and then my chest. I looked back up and raised my hands reflexively in surrender. I'd never been so relieved to be in the crosshairs of a sniper…because this sniper was human.

"Hold!" I whispered sharply. "Hold! Stand down. Friendlies! Command, friendlies inbound."

They looked over at me and saw that I was being laser-sighted. No gorgon wields a sniper rifle. Soon they could see for themselves. The m-deck mirrored the approach of about a dozen men and women, all decked out in dark or camouflage clothing, donning packs and other gear. All were armed with some sort of handgun or rifle. So here at last was the "scattered thermal and infrared movement" that Stoney had asked us to investigate.

We emerged slowly from the foliage, arms out and palms upward in token of receiving. They lowered their weapons, and several of them did the same, silently, mirroring us and proving their intentions.

Their pace slowed as they approached, and I could see them silently communicating with each other using some form of sign language. One of them even threw up a friendly wave: shorter guy with blonde locks under a baseball hat. We waved solemnly back. No words were exchanged, but they beckoned us out of the shadows and pointed us toward Harvill Hall to the east.

Slowly, we emerged, guns still drawn, watching the sky and the surroundings for any sign of gorgons. This would be a feast for them. I counted eleven friendlies, all now retreating back to the hall with us.

Wordlessly, we paced down and across the dell with the red "AP" university logo, and up the surrounding hillock.

Soon, the four of us entered Harvill Hall, where we were met by even more of them. We looked around in amazement.

There were at least four score survivors here, of varying ages: all ragged, all alone, all studying us intently. As we would soon discover, their things were piled throughout Harvill Hall, past the boarded-up windows and reinforced barred entrances: mounds of collected – and discarded – items: furniture, clothing, refuse, waste.

It was messy, and it was dirty. And all of them were covered in the dust from the EMP, just as we were.

The dust was everywhere.

5 | VAGABONDS

I looked around at all of them: so alone, and so confused.

They were all surprised to see us, looking us up and down.

"Shipley. Uh, Sergeant Cameron Shipley. Hiya. Folks call me 'Jet.' We're with a local Blockade, number DN436 over by the zinc plant beyond the Cumberland. This is Bassett, Rutty and Trudy. We're on a recon patrol for supplies and survivors."

One of them, a near-middle-aged man, stepped forward and undid a mask from his face meant to keep out the cold – or the dust. "Hey guys…I'm Preston… sophomore here. Or…sorry, at least I was when all of this went down. We've been here for a while. Some of us ever since they showed up. I'm one of those. Did you guys see what happened a few hours ago? What was that? We know it's winter, but…do you guys happen to know what day it is?"

My eyebrows went up. "Uh, yeah…definitely. December 3rd, 2042."

I wasn't prepared for the response, having mentioned the year. Preston's face went ashen, and his jaw slowly dropped. "2042…?" he slowly squeaked. The others joined him in their dismay, looking at each other confusedly. "We thought…we were thinking…" he stammered.

"Hey, it's OK," Bassett interjected. "Sounds like you guys have been out here a bit longer than anticipated. I applaud you for sticking it out. You guys survived. That deserves some kudos. We'll get you taken care of. Is there somebody in charge here?"

Preston slowly raised his head. "No, not really. We've just been kinda on our own. I guess you could say it's me, but…what am I?" he ended.

"A survivor. A fighter. That's what you are," I reassured him. "Anyone that's left: that's what we all are. And don't let anyone tell you any differently. Now, I don't know what we can offer you, but what we can, we will. You guys are armed, it looks like. You got food, water, all that?"

"Yeah, as much as we can ever muster," Preston replied, still shell-shocked. "We don't go out much by day anymore of course, but we saw that blast, and had to go out and see what happened. Then we saw you guys approaching.

"We haven't really left the university since…," he trailed off. "Well," he stuttered, "we thought it was maybe '38 or 39. But…'42…" He shook his head. "I guess our math was wrong. Most of us aren't from here; we're from Richview Middle School. East of here.

"We were hiding for a long time. A *long* time. We ran out of supplies and decided it would be best to find a bigger campus for more resources…and some adults to protect us. So, we moved over here. There were still some college students here that had grown up. Some are still with us," he motioned around. A few of the older refugees nodded their heads or raised their hands.

Middle schoolers. I couldn't believe it. Middle schoolers, forced to take refuge for sixteen years. That would explain why some of them looked to be in their thirties. Doing the math, that made sense: the ones older than those would have been in high school or even here at APU.

"Many of the previous students left, couldn't stay here anymore. Some branched out east towards the coast. Some ran off to try and find the military and join up. We just didn't feel safe leaving."

Bassett stepped forward and walked up to Preston. "I know days can seem like months in here, and vice versa," he said, laying a hand on his shoulder. You guys have done a great job just staying alive. You're to be commended. Now let's find out how we can keep the pace and build on what we got, yeah?"

Preston brought himself to nod.

"Yeah," Bassett agreed with himself, meeting all of their eyes.

I scanned through the refugees of varying ages. Here I was: Sergeant of a rag-tag army, and yet, no matter how you sliced it, so many of them were my rankless equals. No insignia, no title, no category…but my contemporaries still.

•   •   •   •   •

It was dark now. The dim lights of the campus clicked on. I looked at my watch. 1752. The gorgons were sure to be coming out soon, if they weren't out there already.

Why they were stuck in this little hall, when it was such a sprawling campus filled with various larger buildings, was beyond me. But they probably didn't choose it, and most likely had no other choice than the one nearest them to flee to. It certainly had far less space than the Morgan University Center to its west, which had a cafeteria, plenty of food options, and far more room. But such is life and fate. I wondered how many times they had ever dared to venture out in search of greener pastures, retreating out of fear.

We strode in farther, slowly, quietly; not sure what to make of this makeshift hovel. Behind us, two refugees silently sealed off the doors and moved some large mat-covered chair racks in the way. How they got those over here without making so much as a peep is beyond me. But then again, they had at least three years to do it judging by what year they thought it was.

On every side of the lobby there were erected panels, fastened to the walls, comprised of soundproofing and acoustic foam. Short of a giant voiceover booth, this minimized the reflective surfaces and surely cut down echoing noises and conversation. I saw now how these clever folks survived. Doubtless they ransacked the university audio department and most likely local music stores too.

This tiny, little one-hundred-twenty-foot building in the middle of nowhere. A sad, ramshackle old crumbling hall housing eighty people sheltering in place. *These* were definitely people Bassett could call kids. Prepubescents forced suddenly to be grown-ups, stuffed away in here for years, in various rooms across three floors, and awaiting deliverance; gathering supplies and holing up; avoiding the ever-present threat of annihilation. Amazing. Tragic. At least they got to live above ground though.

We were led to a classroom, room 302. Looking up I could see that many of them were all roughly the same age, with a few notable exceptions. The four of us were sitting before them: it felt strangely like some kind of inquest, with the lot of them scattered at various heights on mounds of random belongings and caches of supplies. On the way to the room there were several smaller rooms in similar states of disarrayed stockpiling. Frankly, it was remarkable how much they had gathered and maintained.

The hall had everything they would need to survive. Internet. Washing machines. Kitchen. Several rooms to hide in. Electronics, wash basins, light plastic plates that wouldn't sound off when they collided. Separate quarters for privacy. Ping-pong tables. Bathrooms and showers. Beds and couches and a horde of blankets. There were fridges and small coolers and portable warmers. There were television sets with makeshift antennas hoping for a signal, with one of the refugees posted up and monitoring it.

But everywhere you looked, the windows were boarded up and they had lamps stationed in various spots throughout. There was no natural sunlight allowed. It was cheerless, altogether gloomy and utterly devoid of freedom.

At various places throughout, virtually everything had a thin film of yellow dust. It was not pollen; though one might suspect that from the surrounding foliage and trees. Besides, it was winter. No: it was all dust from the EMP blast that had made its way through the ventilation system.

Hard to breathe as it must be, they were ready to talk, and more importantly, to ask questions and listen.

One of the refugees brought a portable electric warmer over to us.

"As you guys probably know, these things have been here for a while," Bassett began. The group nodded. "They came in '26, and, well, now there are a lot more of them, all over the globe. We four are part of a Blockade a little over two miles from here. That's where we all live now: underground. There are hundreds of Blockades still left, at least in the states. Don't know about the rest of the world because international communications are sketchy."

"My name is Joseph Bassett." *So, it's Joseph,* I thought, as I munched on dried prunes from my rations. They weren't super sweet, but they were enough. "My associate Allison Trudy and I were stationed in Alpharetta. About two years ago we came across the first of several small gems – we call them amulets – that were eventually discovered all around the globe. They're small in size, and, well, they look like this." He fished in his pocket, and pulled one out. Probably the same one Rutty and I were carrying the day before, holding it up before them.

There was a moment of awe. It was painfully obvious that many of them were clearly pinning their hopes to that which Bassett now held aloft before their eyes.

"This here is just one of them. Discovered south of here by a soldier from our Blockade named Markus Jentzen." Bassett looked at it too. "Over time, humanity began to discover these little buggers throughout the planet. They're comprised of a few elements, some of which don't appear on the periodic charts. Traces of silicate, iron and nickel substrates, but also some others, and we haven't yet identified them. Anyway, they have some astonishing acoustical attributes. When harnessed and focused precisely, audio waves become amplified through them, and escalated to incredibly high values. We think that these came with them to protect them somehow, kinda like, helping them to depressurize or something on their way here. We think they actually reverse-engineered them to shield them against the very thing that we were just able to use against them, which you guys saw."

"The blast wave a few hours ago," breathed a youngish girl with a big scarf around her neck. "You mean that blast, right?"

"Precisely," said Bassett. "The gorgons didn't like it much. Sent them screaming and flailing through the air, and they all took off west."

"Gorgons?" asked another boy, younger than the rest and hunched up against a similar-looking larger man. He was clearly not college-age. "Is that what you call the monsters?"

"Uh, yeah," said Trudy. "See, we call them that because that's what they are: they freeze you somehow with a kind of telepathy or chemical something or other, and then they go in for the kill. Ever read about Medusa, kid?"

"Yeah," the kid replied.

"What's your name?"

"Oliver."

"How old are you, Oliver?"

"Eight."

Eight. Good Lord, I thought. Another baby someone dared to have in the wake of the invasion. Another baby crying shrill cries to attract nearby gorgons. Scary.

"Is this your brother?" Trudy asked, motioning to the older of the two.

"Yep, this is my brother Ro. It's short for Roland."

"Well, Oliver and Ro," she continued, "it's nice to meet you. And we're glad you're okay. Yeah, they're gorgs, that's what we call them, and their time is up. We found a way to drive them off, and we're kinda hoping it's the first step to cleaning house."

Oliver smiled faintly. I liked him.

"There are a lot of us, Oliver," Rutty broke in. "Some six hundred Blockades, all equipped with military equipment, computers, guns, ammo, high tech, as much as we can snatch during the day and as much as we can arrange during the night, like you. We're holed up on the other side of the Cumberland River, and we're out on patrol for food, supplies and survivors. This is the first time we've been up here at the university in years."

"We've got a good store of supplies here," Roland said. "Had a lot of good luck being stranded at a university with a working cafeteria and plenty of frozen food. The ammo and guns we had to steal."

At that it seemed like his face washed in a pang of guilt. *Survival, man. Don't worry about it.*

"But all of us," he continued, "have been here for a while. Had no idea it was 2042." He shook his head.

"I see you have a few TV's," Bassett said. "You haven't seen any news or broadcasts?"

"Nope," Roland said. "Well, nothing of consequence. The occasional patchy signal comes through, but since the networks went down, it's been a piece of work trying to find out anything. We learned to head out during day only by trial and error, and summertime especially, because it sounds like they don't like the heat."

Bassett and I nodded.

"Yeah, they don't," Trudy answered. "That's why that blast was the perfect combo of heat and sound that knocked them on their gorgon asses. Oh, sorry – can I say 'asses'?"

Oliver giggled.

"President Graham is still president, by the way," said Bassett. "And, if any of you know your politics, presidents serve one term of four years, two terms at best. She was elected in 2028. I know some of you weren't even born yet," here he looked at Oliver, "but for those who were, you know she's been in office for far longer than any elected official should be. But she's still there. And there are international leaders who have survived as well. We'll see her now and then, and we know she's alive and still working with the military, or what's left of it. There are top scientists working round the clock in underground bunkers just like our own Blockade south of here, working on solutions. And we have powerful computers trying to find ways to beat them. And we will beat them."

It just occurred to me that the Beast had been working hard all this time on finding a solution. But the EMP begged the question: had it already cracked the code? Was this it? Or would there be more? Is the Beast what figured out the EMP in the first place?

My thoughts were cut short; all of ours were. We all heard it. A swooping noise gusted in the space above Harvill Hall, and a feeling of dread fell upon our hearts. We could hear our hearts beat for a few moments as we stopped and listened. Then another, and another.

My hand instinctively went to my pocket for my sippy as we all looked up. I looked at Oliver, and the poor little guy looked so disappointed. But he was obviously used to all of this, and that was eerie to see. This was a daily occurrence for him. I don't know how close they ever got to being under attack, but his eyes were darting annoyedly back and forth across the ceiling as he subconsciously leaned into Roland's protective embrace.

All this time we had removed our headsets and guns, and they were sitting beside us. I picked mine up and breathed into the mic without donning it, "Command, we have contact. Harvill Hall, APSU." I couldn't make out the reply; I didn't have time. There were a few more swoops overhead. Something was racing through the sky above the university, and it was shrieking.

We all listened. The shrieking sounded at first like bottle rockets, and then coalesced into a haunting dissonance; the harsh unmusicality of it grated against us. I could feel my goosebumps rise. All of this meant only one thing. They were back. And it sounded like more of them.

Without a sound, all eighty of the refugees began to move. A silent opera played out as they methodically, emotionlessly got up and began to migrate out of the room, to various stations and assigned positions, grabbing weapons, grabbing supplies, collecting valuables, donning sneakers they had cast off, etc. But they were all expressionless, all robotic in their motions. Each of them had rehearsed in repetitive orchestral drills just what to do in such a scenario, and they had no doubt done this a thousand times before in their captivity. They were used to this, and it was just another event in their daily routine.

It was both hauntingly beautiful and impressive to watch. But depressing. These poor zombies ambled slowly through the room, mechanical, resigned to their curse that gave them only one thing to do: *survive*. They were so very different from who we were and where we were; but so very similar as well.

We moved back to the lobby.

Bassett put his finger to his lips and then slowly moved toward the main door that we had entered through earlier. There were a few peepholes interspersed in the plywood along the wall, and he motioned for me to head over with him. We arched our legs out silently in front of us, toes first, threading our way between the refugee motion, and reached the peepholes.

I could see them. First one, then another gorgon moving at various speeds over the campus. Most of them were higher up, seeking places to alight upon. After all, that's how they usually operated.

If you've ever seen a shark attacking a seal, it's a sight to behold. I used to watch Animal Planet when there was still cable. I saw so many instances of sharks feeding. Beautiful, breathtaking, and downright tragic if you were a seal. Floating there, comfortable, relaxed, at peace with the world, when all of the sudden, the seal was thrown out of the water by the attack from below. A great white begins its stealthy hunt far below the ripples of the surface.

Completely undetectable by the seal, it goes unnoticed…until it's time to strike.

A horrifying geyser of dark grey, white and red would erupt out of the water as the shark would fly out of the wake with its prey enclosed within its jaws. And then, it was over. Both would disappear under angry foam, and only one would emerge.

Gorgons were the same. They just weren't in the water. They liked to descend from above, at unawares, and then catch you. You were nothing more than a seal to a gorgon, and only one would emerge.

If I hadn't been thinking so much about sharks and nature documentaries, I might have seen it sooner. One of them suddenly appeared immediately outside my peephole, and I was the unfortunate and unlucky sap who had to be right in its line of view. The chills ran down my spine as I jerked my head to the side, out of the peephole circle. I didn't know if it was still there, and I couldn't afford to turn my neck to Bassett. He was unresponsive, so I don't know if he saw it; he appeared to be still looking out, staring through his own.

I held my breath, and I heard every pound of my heart. I heard the sniffing again.

I closed my mouth.

Please don't like dried prunes, I thought to myself, and offered a quick hope upwards that there were no berserkers out there.

The sniffing continued. I could see the dim light from outside filtering through the peephole. A shadow crossed in front of it, flickering with movement.

More sniffing.

In my peripheral I could see Rutty a little farther down against another window. He was flanked by a few refugees. My face was mashed against the wall, as I didn't want to make any other movement, and didn't want to turn it.

He looked at me. It was a strange replay of the night before.
I swear he was mouthing "Come on!" as I was shaking my
head. Less than twenty-four hours had passed, yet here we
were again, hunted by gorgons and hemmed in a narrow
place.

Sniffing.

A wave of anger passed over me. These freaking
aliens. I was tired of running. My gun was cocked – always
was – but I wasn't about to move.

The crowd of refugees were almost in their positions,
and I couldn't see where anyone was or what they were
doing all throughout the building, but across from me in the
lobby, there was one little girl sitting on a thick-armed chair,
seemingly oblivious to the macabre threat looming just
outside. *Obviously,* I thought to myself, *she too had been
born after the assault.* How anyone could have a baby with
all that crying, I had no idea. Having kids post-invasion was
just asking for trouble. But human beings do things for
comfort, especially in times of war. And in such times,
perhaps a baby, life springing from death, was the comfort
they needed. And perhaps she, like Oliver, had been
sheltered in one of the many inner rooms of Harvill Hall,
closed off from the noise and the windows and the
connection to the outside world. Perhaps this was even her
first time in this lobby.

More sniffing. Cold mist coming through the
peephole.

Then it struck me. If I hadn't known better, I would
say the little girl was humming to herself: just with no notes.
She had been taught to hum without actually humming. The
little girl clutched a tiny teddy bear to her chest and sat there,
whimsically flicking her short legs back and forth. I
wondered who her parents were. How long had she been in
here? Had she ever been told about the real threat just
outside these walls? I hoped not. *Ignorance is bliss.*

I cleared my vision, and turned my head back to the peephole, waiting.

After a few minutes, the flickering shadow was gone. The gorgon must have given up and floated away. No sign of movement. I slowly let out my breath. My heart began to slow. I dared to slide my head back into view of the peephole. It wasn't very big, maybe the size of a quarter, but there was only a foot of perimeter between me and sudden death outside. Twelve inches of separation didn't give me much comfort.

I could still see them fluttering about outside. The sniffing had abated, and there were no more close calls. The density of them was disturbing, and I found equally disturbing the notion that I found their movement simultaneously somber and beautiful: as if they were mindless ghostly drones processing toward a funeral of their own. They were all heading east and north now, over our heads, fanning out across Clarksville. I wondered how far north they were going, where the Red River splits off the Cumberland and winds out east.

Bassett and I watched them for a good ten minutes to ensure they were retreating, and didn't leave until the last one had been sighted floating away.

It was so quiet. As I watched them disperse over our heads, I felt a swell of curiosity for the one who had been caught, and was now in confinement. Did the gorgons know him? Would their community miss him? Were they looking for him? I wondered how old each of them was. They were definitely organic lifeforms, and predators at that. But where did they come from? How long would they stay? Why couldn't they just move on to another tiny ball in space? Or had they consumed every natural resource on all the others as well, and soon they'd leave ours a desolate wasteland too?

I shook my head and looked back over at the little girl. She was sleeping soundly in her chair. She had no idea.

My heart sank. Not at the little girl: at least she was sleeping in peace. Why did I actually think the EMP had done any damage? How were there so many of them out there? I suppose it was wishing upon a star that that pulse had driven them off for good.

For now, though, they were gone.

But it was still night, and I missed our Blockade gun towers more than ever.

•   •   •   •   •

Everyone retreated back to roughly where they were when we found them. No more was said, just silent understandings between them. A young woman wordlessly led the four of us to an unoccupied bedroom of the building where we could bunk up, upstairs opposite the co-ed bathroom. She beckoned us to the four bunks inside, and then left without a word, offering a meek smile. It felt oddly like some bed and breakfast with a ghostly host. She had a light headdress on, and a big sweater. It was only 1938 hours, but it was now pitch-black outside, or, at least it would be if I could see it: the windows were boarded up in here as well. The cold, collective residual mist from the gorgons could still be seen (and felt) outside, and a watch was posted. There were rugged and poorly dressed sentinels on each level at the ends of the corridors, armed and posting guard.

It was a foregone conclusion that these people preferred to sleep away the night, and ride out the storm. Looked like that's just what they were about to do. I watched another young woman scoop up the baby girl from the lobby chair, and lead her to another room upstairs. Bassett headed off to the bathroom, leaving Trudy with

Rutty and me. She had removed her vest and pack and was sitting in camo pants and a tank top. Her pig tail bands had been removed, and now her hair fell lightly, messily down the sides of her face. I could just make out the traces of sweat lining her brow and sides of her head. Must have come from while we were waiting out the assault.

We looked at her. She was looking at her gun, and finally giggled lightly, shaking her head. "It's a strange thing, ya know? Look at this thing," she said, holding up her powerful XM5 rifle. "I can't even use it. I love target practice, love shooting. The exhilaration of it. The bang bang bang," she said, simulating sharp movement. "But we can't even use them, or we'll draw them to us. How long would we have lasted, had they broken in? A few minutes. Enough for a sippy, I guess," she smirked.

I offered a faint smile back, and nodded.

Rutty chirped up. Good old Rutty. "Well, enough time to cram it down one of their throats, maybe, as long as you could work by feel and keep your eyes shut, ha! I'd just as soon modify my piece and put a silencer on it, or just get an air rifle and shoot out sippy pellets. Take 'em down that way with a lot less noise." His smile faded. "Still a lotta noise though," he realized to himself.

"What did you used to shoot, Trudy?" I asked her.

"Birds, mostly. Waterfowl, little chippers in the reeds southeast. I'd give anything to go back there with my dad and do some shooting again."

"Where is he? Is he…?" I didn't want to finish the question.

"I think so. I don't know. He and my mom were out on vacation when they all activated, ya know? We were on the phone with them; they were watching it all unfold too. He told me that he loved us…and that he'd find us."

I paused. "Us?"

"Me, Nick and Badger. My two older brothers." She just looked at me. She didn't have to say a word.

"I'm sorry, Trudy."

Her expression didn't change.

"Hey, *que será, será,* right? I mean, we all lost somebody. No sense rehashing it." She was still looking at me.

"How did they die?"

Rutty turned to me as if he disapproved of the question.

Trudy kept my gaze, and clenched her jaw, moving her lips around in irritated restraint. Her eyes eventually fell. "Dad used to take us all shooting. Nick was the best. He and Badge were always competing. Badge couldn't take losing to Nick, but ya know, that's how brothers are. They all taught me to shoot. Took me under their wing." She paused in memory. "I'll never forget the day I brought home my first quail and showed mom. *That* was something." She smiled.

We smiled back in support.

Big long sigh. Pause. "The day the gorgs went live, we didn't know what to do." She looked up, past us, looking at the various refugees slowly moving past us down the corridor, scanning them as if to ensure they weren't eavesdropping. "We ran, of course. But they go fast. I was only eight, but I was fast for my age. My brothers ran behind me, and we made for a Subway."

I remembered then her hesitation to approach the sandwich shop we had found.

Her head was down as she continued. "We were almost there. I swear the bros were making a human shield over me because they were right on my tail, keeping pace. We ran. Aaaand, we ran. Aaaaaaaaaand…we ran. I swear that run would never end. We made it, I don't know how, but we made it. I tripped once, but Badge helped me back up and I still got in. And then, I just…" she trailed off.

Just then Bassett rejoined us. Trudy looked up at him. "I just…turned around, and," she paused, "they were gone."

Bassett, realizing what was happening, crouched down slowly and respectfully, meeting her gaze. He sat next to us on the bunk. Three of us, joined together, taking in this tale of sorrow from our partner, all alone across from us on her own bunk. Trudy, beautiful Allison Trudy, recounting the day she lost everything.

"Badge had turned around," she breathed. "You don't turn around. You *don't…turn… around… you just… don't… look,*" she painfully breathed out, and with each breath, her lip quivered, and her eyes filled with tears. She seemed to be reciting from rote memory what she had been so forcefully taught afterwards, perhaps wishing, through some pained pronouncement, that she could have implanted that knowledge posthumously into her lost brother. I suddenly remembered Jackson, who taught me not to look directly at gorgons.

"You just don't look," she whispered, looking straight at me. "Badge looked." She sighed. "Aaaand, that's when Nick went back for him. Badge was his kid brother after all, so why wouldn't he go? Why shouldn't he go? We didn't know." Her head drooped again. "We just didn't know," she mouthed with a thousand-yard stare into nothingness. A single tear ran down her left cheek.

I realized now that Allison Trudy had perhaps never told that story before. I felt like a prick for inviting it out of her. I didn't need to hear anything else. I didn't need to hear what slow death each of her brothers met with, and how she had to steel herself to remain in that Subway joint for an eternity, washing the sight and memory of her brothers being eaten out of her mind. Fiercely rocking back and forth with her fingers in her ears, whispering assurances to herself, her eyes sealed tightly shut to quiet the macabre violence just outside that door.

She didn't say how long she stayed there. She didn't say what fear or hunger drove her out, or how long she had wandered from place to place, or how she had met up with Bassett in some Blockade far away. She didn't say how she had made it out of Alpharetta. But she said plenty. She had my pity.

"Trudy," I reached out.

Allison Trudy quickly wiped away her tear and walked out, around the corner, shuffling off toward the restrooms. Rutty looked at me. "You shouldn't have asked."

"I thought she wanted to get it out. How could I know?"

Rutty looked away. "You shouldn't have asked."

I looked back towards Bassett. His eyes followed Trudy down the hall.

I shouldn't have asked.

•   •   •   •   •

I had hoped not to bump into Trudy on the way to the bathroom, but I guessed she was still in there. I just needed to hit the bathroom before hitting the hay. It would be a long day tomorrow, and we had to get out and see what we could bring back. We also had to determine if any of these people were coming back with us. There was no way we could house all of them, and they seemed to be plenty armed and equipped without us.

We'd leave that up to Command.

I finished up and headed out from the bathroom back to our room. Nearly bumped into Trudy as she was coming out of her bathroom. Her eyes looked tired. She had been quiet crying, that much was clear.

"Trudy, I'm-" I started.

"Shut up. Don't worry about it," she faintly smiled. "I hadn't told my story to anyone yet. Needed to get it out and have a good cry, I guess. It's all good." She started to turn away but stopped and turned back to me, "And…call me Allison. I never liked 'Trudy' anyway."

"How about 'Ally'?" I countered with a smile.

She didn't answer, but she smiled back.

Nice to meet you, Ally.

We walked leisurely back to our bunks. "Ya know," she said wistfully, "you and Rutty are kinda cute. Nice to be stationed with some guys around my age again." She smiled over at me. "Hope maybe this time I can make some friendships that actually last."

Wow, invite extended.

"Yeah, me too."

•　　•　　•　　•　　•

We were almost back to our room. I checked my watch: 2016. We passed a few noiseless rooms with formless humps swaddled under thin blankets in each one. The doors were all propped open. At some point or another the security badge readers on each door had been disabled, allowing free entry and exit from each room. That at least made it easier to get in and out without having to swipe a college ID card.

It was weird, this hall: eerie, but peaceful, after a fashion. Like an apocalyptic dorm room. The sound of faint snoring could be heard, and I faintly detected the scent of urine. Hey, it wasn't the Hilton.

There were some occasional coughs emanating from various points of the building. That EMP had sent stuff all over, into all of our lungs, and we were just trying to get it all out of our system.

For me, this hall was too naked, too exposed, and didn't have a nice, friendly ring of guns overhead. If those gorgons wanted to join together and bust in here, there wasn't really anything stopping them. There would be a valiant last stand, and then, for these folks, night would always be.

I missed our gun towers. My thoughts suddenly went to Ferro, Pettijohn and Wilkes, and wondered how they were faring southwest of our Blockade. Then with a shudder I realized that the EMP earlier today sent all those gorgons screaming into the western sky, and I wondered if our guys got caught in the crossfire of that horde of extra pissed-off aliens. I wondered about Markus again. All I could do was wish them a feeble good luck from afar. I didn't know them too well, but I had dated Ferro off and on. And Pettijohn was a big guy, man. I had a quick image of Pettijohn as a running back muscling his way through a pile of gorgon defenders for a touchdown. I hoped they would make it back. I was pretty sure we wouldn't be back for the memorial for Hickey and Dupre. We were pretty far away with a big bridge to cross. And that was a lot of gorgons we just saw out there in the night sky.

I felt Ally's shoulder brush up against mine as we slowly paced back to our bunk at the far end. "How long you been part of patrol?" I asked her.

"Six years."

"Right when you turned eighteen then?" I remembered that she was just a year older than I. "Couldn't wait, huh?"

"No, I really couldn't," she agreed. She put her hands in her pockets as she walked. "I guess…I guess you put together wanting to shoot, with losing my brothers, with not knowing where my parents are, and you get one angry vengeful lady."

"Well, nothing wrong with that. But where did the science team come into play if you were so into guns and shooting? When did you get to put your gun down and learn all about," here I playfully mocked her, *"borosilicate glass and simple reflection technology?"* I gave her a gentle elbow nudge. I could smell her mint lip balm as her lip curled up at my tease.

"Don't get cocky, dude. Science isn't something I chose. My dad is a scientist. Maybe I didn't mention that. You can have two interests, ya know. I liked guns, sure. But I like science too. So, at our own Blockade I got to take on patrol *and* tech."

"Oh, so, you've been doing double shifts."

She looked at me sidelong, and I could see a bit of carefree crawling back into the creases around her mouth as we reached our quad and the other guys.

"Something like that," she said.

Rutty was sitting on the same bunk still, whoever would eventually claim it. Bassett was sitting on the lower bunk opposite, and he had the little girl I had seen earlier on his lap. Her young mom was beside her, smiling. Bassett was reading a tiny storybook to her.

For whatever reason this little girl, who only a short time ago was sleeping on the lobby chair, was now wide awake. I was no parent, but I vaguely remember my own parents telling me stories about how I used to frequently get up and ask for water, treats, food, or a story. Anything to not have to go to sleep. Glad to see I wasn't the only anomaly.

Ally and I stopped at the entrance, and I propped my elbow up on a corner of the bunk Rutty was on. Bassett continued, "*Well, that mother, she got older. She got older and older and older. One day she called up her son and said, "You'd better come see me because I'm very old and sick." So, her son came to see her. When he came in the door, she tried to sing the song. She sang: I'll love you forever, I'll like you for always... But she couldn't finish because she was too old and sick. The son went to his mother. He picked her up and rocked her back and forth, back and forth, back and forth. And he sang this song: I'll love you forever, I'll like you for always, as long as I'm living my Mommy you'll be. When the son came home that night, he stood for a long time at the top of the stairs. Then he went into the room where his very new baby daughter was sleeping. He picked her up in his arms and very slowly rocked her back and forth, back and forth, back and forth. And while he rocked her, he sang: I'll love you forever, I'll like you for always, As long as I'm living my baby you'll be.*"

The little girl yawned.

"Alright, Sweepea, that's all you're gonna get tonight, alright?"

The girl silently nodded. It was a respectful act, but I couldn't help but notice again how trained this poor young girl was at keeping her voice from the world. I wondered what her parents had to tell her to keep her that way, and when she would ever be allowed to unmute herself.

The young mom mouthed "thank you" to Bassett, and he nodded back to her with a grin, waving her off with a *no problem* palm of the hand. The mother picked up her daughter and propped her on one hip as they walked back to their own bunk.

"Read me a story, Papa," Rutty jested.

"Ha! You wish," Bassett jabbed back. "I ain't *that* old."

Ally sat next to him, and I sat next to Rutty, putting my arm around him and giving him a quick squeeze. I was sensitive to anything suggesting having a brother, so I was careful to glance over at Ally and make sure she didn't see it. She was looking at the floor, unmoved.

As much as I was in command, that was just a formality. Bassett seemed to know more about what he was doing, and I didn't really care much anymore about chain of command. He was obviously part of a much larger plan with undulating reverberations being most likely felt in every Blockade with communications equipment right about now…and I hadn't known a thing about it or been briefed on it in advance. So, I didn't need to pull rank. In any event, he had been doing some thinking.

He briefly checked his watch. "It's nearly 2100 hours. Tomorrow we're gonna have to set out early," he started. "I think we should get this day behind us. Gotta see what we can grab tomorrow, and then head back. I hate leaving this group of refugees behind, but for now that's what it's got to remain: a station we can draw upon. We're gonna have to leave one of our headsets here. They have chargers for it…but someone's going to need to hear from us and we're going to need to hear back. Any volunteers?"

Rutty raised his hand.

"It'll mean you'll be going in sonically blind, Rut," Bassett clarified.

"I know, it's all good, they need it, they can have mine," Rutty offered.

Good ol' Rutty.

Bassett sighed. "OK, well, we'll take care of that in the morning. I figure Preston might be our point man on that. But let's get on and get back. I've been in touch with Command, and they've asked something pretty incredible of me…something I don't think any of you are gonna like. I know I don't."

I gazed at him curiously. "Oh?"

"Yeah. Well, there's no easy way to say this, so I'll just get it out there." His eyes met ours, and he took a deep breath. "Command wants us to lojack a gorgon."

My eyebrows went up. Complete silence. Even the sound of snoring stopped, as if all ears were bending towards us in that far corner. My cheek flinched. I looked over at Ally. All of this time, she had remained looking at the floor. I wondered if she'd heard it.

The night was coming, and this new plan was outrageous. There didn't seem to be much more to say, either by me or the rest of my team. We were all filled with incredulity, even Bassett. It was a long time before there were words again.

I looked around at all of us: so alone, and so confused.

6 | DIALOGUES

There was nothing more to do except to lie down and take it all in. All of us were brooding on this new assignment: not knowing how in the world we were supposed to surgically insert a tracker into a gorgon without summoning a whole murder of them upon us. *Murder.* How appropriate. Some animals travel in flocks. Some in herds. Some in droves. Some in schools. Gorgons travel in murders, just like scavenger crows.

And we were now going to have to subdue a rogue gorgon and put a tracker in it.

Ally was still staring at the floor. I didn't know if she was lost in the memory of her brothers, or if she had even heard what Bassett had said. She appeared unphased.

Bassett looked at each of us and said "I know this is crappy news. But Command wants what Command needs, right? They say this may tell us something of their movement, as well as what the EMP did to them *and* what they're doing out there in the ocean."

"Bassett," I began, "I know you guys have some experience with this, but how are we supposed to find one without blindly walking into a nest or randomly encountering a rogue like we did earlier today? They're on the move all the time, usually in droves." Not droves. *Murders.*

"Correct. I was thinking of the rogue. And, if we're lucky, we'll find another one tomorrow. But it won't be through searching. We're going to have to draw one to us."

"Draw one to us?" Rutty asked. "And just how-" he stopped short. His jaw dropped. "Oh man. They want one of us to act as *bait.*"

I turned sharply back to Bassett. "No way. Command wouldn't ask us to do that. Stone wouldn't. No way, Bassett."

Bassett paused. "Stone issued the directive. He gave the order."

I was incredulous. No freaking way Stone gave that order. My eyes narrowed as I studied Bassett. "I don't believe you. We're not expendable, and there's no way in hell Captain Stone would throw even one of us to the wolves."

"I said you weren't going to like it. I don't either. But we're thrown to the wolves every single time we leave the Launch, Jet. Whether we go to them, or they come to us, we're in amongst wolves. Always have been."

Impossible, I thought to myself. *How could Stone do this?* I wondered what he was thinking back there all cozied up in Command while we were out here trying to leash his rabid dog for him. There's no way he just untethered his care for us. He'd been out on patrols as well. He'd seen it all. He knew what we faced out here.

"Now," Bassett slowly stated, "there's one more thing too, Shipley. What we're about to do is potentially big. It has potentially the biggest ramifications on the rest of our mission, and could maybe even alter the future for all of us. So I need you to appreciate where they're coming from."

Now he was just being patronizing again. Just when I was starting to like him. That last note had an air of superiority: the same kind I registered when I first met him.

"Oh? And just what is that?"

Bassett stared at me solemnly.

"I just got off with Command. They've informed me," here he looked over at Rutty as this affected him too, "you've been relieved of your command of this unit. Stone has put me in charge of this mission."

I froze, and my jaw clenched at him. I don't know how long we sat there staring at each other. I ground my teeth together. "Well, sounds like you played this hand pretty well too, Joe," I murmured at him with contempt.

"Jet…," he started to plead.

I held up my hand. With a shake of my head and a check in my gut, I got up and walked out of the room. I could feel Rutty start to come after me, but for some reason, he stayed. If he wanted to give Bassett – and effectively, Stone – a piece of his own mind, that was his affair.

For me, I needed space. I grabbed my rifle and headset and walked out.

•　　•　　•　　•　　•

The only thing worse than being angry with someone is having nowhere to go to get away from the person that you're angry with.

Just when I thought I liked him. I kept shaking my head. I know I said I didn't care about rank. But voluntarily stepping aside provisionally to make room for one more knowledgeable about the situation is one thing. Being relieved of command in advance of a suicide mission is something entirely different, and was a sore blow to my pride. I had no idea what Command was up to, but this was highly suspicious and dubious.

I meandered slowly toward the classroom we had all met in earlier. In nearly every room along the way, I casually took stock of the sleeping denizens of this retrofit bomb shelter. It was entirely apocalyptic in nature: a ramshackle hodge-podge of collected artifacts, supposed comforts, loosely organized and wholly insufficient. Granted, there was human company here, and perhaps there was more warmth in this place without the superimposed realization that in the Blockades with our gun towers above we were tiny islands on the very frontier of war; but overall, it was sorely lacking in a feeling of security. Plywood barriers are a poor substitute for gun towers.

I shut the light off as I walked in. All alone there in the dark, I was about to pull out a chemlight and snap it. I was suddenly aware of a tiny Christmas tree in the corner of the room, set there at some point by hands that still held hope. It remained lit in defiance of the dark, just sitting there, quietly emitting peace and hope.

We had always celebrated Christmas, informally, but it had been a long time since I'd seen a decorated tree. This one had all the little twinkly lights. A tiny artificial tree set in a pot no larger than two feet high, on a tiny table in an obscure corner of a room in an out-of-the-way pocket of an aging building in the middle of nowhere.

I walked over in the dark, and sat down at one of the tables in the blackness, close to the tree, my face lit by the colorful, festive glow of red, blue and green. All was quiet.

From the Christmas caroling that lived on in my memory from what seemed ages before, the gentle, gracious words to *Silent Night* began scrolling through my head.

It was all quiet in here. I couldn't hear any gorgons. I couldn't hear any humans. I couldn't hear any *anything* except my own thoughts racing, and that was what I needed, there, lit by the sacredness of that quiet, still, picturesque tree. How I wished for a fleeting moment to wake up on Christmas morning to the sounds of laughter, of joy, of *family.* I missed Dad. I missed Mom. I missed Sissy. I choked back a tear as I just let the lights suck me into a vortex of memories, and spit me back out on the other side into a world full of gorgons.

Then the anger took over.

Stone. Bringing in Bassett. The unannounced EMP. Relieving me of command. Stone was in on all of it. And yet I sensed no change in his demeanor this morning. To my mind, we were always close. I called him "Dad" for crying out loud. I just couldn't shake a sense of profound betrayal.

Bringing Bassett here wasn't a big deal. We'd had exchange personnel before. And Ally came with him, so I was ok with forgiving that. But the EMP? I would have loved to have known about, and dangit, I deserved the courtesy of advance notice of my demotion directly from my "Dad." I wondered if he knew then, when he gave me that smile as we left his Blockade briefing.

A pronounced intake of breath followed by a beleaguered sigh welled up and out of my chest. I cracked my knuckles and just sat there thinking, staring at that freaking tree.

A shadow passed across the narrow window slit of the door outside, soon followed by the door itself opening. Rutty walked in. He flipped the light on.

Rutty looked around, scanning the room, his eyes adjusting to the light, and he spotted me. "Hey man."

"Hey," I said, uncrossing my arms and sitting up.

"Wasn't sure where to look," he grunted with a smile. "Lotsa rooms in this place. You can get lost in big campuses like this with or without a war."

"Yep," I shrugged.

He walked over to me with a halfhearted nod, acknowledging that this conversation sucked, and it wasn't why he was here. He looked around the large instruction room, unslung his gun and put it down on the table with a sigh. "Ya know, I never went to college. Never wanted to, really. Or, heck, I don't know that I even had a chance. But if I did, not sure I'd want to get stuck in all of this rat race anyway."

I didn't have anything to say, really.

Rutty gave up that line of thinking too, and finally came and sat down two seats away. I turned back to the tree. So did Rutty. "Makes you miss the old times, doesn't it?" he asked. "Man, I miss Christmas. Weird being stuck in a world full of gorgons with no 'fa la lalla la…'"

Stop reading my mind, Rutty.

"Remember the big house on that patrol where we found all those toys, and that huge chest?"

"No?" I said. That didn't ring a bell.

"Yeah – it had that massive toy chest and they had one of those Godzilla toys that you were so into back then. Remember that? You could press a button and it would shoot out its atomic breath or whatever you call it."

Suddenly I was three years younger and holding that Gozilla again. "Oh, man, oh, wow," I exclaimed slowly. Yes, I sure did remember that. "That was something else. Those parents sure splurged on those kids. That was a ridiculous toy chest," I said, laughing softly. "You could put a VW bug in that thing." Rutty laughed with me. "I wonder how long they got to play with those before everything went down."

"Yeah. It was like walking into an old Christmas morning in that house though: remember how mom and dad used to just *load* the tree underneath? Even with wrapped boxes that had no gifts, just so it would look like so much more?"

"Yeah, I remember that. They loved to show bounty. And…I think also to mess with us a little." That was a good memory, and I loved sharing it with Rutty.

We sat there alone in this vast college lecture hall. I briefly wondered if things ever settled down, would I pursue a college degree? Would things ever settle down? What degree would I even pursue anyway? I was a glorified grunt, really. All of that seemed wishful thinking, and all I really wanted right now was a little holiday spirit.

Rutty gave some time for all the nonsense to clear the air. "Look, buddy, I know all this sucks. I just wanted to say I'm sorry. I asked Bassett after you left if he knew about this before now too. He says he didn't. Take it or leave it. I honestly think he just got the order. I'm sorry you didn't."

I thought about it and exhaled loudly. "No," I began. "Broski…I don't think this is about Bassett at all. He strikes me as an entrenched war dog just following orders, and he seems to know what he's doing. I'll give him that. But look what's happened in a single day now that he's in the picture. The amulet. Losing two, maybe more, of our guys. The EMP. The demotion. Something's crazy with all this."

"Dude, no one's demoting you, it just sounds like Bassett's been moved to point on this one."

"I hear you. To me, that's still a demotion below some new guy who clearly likes to 'hold his cards close to his chest' a lot, while yours truly is being shown to my seat at the kids' table."

"Well then maybe you and I should put his name in the hat for the bait then," Rutty offered playfully. "I mean I know you don't want to serve up Trudy, and you love me too much."

I looked over at him.

"*Right?*" he asked nervously in jest.

"I love you too much, man," I assured him, with a laugh. "I won't be serving you up as bait. I have no idea how Command even wants us to do this. *Bait.* Good grief." I shook my head. So did Rutty.

"Ya know, in all my years with all this garbage, never once did I think Stone was dealing under the table." I stopped. "Crap, look at me. Now *I'm* the one talking in cards."

"Hey. A house of cards either stands or falls, man. And it ain't fallen yet, so…we just do what we do and go where we go and trust that we'll make it back each night for some more crappy eggs the next morning."

I couldn't help but laugh: that's what Rutty always gave me. Laughs. He was the younger brother I never thought I wanted; he reminded me a little bit of Sissy and a *lot* of dad; a little slice of home and family.

"Thanks buddy. I know it's early, but merry Christmas." I fished my sippy out of my pocket and handed it to him.

"Ah! Get that outta my face!" He slapped my hand away. Luckily, I had a tight grip on it, and it didn't go flying off into some far corner to be discovered by the little girl as candy on the floor. That would be truly awful.

What a world we lived in.

Rutty looked at his watch. "2142," he said. "We should hit the hay if we're gonna head out as early as Bassett thinks we're going to tomorrow. I don't know what kind of food these guys cook up but I sure hope it's good. Gotta get one last meal in me before I willingly surrender all my communication with this world."

"You okay with that? I mean, really?" I asked him. Giving up his headset would cripple him in terms of communications, and if we got separated, we wouldn't know where he was, and he wouldn't be able to tell us.

"Yeah, it's fine. For the cause, right?" He pounded his fist on his chest and made a "V" for victory. "These guys could use it, and I ain't never gone rogue yet, except for that one time in my hideout at the plant. Just," he paused, "let Trudy walk in front of me; that'll keep me *really* focused."

Sly dog.

He smiled and laughed, which turned into a yellow dust-laden cough, his lungs still clearing out the gunk from today.

"Man, you better take that sippy before I do you myself, bro," I laughed a threat his way. "You know her real name is Ally?"

"Ally Trudy? No joke?"

"Well, *Allison.*"

"Allison Trudy. Hmm. I like the sound of that. Cameron and Allison. Ally and Jet. Sounds nice," he said, walking towards the door. He winked.

My lips involuntarily curled up in a smile.

"Night, bro," he said. "See you back at the bunk. Get some shuteye soon. I'm gonna go connect with Preston and give this up, probably walk him through it a bit."

"Alright," I waved him off.

Rutty was almost out the door, and then popped back in. "Merry Christmas, man," he said.

I had already looked back at the tree and was hypnotized by the multicolored glow. "You too, buddy," I said wistfully, not looking back.

•   •   •   •   •

I stayed in there for another five or so minutes and then began a slow walk around the perimeter. I had my gun, I was pacing around the place, and occasionally I'd pass a room where some refugees were still awake and peering out of doors at me. All roughly my age or younger, all with the same disinterested and bland look of survival on their faces. Some waved. Most didn't.

The top floor of the building wasn't all that special: multiple rooms and closets, offices here and there. I walked down to the bottom level and visited the foyer again, slowly revisiting the dreaded peephole where I saw the gorgon on the other side.

I peered out into the night sky, and there was nothing. I waited for a bit to see if there was any movement. All was quiet outside and in, except for the occasional murmurs and sudden slight noises emanating from various places within the building as people either slept, or prepared to. All clear outside.

"There you are," came the low, gruff drawl behind me. My gut tightened and I blinked slowly, turning myself around. In a reflex, my jaw clenched.

"Bassett," I greeted him.

"Can we talk?" He went over and sat on one of the chairs in the lobby near where the little girl had been swinging her legs so carefree earlier. Bassett eyed me curiously.

I guess we're talking, I thought. I figured I should go first, so I could beat him to the punch.

"Listen," I started, "don't worry about the whole chain of command stuff, I get it." I held up a hand and sat down in a huff across from him, one seat down.

Bassett looked at me and exhaled heavily. "Jet, this wasn't my idea. And I know how you feel-"

"It's not a pissing match," I dismissed him.

His response was surprisingly brisk and alarmingly loud. "That's right, it ain't, Sergeant! I've been replaced dozens of times. Hell, Trudy practically replaced me, leapfrogging to Lieutenant. It just comes with the territory - and if I had to make the decision, I would have done the same dang thing."

I could feel the heat under my cheeks.

Bassett sighed, threw out his knuckles, and craned his neck like he was trying to work a boulder out of it. "Look, I-I just have some seniority in this area, and I guess that's just what Command needs right now. I know none of this makes sense yet, and you just met me but Jet, that's why I said I needed you to trust me on this."

I remained silent and just looked at him. "I said it was fine. Alright?"

Awkward silence.

Bassett got up and paced the floor for a minute, staring backwards up the hall away from me. I didn't look up at him.

"Ya know," he said with a stifled chuckle, "I'm fifty-two, and you remind me a lot of how I was at your age." He turned back toward me. "I'm old enough to be your father, for crying out loud. You may not like me, Jet, and I get that, but we're a lot alike. And we both want the same thing. We're just having to go about it in different ways now. I think Command is under pressure from the President, and this new thing we all have with the amulets, well…" he trailed off.

"What about the President?" I asked.

Bassett slowly walked over to me and sat back down. This time he picked the chair directly across from me.

"I'm not sure. But I know that the President has been talking to the Blockades directly. She was talking to ours in Alpharetta, right before I got my orders to come here. Man, I *liked* being home. *Georgia* is my home. But like you, I had to follow orders, and I was sent here by my own Command. I think the President and what's left of the military are working on something big, and I think these amulets are, frankly, the key. And that's why things seem to be moving a little fast right now."

"What's moving fast?"

"You want a list?" I swear he was going to start counting his fingers. "Trudy being rushed in science back home working on the masks. We then get shipped out up here. We're then sent out with you to uncharted territory across the Cumberland. We're asked to give up communications for one of our own. We're told to make ourselves bait. We're told to find and track a gorgon. I'm put in command. This is all happening a bit too fast for my taste too, believe it or not," he chuckled helplessly.

I'm so terribly sorry you had to be inconvenienced with taking over my command. Let me know if there's anything I can do to ease your suffering.

"I think that there's some new intel, either human or sigint, that has forced the hand of the upper echelons, and that we're simply being asked to keep pace. I don't know what it is. All I know is that I would have preferred to stay back on my home turf, and that's hundreds of miles away. This was not a power play; I want to assure you of that. I miss my wife, man."

I looked beyond him at the wall. I could feel him continuing to watch me, as if he were desperately awaiting sign off.

I swear an eternity passed. I coughed a bit from the yellow dust.

"Look, Bassett, I don't want a rift. If Command wants you, Command wants you. It's fine. I'll fall in line," I assured him as I turned my gaze to meet his. "I just hope we get somewhere fast with this tomorrow. Being thrown to the wolves is one thing. Being hand fed to them on a silver platter is another. I also don't like being kept in the dark, and that's happened twice now. So, I gotta know from the outset this time: what's your plan?"

"Honestly," he breathed, "I'm still working that out. I don't think I'm gonna get much sleep tonight. Part of that was spent wandering around here looking for you guys," he quietly laughed. "Rutty came back right after Trudy dropped off, and I thought I'd come find you and sort this out before the op tomorrow. It's already nearly 2300. I've modified some of our own GPS trackers. That's what I was doing while you two were out. None of us want to get within fifty feet of those things. Preston has some rubber bullets. Rutty's got his RPG shooter. My plan, if we can find a rogue, and even if not, is to bait one, lure it, and fire at it, knocking it out; that way we don't kill it. Then, why, we'll wait and see if there are any more of 'em. When it's all safe, well, we'll send in the lojack team. Low and slow, snipe n' dive for cover before it tries to do its thing."

Bassett sat back, casually picking at a splinter in the wooden arms of the chair. He was lost in thought, presumably playing back in his head the scenario he had just laid out for me. I didn't envy him for having to think this one through fully.

"Alright," I said, interested. "That still doesn't answer the question about the bait."

"Oh, that part's simple. Trudy volunteered." Bassett sniffed nonchalantly.

My heart sank.

No more words were exchanged, unless loud sighs count as words. Eventually we both made our way back up to our room. There were Trudy and Rutty, on their respective bunks, snoring away.

There was nothing more to do except to lie down and take it all in.

7 | BRIEFING

How did it come to this?

I couldn't believe it, and didn't want it to be true. Trudy. Ally. *Bait.* How could she volunteer for this, when we had lost so much already? Did she not have anything more to live for? She seemed so happy and carefree when I first met her: bubbly and daring. Now it seemed she was just daring and suicidal. I felt I had to talk her out of it. If anything, *I'd* be the bait.

It's incredibly hard to talk someone out of something when they're asleep. I couldn't wake her; we would all need to be up in a few hours. I was a cranky wake-up: I know how it feels. Less than twenty-four hours ago I was throwing pillows at Rutty. I didn't feel like instigating a pillow-fight with Ally: it felt like we were just getting to know – and like – each other.

It would have to wait until the morning.

In the dim light coming from the hallway, I saw Bassett place his boots under his bunk, plug in his headset to charge it, climb up to the top bunk, and lightly position himself on his side so as not to shake the bunk and wake Ally. Before long, the sound of snoring increased. We were all tired.

I was tired; but not quite ready to drift off to sleep. So many thoughts were pouring through my mind, and my heart was racing.

•   •   •   •   •

I woke to dim morning light filtering through a crack between the boarded-up windows. For a moment I forgot where I was, and half expected to look over and see Mom, Dad & Sissy's bunks. But no – that was yesterday. Ah! I remember. Harvill Hall. The refugees. The demotion. Ally's story. The Christmas tree. The ridiculous mission we were about to take on.

It was December 4th.

It was Go Time.

I suddenly had a coughing fit and turned over quickly to cough into the pillow. We were trained to do that to keep the noise down. As I laid with my face buried in the pillow, I remembered the rest from yesterday: meeting Bassett and Trudy, the riverbank, the heron, the EMP, and the disclosure.

Things were moving fast. Or, at least, they were about to.

The others woke up coughing too. Stupid EMP detritus. We all looked pretty comical: lying there with our faces buried in pillows retching our lungs out.

Rutty got up and didn't say good morning. He scratched his hair and sauntered off to pee. I looked at my watch. 0532. What was it with waking up earlier than home when you're out on patrol? We hadn't even set an alarm. I never understood that. *No rest for the weary,* I thought.

A middle-aged man must have passed Rutty in the hall, because he leaned in. "Hey, gang, I'm Jesse," he whispered. "Want some breakfast?" Then he smiled: much too unsettling for my taste, the time, or this predicament.

"Love some," Bassett replied, as I simultaneously grunted "Sure, thanks." We looked at each other. "Morning," I said to him.

"Morning, Jet," Bassett greeted me, scratching his hair and yawning. It was still fairly dark out, but the sun was riding over the hills to the east, and our room was on that side of the building. There were no peepholes up here, but I was glad to discover that there had been no intrusions overnight. We needed sleep. If for no other reason than to clear out our lungs. I wondered how much coughing we had all done while sleeping.

I checked under my bunk. There was my rifle, my pack, and my socks. I didn't like to sleep with my socks on, and it was important to air them out being inside of those stuffy boots all day, or I'd get sores.

My thoughts went to Ally. I looked over at her bunk. Unoccupied. The women are up early while the men slumber…how long has *that* been true? I wondered where she was.

"Where's Trudy?"

Bassett shook his head. "Don't know. Maybe the bathroom," he yawned again, "I heard her get up about an hour ago. I didn't get much sleep. Going over scenarios in my head."

Oh, you poor Baby In Charge, I thought.

I got up and followed Rutty to the bathroom.

●　　●　　●　　●　　●

Didn't find Ally. But I walked back to the room, and she had returned. She was dressed, and was on the floor stuffing her pack after lacing up her boots. Rutty was still in a stall in the bathroom, and had probably fallen asleep on the toilet. It's fine. He'll collapse onto his face and wake up that way and be no worse for the wear. He's done that since he was a little boy.

"Morning, Trudy," I greeted her. Just then I caught a whiff of freshness, and women's shampoo. All coming from this beautiful woman whom I had just addressed formally.

She looked up at me curiously, and cocked her head. I flashed my eyes over to Bassett who was rummaging through his pack too. I held my hands up. I didn't know if she was ok with me calling her Ally in front of Bassett.

"Morning, *Shipley*," she retorted formally in return.

I chuckled and rolled my eyes. "Time for breakfast in a few. They have it ready downstairs, but I can't smell it."

"Neither can I," she exchanged, "they're doing right to mask the scent and keep it contained for sure. A little like what someone else seems to be doing."

Bassett detected something in her tone of voice, and looked around at her. And then he looked at me.

I was confused - I wasn't trying to keep things secret, and there was nothing to keep secret anyway, so I was a little annoyed at the accusation that I was concealing the fact that I liked her. Just because I called her Trudy and not Ally? Sensitive much? *Women.*

"Hey, it's fine, *Ally*…ok?" I asked firmly.

She rolled her eyes in return and got up to walk out, throwing her pack on her back. "*Men,*" she breathed accusingly. At least great minds thought alike.

"Wait, what?" I asked, following her. She walked briskly back towards the bathroom, and back inside. I turned around and saw Bassett exiting our room to head down to breakfast. He was shaking his head and laughing grimly.

I tried to keep my voice quiet. "I wasn't saying anything, I just didn't know if you wanted me to call you 'Ally' in front of Bassett. In front of Joe."

She stopped just inside the bathroom. I followed her. "You think I'm with Joe?"

"What? No…I just…no! I don't know…?" I mumbled weakly.

"Well, I'm not with him, OK? I just thought it would be nice to have a little more familiarity around here what with all the cold crap we always have to deal with. Sorry you didn't see it that way. Especially after you make me open up to everyone last night with my whole life story!"

There was obviously some hurt there. "I should've thought more about that. I'm dumb sometimes." *OK, that was not a smart move. Stand by for incoming.*

"You're right, you *are* dumb." She turned around against the far wall and crossed her arms.

Saw that one a mile away.

"Look, Ally, I'm sorry," I said in a huff, as I walked past a closed stall door toward her. "Rutty, get up!" I said as I banged harshly on the stall door, not taking my eyes off of Ally. There was a startled murmur from within the stall, followed by Rutty's head popping up over the stall shortly thereafter, watching us. "I didn't mean anything by it. Call it decorum or whatever you want: I was just trying to keep things in line."

Rutty wiped some sleep out of his eyes as he glanced over at Ally. He disappeared back down, flushed, and momentarily emerged from the stall.

Ally let out a sudden and quick exhale, uncrossed her arms, and just looked away for a second. "It's fine." She took the pack off her back and rested it on the bathroom counter, re-crossing her arms.

"No, it's not. I get it. I heard you volunteered."

She clicked her tongue.

"Bassett told me last night." Now she rolled her eyes. "I don't know why you did it, but…it was brave. And…," I searched for the right encouragement to toss her way, "we're going to take care of you."

She looked at me doubtfully and raised an eyebrow.

"I promise. I don't like that you volunteered, but I promise we'll take care of you. *I'll* take care of you."

She sighed again. "It just seems that anytime I find something good in my life I don't know how to hang onto it long enough to actually remember it later."

"Find what? What did you find?" I looked over at Rutty, who rolled his eyes and shook his head at me. What was I missing?

Ally walked right over to me. "You are *such* a knucklehead." And then she grabbed me hard and kissed me.

I hadn't been kissed like that in a *long* time. I can't remember how long it's been, but I could taste her mint lip balm. Our lips locked, and I embraced her. I could smell her hair up close now. I don't know how long it had been since she had showered previously, but thank God these college showers had actual shampoo and soap. I was definitely appreciating it now. No trace of yellow dust on this woman. I came alive inside as she wrapped her arms around me, and my heart fluttered.

And suddenly we were both aware of Rutty smiling and watching us with raised eyebrows, nodding.

"Aw," Rutty said. "So sweet. Shucks, you two. I had a feelin' about you kids."

"Get outta here, ya punk." He recoiled with a snort, and went to wash up.

I turned back to Ally. "I'm sorry. I won't call you Trudy again, platoon or no platoon."

She smiled warmly, hugged me tight and didn't let go. "Good," she began. "Because platoon or no platoon, I don't know what I'm really volunteering for, and I kinda need to connect right now."

Connect, huh? My mind raced.

"I hear you. And I'm here for you. Once Rutty leaves, that is." Rutty snickered behind us.

"There's nowhere private in this whole place," she said. My heart raced. *Is she thinking what I think she's thinking?* "We never had a chance at time anyway," she said with an air of futility.

I pulled away from her. Too soon. I leaned in for another slow kiss, and she received it. I ran my hands up and down her back. The thought of making love to this woman was all too alluring. How long had it been? "Ally, I- I don't know what to s-"

The door opened sharply, and there was Bassett. Ally looked past me, and I turned around to face him.

"Hey, uh, Bassett," I said regretfully, letting him know perfectly well that he had just ruined everything.

Bassett grinned. "When you two lovebirds are finished, would you care to join me at breakfast so we can figure out how we're going to accomplish this kamikaze mission today, please? Thank youuuu," he trailed off in a sing-song fashion as he walked back out.

I'm sure Ally was thinking it too: *If we must.* I could feel my heart slowing, re-emerging into life as we know it from the warm throes of young love.

Bassett left. I looked back at Ally. I clenched my lips together, and looked at hers.

"It's alright," she said. "It's OK, really. He's right. I'm gonna make it through this, and we'll have time when I get back."

I reluctantly nodded. "Just get back."

She stared into my eyes. And just then, I was afraid. No, *terrified*, that she wouldn't.

• • • • •

We turned around to face Rutty, who had a big grin on his face. He gave me a quick flash of his eyebrows in mock-commendation of my apparent score, and then giggled. He strode to the door of the bathroom, opened it for us, and then gestured graciously as a doorman for us to walk through.

I shook my head, and Ally and I walked past him to the cafeteria.

When we arrived, the room was empty. We heard noises, and followed them around the corner to the small kitchen. The door was closed. We walked in and found five people in there, including Bassett, Preston and Jesse. Two women were also present. I guessed that they eventually migrated here too, from an elementary or middle school, after the gorgons came. I wondered briefly what it was like going through puberty in confinement with all these people around that you were forced to live with. All that teen angst. *Ick.*

The exhaust fan cavity from the stove had been pulled out, and the cavity boarded up. Instead, a new range hood had been installed over the stove, redirecting to a large filtering device perched atop a vending machine. *So that's how they're diverting the scent away from the outside. Genius.*

On the stove was a pan of eggs and bacon. Real eggs. Real bacon. My eyes went wide. I stole a glance over at Rutty, and his were wide as baseballs as well. Same with Ally's.

Bassett looked up. "Welcome," he whispered. "I say we dine in style before we head out on this ridiculous mission, what do you fine folks say?"

The kitchen was cramped, but we filtered in. There were no chairs, and we just leaned back against the countertops. Across from us there were a few vending machines with a varying assortment of dry goods, juices and sodas. Preston reached around and extracted a small box from the counter behind us, withdrawing a few dollar bills to insert into the machine for our selections. Someone had broken into the university safe, or perhaps found some petty cash. Of course, they couldn't break the glass to get to the contents of the vending machine: that would have been too loud and noticeable.

He handed them out to us. All of this was done silently. It felt like some solemn ancestral ritual.

Being handed those dollar bills reminded me of receiving an allowance for chores. Felt funny. I made my selection, and chose a Kern's Peach Nectar from the machine. I didn't know how old it was, and wasn't going to look. When it dropped, it made a thump, but not so horrible as I would have expected. The retrieval area of the machine had been lined with sound-dampening foam. Ally and Rutty made their selections too. I proceeded over to the other machine and got a bag of Funyuns. No crazy sounds with the issuing of those. I hadn't had Funyuns in I don't know how long; they were going to go down proper after this meal.

I turned around and noticed the collection of stuff on the stove. There was sausage, bacon and eggs. All cooked and ready to go! I was blown away. One of the ladies present handed me a plate with food already served on it, accompanied by a tender smile. She looked to be about thirty. I mouthed "thank you" to her, and she mouthed back "you're welcome." Then she leaned over and whispered, "I'm Ruby and that's my younger sister Vera," motioning to the other woman.

I nodded and waved silently. "Thank you so much for breakfast."

I turned to see Rutty nodding a quick "wassup ladies?" to both of them. He was faster than I on the field, for sure, but here, he looked silly, like he was trying to keep up. And these ladies were a decade older than him. I gave him an elbow in his ribs to let him know I was on to him. It didn't dissuade his interaction with the women.

When we were all served up, we just ate in silence, with the occasional yummy noises and gratitude directed toward Ruby and Vera. I don't remember the last time I had had warm, crispy, fat-laden bacon… and actual eggs that tasted like actual eggs. Someone had a chicken somewhere, I guess. It seemed a feast. I could tell by the looks on everyone else's faces that they felt the same. You would think for a minute that the war had ended, and we were all dining in celebration.

When we were all done, Preston directed us out and to one of the adjoining side rooms. It had a few round coffee tables, a large table to commiserate at, a whiteboard, a corkboard, and a large TV on a wall shelf in the corner. It was on, but played only static. It even had a folded-up ping pong table. If you wanted to hole up and plan a top-secret suicide mission against an alien species that could freeze you with their eyes, this was the place to do it.

Two floor-to-ceiling windows flanking each side of the room were all boarded up.

Vera and Ruby left a pitcher of water and some glasses for us. I watched Rutty give them a little wave goodbye. To Vera especially. I sat next to Ally at one table, along with Rutty. Jesse and Preston sat at the table behind us. Bassett was up front preparing a few things.

We waited a few minutes and then watched as ten of their guys joined us. Varying in ages, the oldest looked to be about sixty-two or sixty-three – maybe she had been a teacher here – and the youngest was clearly a zit-faced freshman, younger than Rutty. They slowly filtered in, giving us half-hearted smiles and grave acknowledgement that something big was being planned. Vera was back again too. They took up varying positions in the room, sitting on the chairs in the back, or up front by the door we had entered. Some of them were left standing. One of them was the kid with the blonde locks and baseball hat I had watched greet us yesterday at dusk on our approach.

I looked at my watch. 0649. Man, it was early. I moved my gaze up to the boarded-up window. Along the cracks I could see morning sunlight starting to try to jab its way into the room. I didn't know where we were in the building anymore, but I presumed that we were still on the east side from the light coming through.

Once we were all in the room, Bassett took over. He scanned the room and then cleared his throat, standing up towards the head of the room in front of the TV shelf.

"Thank you, guys, for breakfast," he said quietly to Jesse, Vera and Ruby. They nodded. "Uh, OK gang, I'm Joe Bassett, Staff Sergeant, Eagle Patrol, Blockade DN282 out of Alpharetta."

I didn't know he was a Staff Sergeant. He outranked me after all. And Ally outranked all of us.

"I'm here with my associate Lieutenant Allison Trudy, also from Alpharetta, along with Sergeant Shipley and Private Shipley, our brothers out of Blockade DN436 here in Clarksville, on local patrol and recon for supplies and survivors."

He straightened up.

"So, this is our mission. We've been instructed by our Command to put a tracker on a live gorgon, and that's not going to be an easy feat." There was genuine astonishment in the room: some of those gathered had not heard yet that this was the mission.

"This operation is being conducted in tandem with other units as manpower is available. Now, our Command has their intel and rationale for this, but right now we're flying blind as to what that exactly is. However, I do see the logic in it, especially if we want to find out what's happening out over our oceans.

"Until now, from usable military intel that we've received, the enemy has been preventing us from venturing toward the coastlines of any of our continents." Here he backed up to the whiteboard and began to draw out a map of the United States, plotting a star in the southeast region roughly where we all were. "For the western hemisphere this is definitely true, and my associate Lieutenant Trudy also came from Alpharetta where they hit us hard and pushed us all inland.

"President Jean Graham is alive and well, and has instructed our military forces – what remain of them – to attempt to track a live gorgon and determine its movements. We need to find out exactly why we are being forbidden from exploring beyond the coasts. Preston, Jesse, and the rest of you: my team here is aware that back home we've made a pretty darned big development with the gorgons, and research teams have actually devised some makeshift reflection technology to shield us from the gorgons' preferred method of immobilization.

"Allison Trudy was part of that team, and she helped develop the visors that work to deflect the, well, the *whatever* it is that they do that wrecks us." He motioned to Ally.

Ally cleared her throat and twisted around to face all of them. She looked them over, and then down at me. "Lieutenant Trudy. Hi. Uh, yeah, that's right. Up until now we were at the mercy of the gorgons, fighting blind, quite literally, not knowing how to engage them without summoning more of them to us in the process. Kind of like a Catch 22. And, when and if that *did* happen, not really understanding how to prevent them from immobilizing us. Well," she paused, lifting one of the new visors out of her pack and holding it aloft, "we actually have some defense now. Take a peek."

She passed it to the nearest refugee standing along the wall, and each in turn inspected it and looked through it around the room.

"It's not foolproof yet, but it's new technology that can actually somewhat deflect whatever they're using against us to freeze us in our tracks, and…you know." She gulped and shrugged her shoulders. "The technology is based on radio waves that are emitted from the helmet that can actually disrupt the telepathy, or telekinesis, whatever it is, that the gorgons use. It's pretty complicated, so, for now, suffice it to say that they work…to a degree. But they are the first step toward full-blown shielding.

"The other thing is that we actually have one in captivity. Our team managed to capture one of them."

There was a collective yet subtle gasp from the inhabitants here. Such a feat strained credulity and seemed wholly impossible to them. In surveying their expressions, some of them were smiling through their doubts, looking at one another with hope and newfound possibility. *Could it be that the tide was turning in this war?* That was the question I knew they were all asking themselves. Ally continued.

"It's being monitored and studied by a science team back home. Sedated for the most part, but always under restraint, with blinders on, so that it can't see us. I was part of the team that was studying it."

"You've seen it up close then?" asked Preston.

Up close, I thought. *That's an understatement.* I looked again at her injured hand.

"Yes, I have. More than I would have liked to, honestly." She held up her hand. Clearly visible for all were the bite marks from that gorgon. She then recounted for them the story she had told us: about the discovery, the team subduing it, the injury she incurred, and the loss that Bassett incurred: his sister.

"We sedated it, and I've looked inside what are probably its ear canals, I've taken and studied saliva samples, scraped off some of its skin for microscopic slides, and looked at its blood cells. It's flesh and bone, just like us, but obviously with some extremely alien differences. There are several teams working on them, more than I have.

"But that was before we were moved. Bassett," she gestured to Joe, "and I were only recently dispatched to Clarksville, and I was pulled off the science team back home. But they're making progress and learning more every day about it, and their kind. Which, I guess, is what led to our new assignment here." She sat down.

Bassett continued. "Now, you all saw what happened at 1330 yesterday. That EMP was triggered by me, in a satlink to an outpost about three miles southwest of us. It came from our Blockade, DN436 just outside Clarksville by the zinc plant.

"When the enemy first showed up in 2026, our entire military system was scrambled. You could call it an intergalactic *coup d'etat*, sure. They were everywhere. In a few weeks we were scattered and in hiding. Military was defenseless; rendered obsolete in a flash. Random pockets of resistance sprang up all over the world: underground coalitions were formed, and we learned. We studied from areas of relative protection. We observed their patterns: not just daily, but monthly, seasonally, annually. They all seem to disappear for the most part during the day, as well as nearly completely in the heat of summer.

"In these prized moments of respite through all these years, the government – what's left of it – has been able to make great progress, establishing command posts, Blockades such as ours, and underground bases. We've also recovered nearly five hundred of these so-called 'amulets' that arrived when the gorgons did." He fished one out of his pocket and held it up for them. Again, murmured astonishment.

"How exactly these came with the gorgons is anyone's guess. But what we *think* they are is some kind of a sonic emitter device. Now, none of us have ever seen any kind of alien ships, or large transport ships. No UFO's. These things just all kind of floated down into our atmosphere, and communicated. Their communication happens through audio waves, through the air. We *think* that they used these to protect them in transit to Earth, and also while entering the earth's atmosphere.

"We've all traveled up in planes and some of us have gone down on deep dives where the pressure changes, and we need to pressurize or depressurize to accommodate, and not have our ears burst. Since we've learned that these things can't see so well, it's a highly educated guess that they are nearly entirely audio-based, and these amulets probably were used to provide some audio discomfiture and allow them ease of passage without their ears popping and their brains exploding from the pressure.

"But what was used to protect, it seems, can also be used to attack. We've found a way to turn their own technology against them. The EMP I triggered yesterday was coupled with sonic waves focused at high frequency through a few of these amulets. The tech team has created what they call a DTF, or 'dissonant tidal flood.' The broadcast signal is amplified so high, we can't really hear it, but the gorgons can, and oh boy does it do some damage.

Yesterday, our team here saw what it did to those things. They were *writhing* in pain. They recoiled and screamed and took off away from that signal. Many of them were killed, or lay dying. We discovered a gorgon graveyard shortly afterwards with a score of them lying there with their ears covered in blood, convulsing from the inside out. That was our precise objective: exactly what we wanted to happen. We just didn't know how well it would happen. It seems in their haste to consume us, they should have hung onto these devices and kept them close.

"Now, President Graham has overseen much of this, and there are no plans to vote her out, because democracy died with the people, and with Congress. But she's aware of our progress, our plans, our objectives and our missions. She's been at the heart of it, though you may not have seen her. Trudy and I are up here at her behest. That DTF was authorized by her. Now her security force keeps her on the move, visiting the different blockades and relaying orders and instruction. But also comfort and assurance. The President wants you to know that The United States is not leaderless nor impotent. And the day will come when we will strike back, harder than yesterday, and harder than that DTF."

Bassett was speaking harder and more triumphantly now. His hands were raised and for a moment he struck me as a powerful senator or political figure, enthralling the masses under his spell. Indeed, he paused for a moment, seemingly waiting for his thunderous applause. But there was none, nor would there be in these audiences. Applause meant noise, and noise meant death. So, on we went in silent agreement with him, nodding. It was some comfort that he knew that, because he lowered his hands.

"Our assigned mission is to capture and release another gorgon, after implanting it with a tracker. Using the mask technology that Lieutenant Trudy just demonstrated, as well as the amulets that we have recovered, we're going to find one. Knock it out. Implant the tracker. And let Command take it from there. What they learn from its behavior will then determine where we go after that."

I glanced at the clock on the wall. 0705. The day was moving along.

"We all know that the gorgons are attracted to sound. Sound has been our enemy, our Achilles' heel for many years now. Well, we're going to make it our weapon. But first, we need to make use of it another way. We never know where they'll be or where we'll bump into a gorgon next. So, our brave, dear Trudy here has volunteered to act as bait, to lure one in. We all hope and pray that it's not a berserker – those are the ones that are meaner than the rest and they have some kind of chemical imbalance that makes them act like a crack addict – but we've got to get their attention in order to grab one and track it.

"So, she'll start screaming, draw attention to herself, and then lure it in. If she screams, it'll come. Sergeant Shipley and I will subdue it along with those of you who want to help. But let me issue a warning: we only have two of these masks. The rest of you will have to fight blind. There is a high possibility of loss of life in this mission. We are commanded to do this; you are not. So, each of you must decide now whether or not you want to serve. You will of course be held blameless if you decide not to. Anyone who wants to stay behind, now is your chance to walk out."

This plan could actually work. That's what Rutty and I had done in the zinc mill last year. There were some scattered murmuring and sighs, ending in quiet resolve.

No one left.

"Alright," Bassett continued. "Private Shipley here will be our potato shooter. He's going to use rubber bullets from your stockpile to knock it out cold, and hopefully not kill it. The rest of you, if you're willing, will act as guards, forming a perimeter and ensuring that the skies are clear. We'll need your eyes and ears to make sure there are no more of them, so we can get this thing implanted. And then? We send it on its way, and we'll see just where it goes and what it does. From there, we let Command and The President do what they do best."

He paused, looking us all over. I could see him scanning the rows of people behind us. I watched as he appraised their value and estimated their courage: even the old teacher. I looked at them too. They were gunning for a fight, but peer through the creases, and there was definitely fear behind those steely eyes.

"So that's it." He looked at the clock. "It's 0710. At 0730, we meet back here for final briefing and launch. Our team has what we need here. If you're still in here, it means you're on the assault team with us. Feel free to return to your rooms and grab whatever you think you'll need. Armor up. Hug your loved ones. Good luck." He nodded.

Something about the way he said 'hug your loved ones' suggested finality, and I glanced around the room to see if it had hit anyone else the same way. It sounded so…final. And then, he put his hands out, palms upward, in token of receiving. In grave agreement, the whole room, myself included, echoed that simple and gracious gesture back to Joe. Come what may. We're ready to do this for all of humanity.

That was it. He immediately glanced our way and clenched his lips in solemnity. I think I knew what this moment meant to him… and to us. It was all or nothing. We nodded back.

We were about to head out on a mission. Not one where we *might* see a gorgon. Not one where we might have to run *away* from them. No, this was a case of *would* and *toward*. This was a suicide mission. I didn't have much hope that we'd all make it out of this.

I glanced over at Rutty. He was lost in thought, staring at the floor and picking at his lip.

Bassett strode to the side of the room and began quietly talking with Jesse and another tall refugee, a man whose name I didn't know.

I just hoped that Ally would make it. I looked over at her, and she looked at me and squeezed my hand. Man, she was beautiful. Why, oh why, did she have to volunteer? A bunch of the refugees were now streaming out of the room past her, and as they did so, they invariably would squeeze her shoulder and whisper "Good luck."

The older teacher lady came up next, and her face creased into a thousand smiles as she mustered "You got this, sweetheart. We're all with you."

It was sweet, and we all felt the same way. But I just couldn't shake the fear. I had just met her. And I think I'm falling in love with her. This is too soon. A question lingered in my mind: "How did it come to this?"

8 | LOJACK

There were few words. Maybe there was nothing to say anyway.

We all made ready to leave. The refugees had now gone back to their rooms or other areas for supplies, and to arm themselves. One of the men who left the room was met by the young mother of the little girl outside the hall. I watched them embrace. The father scooped up the little girl into his arms, and then the three of them vanished from my sight around the corner.

As promised, Rutty surrendered his headset to Preston, and showed him the ins and outs of it.

Ally looked into my eyes. "Well, this is it," she said.

"Don't say that," I growled, taking her by the hand. "You're gonna be fine. I promise you. We got-" I looked around, "like a dozen people covering you. We'll take care of you, I promise. You know, you don't have to do this, Ally."

The quickness of her response surprised me. "Oh yes, yes I do." She nodded repeatedly, briskly. There was a story there, apparently.

My eyes narrowed, and I squeezed her hands in tandem. "Why?"

She shook her head now. "Tell ya what," she said, as she stole a quick look over at Bassett. "I make it back, I'll tell you the whole story."

I glanced over at Bassett too, and then returned to Ally. There was little I could do to persuade her to let someone else go in her stead. And how could we ask any of these refugees to do what we've willingly enlisted ourselves to do all these years anyway? We were part of the remaining Army infantry of the United States. These were just scared and starving middle schoolers and college kids, frozen in time: hiding for their lives and just hoping to shoot straight when the time came.

As if she guessed my thoughts, she turned to Rutty, who was standing nearby with his head bowed, and said "Just shoot straight."

Rutty looked up and nodded. He reached out and handed her a stick of gum. "This might help."

She let out a clear, appreciative laugh. I could see her eyes moistening. "Thank you, Rutty. What's your real name anyway?"

"Rutty. That's all. Rutty R. Rut," he joked.

She snickered. "OK, if that's the way you want to play. Thank you, Rutty."

He grinned back at her. "Gonna go grab a quick bite. Be right back."

Ally then turned back to me as Rutty made for the door. Her hands released from mine as she managed a *this is it* smile. I let out my breath, and then returned the gesture, nodding to her. We embraced, and I could smell her mint lip balm and sweet shampoo. I wasn't ready to let go of her.

Rutty was at the door. He suddenly turned, and in a halting, pronounced whisper, he said, "Hey Trudy!"

She turned towards him.

"Wyatt – Rutledge – Shipley," he enunciated clearly, and then he smiled gleefully. "Or…just Rutty."

Ally smiled back at him. Rutty left.

•　　•　　•　　•　　•

0722. The time was drawing near.

We were now all assembled in the conference room.

There would be sixteen of us on this mission: myself, Ally, Rutty, Bassett, Preston, Jesse, the older woman (who I found out everyone affectionately called 'MeeMaw'), and nine others, all ranging in age from eighteen to sixty-three. I hadn't seen all of them behind me in the meeting, but I recognized the tall, unnamed man talking with Bassett earlier. He introduced himself as Riley. The others were that blonde kid Fox, along with Witherspoon, Heck, Abbey, Dunbar, Lundmark, Rothwell, and St. Marie. Everyone was standing together up front, huddled around the whiteboard.

"Alright, gang," began Bassett. "Here's my plan. I'm open to feedback. The gorgons were last sighted heading mainly northeast. But we know they could be anywhere right now, so we have to just anticipate that. What are your names again?" He motioned to three of the refugees.

"Abbey. Heck. Rothwell," they sounded off.

"Right. These guys ran recon, and I agree with them that the best course of action would be to head straight south to the Woodward Library." He was drawing feverishly on the board now, scribbling out the terrain, as well as the inside of the library. "There's lots of places to hide in there, between rows, and in different offices. Whatever we do, we want to keep them away from Harvill. Our shooter team will go in first. That's Private Shipley and Witherspoon. The exit is facing us. Rutty and Witherspoon will go first with the recon team to post up just inside the doors and give the all-clear. Rutty will have the RPG shooter and a sidearm; Witherspoon will have an assault rifle and a sidearm as well. Witherspoon tells me he's a good shot." Witherspoon nodded. I recognized him as the father of the little girl, and also the one who laser-sighted me with the sniper rifle the day before.

"St. Marie, Lundmark, and Dunbar, you're our aerial defense force outside. You'll have to stay hidden, and let the gorgon pass you. Don't worry about anything you hear *inside* the building; your job is to keep more of them from coming, and shoot 'em out of the sky, got it? We can only handle one of those things at a time. Whatever you do, don't post up across from each other. We don't want any casualties from friendly fire. Stay hidden, together, on one side."

They nodded.

"Trudy is going to go last, and she's going to let out one heckuva scream. That ought to get their attention. Then she'll take off for the library and get inside. Rutty and Witherspoon will let Trudy pass, and they'll let the, hopefully *one* gorgon, pass as well. Our guys won't have much time, because Trudy needs to get hidden quick, and we're counting on the inside of that library to be unfamiliar territory to it, so I'm guessing it's going to have to slow down, survey the area and start sniffing. That's when we'll fire on it to knock it out cold. Rutty, you've got to hit that thing square. If you don't, it's up to Witherspoon to take it out at the knees, or the shoulders, *something* – but, and this is key, you must use non-lethal force! We need that thing alive. It has to be able to fly away from here." Rutty and Witherspoon nodded.

"At that point, it's a full court press to get in there, subdue it, and implant the tracker. Trudy gets a mask, because it's going after *her*, and this is *her* game. The other mask is going to have to go to Witherspoon, because he's our last line of defense to take it out before we send in the squish squad." Rutty didn't look pleased by this. "That's why you've got to hit it, Rutty. You don't, and that thing will be flying around in there pissed and go after anyone pointing a gun at it.

"I cannot stress this next part strongly enough: until that thing has been immobilized, do *not* engage. I repeat to all of you: do *not* engage. Stay back. The recon team will have this blanket," he pointed to one on the ground by the door, "and they'll cover its head just in case it's not out cold. But you've got to hang back until that's done. We've all seen what they can do if they see you, and you see them.

"Sergeant Shipley and I will post up around the corner from the door, for any incoming. So will Rutty and Witherspoon and the recon team. Preston will be back in Harvill with one of our headsets, so he'll be able to hear what's going on from over there. If this falls apart, it might turn into a pretty pissed-off swarm of them, and Preston will need to know that and take evasive. He's still in command of Harvill.

"And here's the tracker." He pulled out a tiny device in capsule form, transparent to the mid-point, and flickering with a dim flashing green light. "This is it. It's a little guy, but it's GPS-locked to a diameter of about twenty feet accuracy. Command is already reading it hot. We'll undoubtedly get some signal interference from inside the building once its inserted, so we'll have to work fast to get it in, bandage up the gorgon, and then lug it back outside and deposit it fast, so we can all return to Harvill unmolested.

All told, it should take less than five minutes to cut out a chunk of its arm, implant it, sew and bandage it up, and then take it outside. And we've got to do all of this quietly," he said, scribbling marks of where and how on the whiteboard.

"Aside from the physical irritation and swelling that'll subside within a week or so like the rest of us, it shouldn't know what we did, nor why. But Command will have a fix on it and be able to have eyes on it from above. Then we all high-tail it back to Harvill, and link up with Command. There and back again. Here-there-here. That part isn't complicated. The complicated part is everything in between. Another thing: they stink like hell. Horrible stench. Just be ready to vomit."

Bassett paused.

"I don't have to tell you all that we have our work cut out for us. Should that gorgon be a berserker, we're going to have one heckuva time subduing it. And should there be more than one of them, or a group of them like we saw last night, well then, God help us. What we're about to do is going to happen very, very quickly. This could be our end right here. It's up to us to ensure that doesn't happen. We *have* to take this thing alive, or this whole op is for nothing."

The room somberly nodded.

"Let's take a few breaths. We can do this. There are a lot of things happening right now that could turn the tide of this war. This is one of them. Report to the south exit in three minutes."

All of us breathed a quick collective sigh. There were various embraces and words spoken. Some kissed. I noticed Witherspoon hugging his wife and daughter. I wondered if the fact that he was a father played into the decision-making that granted him the other mask.

But his wife was in tears, and she was speaking rapidly under her breath at him. He tried to console her as she held up her daughter before his eyes and pointed at her.

It was obvious what she was doing and saying. *Your daughter needs a daddy, so why are you doing this?*

That was a good question.

Why was Ally doing this? Why was Rutty doing this? Why was Bassett doing this? Why was Command?

Why were *any* of us doing this?

•　　•　　•　　•　　•

0727. Silently, dutifully, we all made our way to the south exit on the first floor of Harvill. That door had a swinging metal sheet over the window, allowing anyone on the lookout there to simply swing it inward and see what was going on outside. It was plenty light out, although cold. I looked at my watch. Forty-eight degrees. Not too cold.

As planned, we mustered in the hallway, and Bassett asked Rutty to say a prayer. He was honored by the request to pray.

Rutty pulled out his cross necklace and began, slowly. *Our Father, who art in Heaven, hallowed be thy Name. Thy kingdom come; thy will be done on earth as it is in Heaven. Give us this day our daily bread, and forgive us our trespasses, as we forgive those who trespass against us. And lead us not into temptation, but deliver us from evil.* Rutty paused and then repeated. *But deliver us from evil*, he whispered with much more emphasis. *Amen.*

"Amen," we all repeated silently.

"Amen," I breathed. I heard Ally do the same. She was right beside me. I had my right arm around her, and I could feel her trembling, despite the fact that she had on several layers more than she had on the day before, including the mask. The refugees must have loaned her some extra clothes to protect against any gorgon attack. After all, she was well-acquainted with their claws. I turned to her and took her face in my hands. "You can do this. You got this," I assured her. She said nothing in return, but slowly exhaled. I heard her breath catch, and she swallowed. She tried to smile but her lip quivered. "You got this," I repeated, and I kissed her warmly. "I'll be in there waiting for you, and we'll take it out. I promise you," I said feebly. All I could do was offer a verbal promise, but she knew I couldn't guarantee fulfilling any of it. I pulled her close and then I, too, trembled. "I don't wanna lose you!" I declared to her; my face pressed up against hers.

Now it was her turn to encourage me. "You won't. I smeared myself with Christmas fruitcake this morning. No one likes fruitcake, not even a gorgon."

That was an awful joke. *Awful.* But it did the trick. I snickered in her ear, and we pulled apart, looking under our brows at each other. I kissed her on her forehead and made ready to leave.

•   •   •   •   •

0730. Go Time.

Bassett looked us all over and nodded. He spoke softly into his headset, "Command, Blockade DN436, we are go for incursion and capture."

"Confirmed," came the discreet reply. "Good luck to all of you."

Ally retreated to the back of the line, squeezing my hand lightly as she passed by me. With everything in me, I really didn't want to let go.

Bassett looked ahead to Fox who was serving as door warden, and nodded to him. Fox opened the door.

A breath of cold morning air wafted in. Time seemed to slow again. I watched as Rutty and Witherspoon slowly filtered out. Rutty was brandishing his RPG launcher and a Glock 19 handgun. Witherspoon had his M5 and a Colt. I could see some extra mags in both of their back pockets. Witherspoon was wearing the other mask. They slowly filtered out, surveying the sky and the terrain for hostiles.

I checked my rifle and my Beretta. Good to go.

It was a hundred and twenty feet from the Harvill exit to the Woodward Library entrance due southwest. They slowly filtered out across the grass. I could practically hear everyone's heartbeats thundering, we were all so closely packed in that corridor watching them head outside. The quiet was deafening. They had a short hill to ascend, and then they were past a group of transformers and inside the building. We saw them close the door silently behind them, and gave them one minute to post up.

Bassett was glued to his watch. I looked at mine again. 0732.

With military precision, we were sticking to Bassett's timeline and orderliness. The recon team went next, stealing across the grass and keeping their eyes peeled. Abbey, Heck and Rothwell were soon also inside the building. Our numbers were diminishing. Five down. And then there were twelve.

With that, Bassett and I were next, along with the aerial defenders. I looked back at Ally. She was further down the hall, and was doing quick jumps to warm up and get the adrenaline going. She had slipped on her mask.

0733. No time to waste. We ran out, cover formation with each other, flanking the rest of the refugees in the middle. Seven more to the library. The aerial defenders posted up to our west, under the fading trees.

And now, there were three. Preston was left alone with Ally and Fox in the Harvill hallway. I saw the flap close.

Bassett and I entered after the refugees, and we hit the lights right after that. No sense in helping them find their meals with extra light.

Once inside, I made a note of our team and theirs inside Woodward. Those who were close enough, I could see their eyes: wide circles of adrenaline, and ringed with fear. Mine were too: I knew it. A few of them had scarves over their mouths to keep out the cold – or was it to shield the sound of their breathing for when the gorgon got inside?

My heart was thudding inside my chest.

I practically collided with Rutty who had taken position behind a row of bookshelves. I quickly clapped his shoulder and said "Hey bud" to him as I moved around the corner behind farther shelves.

No sign of the enemy yet, but it was too early for all of them to disappear, and we spotted that rogue yesterday morning, early, behind that shed. Their numbers tended to thin as the day progressed, but no: they weren't gone. They were out there. I cracked my neck from side to side. "We're in, Preston. Awaiting go, Command."

"Copy," came the confirmation from Preston. "Copy," echoed Command.

The rest of the refugee team filtered out into the stairwell opposite us, awaiting the signal. Bassett and I posted up around the corner behind some bookshelves.

I had never been on any kind of Navy Seal team or mission, but this reminded me of old movies that I had seen, when Hollywood was still hopping and churning out action movies. I remembered the documentary of a Seal team infiltrating the compound of the terrorist Osama bin Laden, and how quick and noiseless it was. They had had their slip-ups, sure, but overall, the missions were always silent incursion to get in, take care of the bad guys, and get out. The only way ours was different was we were bringing the bad guys in *with* us. I shuddered in the cold of the morning, despite my underlayment and fatigues.

We were all ready as we ever would be. My eyes darted around the room, checking and re-checking positions, and making a mental note of where we all posted up. My mind was on high alert, amplified by the fact that the main course was making herself the bait, and would be screaming across the lawn any minute, pursued by ferocious predators.

I nervously looked at my watch again. 0735. Every blink of the seconds dots seemed louder than my own heart. Any minute now we would hear Command speak the words that would set this in motion. I looked back at Bassett. He was readying a small kit with the tracker and a few surgical instruments, scalpel, bandages, etc.

"Come on, come *on,*" I said.

0738.

"DN436, Command, you are a go."

And there it was. Bassett heard it, I heard it, and I assume Preston heard it. "Roger," I confirmed to him. My fingers reflexively tightened around the grip of my M5. My other hand quickly went to my holster to ensure that I had packed my sidearm. In that moment I couldn't remember what I had been issued. Was it a Colt? A Beretta like I used to have? A Glock like Rutty's?

My thoughts were cut short as a horrendous scream sounded from far outside the building, and it was getting closer. Impulsively my body started to go for the door, and then I stopped myself. Ally was ringing the dinner bell somewhere out in the narrow space between buildings. I moved to look around the corner and out the window. She was standing out in the middle, screaming her head off and firing her sidearm into the air. I saw her turning wildly around, looking in all directions, and then she stopped, looking east. Something had caught her eye. She screamed again. This time it was no attention-getting shriek, but one that comes from the depths of one's soul, crying out in terror for one's life. And she was flying for the library door.

"Oh crap, oh crap, oh crap!" I cried, retaking my post. I leaned against the wall. I could see Rutty there with Witherspoon. How long does it take to get over here at a fast clip? We did it in a matter of seconds. But she was sprinting. Where was she?

The door to the library flew open and shattered. Ally's muted and terrified scream suddenly became frighteningly clear, like a claxon in our ears. Her voice filled the entirety of the Woodward library and did not die, reverberating throughout. I looked back through the window. There they were. *Oh no.* There were *three* of them! *Three!* One of them was a bit bigger than the others. They zoomed past the window and then slowed at the door.

I could feel Ally's thudding footsteps *whoosh* through the library and past the front study area where Bassett was. From the recesses of the opposite end of the floor I heard her scream "Jet! Jet!"

"Hold!" whispered Bassett to everyone. "Hold!"

Ally disappeared into a room on the far side, kitty corner to the entrance she just barreled through. She had stopped screaming. There was no more point to that.

They were in here.

I could hear her deep, stunted breathing from afar.

And I could hear their hissing, closer. It was coming in rapid and noisome exhalations, gurgling with venom and surging with hunger. They were right around the corner from me, halted in the open space past the entrance corridor. I couldn't see them yet, but I knew they were there.

I peered over the row of books directly in front of me and could see them. *No,* I breathed to myself. *NO.*

One of them was a berserker.

It was twitching helplessly, spasming with a kinetic energy. *No, no, no!* Sweat dripped into my eyes. And then my sight was drawn towards the far door of the stairs. One of the refugees was in there, desperately peering out at the gorgons. The thought occurred to me that they may have never actually seen one before. What a horrible fate that they should be included on a mission so dire, and possibly so fatal.

We all paused. Why were we paused? *Of course:* because there were three of them. What do we do now? There are *three* of them in here with us! A chill ran down my spine. I couldn't see Bassett, but he must have been thinking the same thing.

That's when the sniffing began. They were searching for us. And they were going to find us. That berserker was *going* to find us. We could see the cold mist filtering out across the library floor.

At that moment one of the refugees proved their worth. It was MeeMaw, taking the lead. The door to the stairwell slowly opened, and she fired. In her mind, we could deal with one of them, sure, but *three*? No way.

MeeMaw continued firing. The gorgon who was hit let out a spine-chilling scream of agony. The other with him, and the berserker, recoiled as the darkened library was strobed in flashes of deafening thunder. They covered their ears. The smaller gorgon actually observed its mate falling, curiously watching it spill onto the floor. It lowered itself to him. Stunningly, it began to try to eat him while still covering one ear. Revolting. My stomach churned.

That's when I saw Rutty lean around his bookshelf and see the first gorgon drop. He whipped into action, slinging his torpedo launcher, drawing a Glock 19 and firing repeatedly at the downed gorgon, and the other one with it, while keeping cover behind the bookshelves. He was partially shielding his eyes. The gorgons' flesh exploded at varying points with bursts of light coupled with translucent fluid splashing onto the ground all around them. It was a grisly scene. Witherspoon began to fire as well. In a matter of moments, there were two gorgons down. The berserker disappeared into the shadows.

"Hold!" Bassett yelled over the din. And he was right – we needed one alive. "Hold!" he yelled again.

We froze. The shooting stopped, and the smoke swirled throughout the library shelves.

The berserker had pulled back into the corridor as the madness unfolded, slinking into darkness while shielding its ears. The noises were too much for it, apparently.

There was mist and smoke everywhere. It was hard to see: I could dimly make out Rutty up ahead holstering his Glock, and readying the launcher. Witherspoon had retreated from him, and was going around the other side to fire on the gorgon just in case Rutty missed. It got eerily quiet. I guess everyone was trying to see where it went. I could feel my own eyes mad with haste, darting around in a pinball search of the room. Where Ally was. Where everyone was.

Up ahead, Rutty turned slowly around and pointed the launcher towards the door, quietly kneeling beside the bookshelf. But the gorgon beat him to it. At just that moment, it saw him, and it shot across the library in a blaze of shrieking fury, careening into him in a horrible explosion of wood, metal, papers and clamor. *Dang* they were fast. Rutty flew back, and the rocket launcher was knocked from his grip. Witherspoon was sent flying backward as well, into the adjoining shelves of books. He quickly got back up and drew his weapon, pointing at the berserker. It saw him over the row of books and made a strange sound, looking right at him, humming. It was trying to freeze him. But Witherspoon had the mask on!

Rutty was to its left, and could see it targeting Witherspoon. "Hey! Hey!" he called out in a reflex, avoiding its stare. He went for the launcher on the floor to his right, but it was trapped under the weight of a fallen bookshelf. Just then the thing looked at him, distracted from Witherspoon, and it pounced horribly upon him.

I watched Rutty slide oddly across the carpet as the weight of the gorgon dragged him backward. It was on top of him, twitching and flailing. He had his eyes closed. I couldn't pull my eyes away. "*Rutty!*" I found myself shouting for him, and then covered my mouth. Why weren't we going out to help him? Why wasn't I? Of course: no blanket over its head. And it was a berserker. No one would go out to help him, and he was the one with the RPG. I didn't know what to do, standing there second-guessing myself. Everything had fallen apart.

Why wasn't I running out there to help him? *Why???* Ally's brother Nick had run out after his kid brother Badger. Bassett had tried to save his sister. *What the hell was wrong with me?*

And then, all of a sudden, he looked. My little brother looked up at his assailant! Waves of horror poured over me. It was only for a flicker of a moment, and maybe he thought that would be okay. It was enough. The berserker gorgon just hovered there, staring down at him, humming.

A deep chill ran up my spine. *You just…don't…look.*

I could see Bassett out of the corner of my eye lift himself up and over the study area table, to observe what was happening. He had grabbed an industrial-sized fire extinguisher. Every sound in that library became muffled.

Rutty was fighting the gorgon. He was huffing and coughing. The berserker wasn't fighting back: it was disturbingly calm, hovering there above, watching him. The vapor was wrapped all about the two of them. Rutty threw as many punches as his little body could throw, but then they started to slow, like molasses through his veins. Something was slowing him down on the inside.

He made a sound: I couldn't tell if it was a whispered prayer, or an inadvertent grunt. In a reflex, he swore, and his body involuntarily and softly coughed. I watched, transfixed in horror. My little brother turned a pale shade of blue, and, against his will, his green eyes were held fast to the gorgon. I heard him gulp feebly. And then I heard no more.

The violence was calmly brutal and brutally calm. A wisp of breath escaped his lips, and then he lay still. The gorgon opened its mouth wide, buried Rutty's head in its maw, and chewed. I will never forget that crunch. *Never.*

Something in me spasmed, and I screamed involuntarily from the well of my soul. It was almost as if I was held captive by its stare too, rooted to the floor in horror. Something flashed slowly past my eye, to my right, and it crashed into the gorgon, wielding a heavy red tube through the air that came sailing straight into the gorgon's temple.

Simultaneously, the creature was so intent on devouring Rutty that it never saw Bassett's fury. It turned to face me as I screamed, but that fire extinguisher knocked it out cold. And me: I couldn't take my eyes away from my baby brother, lying there mauled. I couldn't help Bassett. I couldn't move. I couldn't do anything.

Rutty lay there, under that berserker. *Dead.* My gun dropped from my grip and fell to the floor with a dull thud. Everything around me swam. I heard Bassett breathe out "Oh no," and look Rutty up and down. The blood was pooling around all of them, spreading out across the floor.

Dead.

Wyatt Rutledge Shipley was gone. I don't know how I did it, but I joined my gun on the floor, falling to my knees with a sound that they told me later was the most tragic sound of despair they had ever heard. Some had to cover their ears. My hands, for some strange reason, were extended outward with palms up. I dimly registered it was so, but I was not receiving this. No, this was incredulity fused with wrenching outrage.

Everyone poured out of their respective places and converged on the beast. They heaved it off of Rutty and then heaved their own weight upon it, throwing the blanket over its head. And then Witherspoon returned and pulled his mask off, observing the ghastly scene with his own eyes. He turned away and vomited. Ally threw up too. Pretty sure I did as well. And it was not from the gorgon's stench.

I couldn't hear what anyone said. Bassett looked like he was shouting toward me. There was blood all around him. Two of the refugees came over to me and cupped their hands over my mouth and my eyes. They tried to turn me away, but I was deadlocked in despair.

Desperately they tried to mute my screams. So many hands over my mouth. Then a cloth and some kind of sweater. They held me tight.

I saw Ally. She, too, was weeping uncontrollably. She ran to my side and took my hand, and I could see her rhythmically taking deep breaths, and I guessed that she was encouraging me to do the same. I tried. Her lips were moving soundlessly, indecipherable through my gags and screams.

The rest of them were scattered throughout the library, watching the windows, posting guard at the front door. Something was coming through on the headset repeatedly, from either Preston or Command, but I couldn't tell. My head was swimming, and my vision was blurry.

Rutty was gone. That awful monster had beheaded my brother.

Through my sobs I dimly heard Bassett working on the gorgon, and yet talking with Command in a halting, stunted, choking voice: "Man down, Command. Private Shipley is down."

But Ally was there. She was holding me and covering my mouth: that's all I remembered. There were few words she could even say. I couldn't hear them.

Maybe there was nothing to say anyway.

9 | ONWARD

Things would never be the same.

It was all coming back to me now.

I had a throbbing headache as my eyes blearily willed themselves to open, and everything around me slowly emerged from a fog of memory and oblivion. Blurred shapes became tangible, and as I looked around, I realized that I was back in a bed in Harvill, in a quiet room, under a blanket. Everything was white: the color of purity, silencing all other colors in its peace: especially the color red.

It wasn't my room, but it was somewhere.

I sighed and laid my head back on the pillow, on my side. And that's when I saw it.

On the little table next to my bed, two headsets lie there, seemingly intertwined in cold harmony. One was definitely mine; the other was Rutty's. It was all I had left of him. Preston must have laid it beside me.

Ally walked in. She noticed that I was coming to, and she came over to me and sat down, embracing me. No words. One of those embraces where there is a shared understanding of the journey one has been through. One of those embraces where you can't help but let it all out and sob; and that's just what we did, together.

I could feel her body shaking, tremors running through it, before I felt her first tear on my cheek. Or was that my tear? Either way, we had both lost someone special who would never return.

The tears subsided. She told me that the mission had been a success. Bassett had successfully implanted the tracker in a berserker, and silently, with the help of all of them, they had heaved its putrid muscle-ripped body outside, back onto the grass. Time would only tell what we would or would not learn from this pathetic and useless mission that took the life of my little brother, the last bit of family I had.

When he died, they had scooped his body up – what was left of it – and wrapped it in cloths that they had found in a library supply closet. They weren't going to leave him there to fill the belly of a gorgon. All of them had bravely stayed behind, despite the ever-present threat brought on by all that noise, and tended to him with honor. The gorgon: they heaved it out onto the grass irreverently to make its own slow recovery; something it had denied Rutty. Ally said Fox ran out and kicked it in its side while it was out cold. It woke up a half-hour later and took off.

Rutty was brought back to Harvill Hall in a big laundry cart, but he was soon going to stink, and they couldn't afford to keep him there; they would have to bury him as soon as possible.

As for me, a few of the refugees and Trudy had thrown me over Riley's back and taken me nervously back to Harvill, watching the skies under the protective cover of the aerial defenders.

"What time is it?" I asked her. My watch was too far to reach.

"Almost ten," Ally said, stroking my hair as I lay there. "Command wants us to head back at 1300. Also, there was some kind of explosion a mile or so north of here, about an hour ago. We don't know what it was. One of the guards thought it was actually some kind of missile, but we don't know. There was a big blast, and a plume of smoke. The gorgons converged on it pretty quick: they saw a bunch of them zip across the sky in that direction. Command says they have no information. Smoke's still rising from there."

"A missile?" I asked. I shook my head. No idea. It was so hard to believe that it had only been a little over twenty-four hours out here. So much had happened in a single day: it boggled my mind. But then again, my mind was in no state to process things clearly.

Ally offered me a glass of water. I sat up and drank it with an eagerness that surprised myself. I was thirsty as all get out. I gave her back the empty glass.

We sat in silence for a few minutes, and then a thought slowly dawned on me. "Rutty would have liked to have died in a library. He loved books, he really did," I said through tears, looking up at Ally. "He loved books."

She nodded.

•　　•　　•　　•　　•

There was a shadow at the door, and the floor creaked. We both turned to see Bassett standing there. He said nothing. Neither did we. He came in and slowly sat down on the floor opposite us, his back sliding down the wall. He looked tired and spent.

"Jet, I-" he started. "I don't know what to say. Words won't even do it justice. I'm *so* sorry, brother." His eyes were wet.

I looked at him. This was his mission, and he was in command. But Command gave him this charge, and I didn't blame him; how could I hold him responsible? After all, he was the one who knocked it out cold and stopped it from reveling in its kill. He was the one who came up with the plan on how to get it all done, and like it or not, we were all part of that plan…including Rutty. And he was the one who implanted the tracker. We accomplished our mission.

"Joe, don't. You have nothing to be sorry about," I assured him. "Rutty saved Witherspoon. You saved Rutty. We got the gorgon. I'm the one who is sorry. I just… stood there. I…," I ended, wanting to say more, and not finding the words.

"Hey," Ally interrupted gently. "Don't do that. You know as well as we all do that there was nothing *to* do. There was nothing we could have done except to close our eyes. You guys didn't have a mask, and you couldn't look at it or you'd have ended up just like Wyatt," she said through tears. I loved that she called him by name. "You can't engage them, you know that."

She was right, and I knew she was right.

I looked back to Bassett. "It's OK," I said. I took a deep breath and laid back down. "What's the plan now?" I asked blandly, staring up at the ceiling.

No one answered for a while. But then Bassett cleared his throat and took a breath. "There really isn't one. We're heading back. Stone figures we did our job, and we could all use a break. We're to return at 1300."

It was just then that I realized that we'd be in time for the memorial.

Only this time, it would be for *three* people. Maybe even more.

•   •   •   •   •

At some point, I don't remember when, I had risen and showered. The tears came, fused with a life full of memories, all blending imperceptibly into the hot spray. I could only quietly lament my kid brother, and send him off to the skies of my mind. I was still in shock; left in incredulity. I'd lost partners before. *But not like this.*

I toweled off and got dressed, numbly. Before he left, Bassett had said that they'd all be in 302. No one felt like eating. I certainly didn't. So, I met them there. Preston, Riley, Jesse and a few others were there. MeeMaw saw me enter, and came up to me, taking my face in her hands. She hugged me. I shrugged off a feeling of brief annoyance, and accepted her embrace. She was only trying to help. MeeMaw walked out.

I looked at my watch for the first time since the attack. 1102 hours. Bassett informed those there that a few of the refugees were just outside, digging a hole. They were doing it extremely quietly, and under a thick cover of trees to the southwest of us which hugged the building. There was a guard posted to protect them in the work. There were fewer sightings now that the day was getting on. For that, I was truly thankful, because it would soon be time to bury Rutty.

I didn't want to help. I didn't know if I would make it through it. I honestly was beginning to feel embers of anger stirring within me. A slow sludge of dissent and contempt was taking root, and I wanted to give Command a piece of my mind. I wanted to give Stone a piece of my mind. And frankly, I wanted beyond measure for this operation to succeed: to yield *something* we could use.

The truth of the matter is that I was angry at the God that Rutty served and prayed to. I remembered the last line of his prayer: deliver us from evil. *Deliver us from evil*, he had prayed twice. So where was God? God was not there, and he had delivered Rutty from *nothing*. I was angry and wanted to give *God* a piece of my mind. I remember looking up in the shower, at the cold porcelain tiles overhead, and that's all of God that I could see. Cold, porcelain tiles that would not answer back, would not explain themselves, and would not deliver us from evil.

That was not the worst part. The worst part were my last words to him. *Hey bud*. So casual. So flippant. So… nothing.

I wasn't even allowed to say goodbye.

•   •   •   •   •

Ally found me wandering around Harvill, ambling, unsure of where to go: in a fog. I couldn't stay in our bunk forever, as that had Rutty's clothes which had been washed, his boots, weapons, headset, and everything else of his in there. Even the books he had brought. There was a giant bite out of his upper fatigues, and they were punctured and shredded near the top. He had been mauled. I shuddered and walked hastily out of there, grabbing one of his books to hold onto on the way out.

Somehow, Ally persuaded me to go outside and attend the burial. I could have only done it with her help.

As I walked outside, I could still see traces of black smoke wafting eastward away north; testament to whatever explosion Ally had reported had happened around 0900. I would ask Command about it later.

All sixteen of us on the mission were there. Sorry, what am I thinking: I mean all *fifteen* of us. We cautiously walked outside, passing more refugees flanking us as we exited the building and processed to the left. They were carrying Rutty's body before us, wrapped tightly in white linen, around the corner of the building. I don't know who had done it, but someone bravely assembled what they could of his head, which they had extracted from the gorgon's mouth, and it was in there with his body, in the right place. People can really rise to the occasion, and a sudden feeling of overwhelming gratitude washed over me for them honoring him as they did. I hadn't known any of this before. I choked back a grunt, and I could feel the tingles and the tears intermingling inside me. My eyes began to well. I gripped his book violently in my hand. I could feel it curling.

They had waited for another half hour after the berserker had regained consciousness, of course; it woke up groggily, gripped its own arm and appeared to wince. Programmatically, it just did what they do; hovered there, sniffed, then floated away looking for more food. *Punk.* Twitching and snarling, it darted up over the library and went off north. The coast was clear now.

We passed under a cover of fairly naked winter trees adjoining Henry Street, and there was the grave. It was dug in silent haste, but it was sufficiently deep. I don't think it was beyond a gorgon to go grave-robbing, and we didn't want to take that chance and so dishonor our loss.

Wordlessly, silently, we wiped our eyes. We all lifted his body gently and graciously, and then began to lower it in. Two of them had decently jumped in the grave to receive his body, and lower him in lightly from there. I looked up at Bassett. His face was a twisted red mess of angst, and his brow was furrowed. I knew he was also thinking of Steph. I scanned the crowd. All of them were the same. In fact, MeeMaw had cupped her hand over her mouth and was desperately trying to hold back tears.

She couldn't do it, and briskly walked back inside Harvill, past our gunners.

Gunners at a funeral. *Good grief.*

Wyatt Rutledge Shipley was committed to the earth now. My little brother was truly gone, committed to the earth. In went the dirt, gradually, softly, bit by bit, and with each scoop of that shovel my heart swelled and overflowed with grief.

Good grief.

Scoop, scoop, scoop. Down went the dirt, down went the memories, down went the heroism, down went our friend, the last of my family, in solemnity and grief.

Good grief.

Good because he died a hero. Grief at the loss of someone who was part of a mission that would yield results of which we were not even assured. Grief at how young he was. Grief at this long war, and the continuing toll that it exacted on all of us.

I couldn't see anything. My vision swam. I could feel Ally rest her head on my shoulder, and I squeezed her hand tight, though mine trembled violently.

With each heave of my chest the sadness and grief contorted my face and my breathing into raspy gritted breaths, I could feel my body surge with adrenaline and wrath. My entire form started to rack with rage, and I could feel my head shaking. It was cold out, but not that cold. No: this was my body steeling itself for revenge. Preparing itself for payback. It was all I could do to restrain myself. My mind drew up irrational mad battles upon glorious battlefields wielding multiple guns, firing in every direction as gorgons plummeted from the sky to join the fiery earth below. Gunfire sprayed from me as a halo: shielding me and delivering this sad planet from the fate that had for too long bound it in chains. And what was that I was shouting on that battlefield? *Why? Why? Whyyyyy?*

Or was it, *Wyatt! Wyatt! Wyatt!?*

I would have my revenge. But it would not be this moment.

The last earth was piled on. I nervously knelt down – or was it that my knees gave out and I collapsed? – I was trying to kneel at least. But I accidentally fell over on my butt. No one laughed. Ally reached down for me and steadied one arm.

Shaking, I got to my knees, reached out for Rutty's grave, laid the book I was holding on the top of it, and slowly stood back up.

It was then that I remembered his words in the darkened room the night before:

Man, I miss Christmas. Weird being stuck in a world full of gorgons with no 'fa la lalla la...'

The refugees and Bassett held their hands out, palms up. I couldn't bring myself to do that. I just couldn't. I wasn't ready to receive his death, willing or unwilling. I resolved then that I would celebrate Christmas with him, however I could. And it would start right now. I turned to Ally and said "Come with me, please? I really need to show you something."

And with that, we turned and walked back inside.
Good grief.

As we strode back inside, suddenly my mind was taken back to a memory of Rutty turning fifteen years old in our Blockade. Some young girl – her name, *Carrie Franklin,* suddenly came rushing at me from out of the past – had serenaded him with a sweet acoustic guitar song called 'Fight on, Fighter.' I could hear the dim but powerful strains echo through the vaults of my memory as we walked in silence.

And then I swallowed hard as I realized: that's *exactly* what Rutty did in the library under that gorgon. He fought on, the fighter that he was. He fought. *He went out fighting.* Ally had no idea why I melted right then and there, sobbing in her arms.

The song had come true. I vowed through my tears, right then and there, that I would fight on for him. Always.

Fight on, Fighter.

•   •   •   •   •

There we were, in the dark of room 302, as Rutty and I had been the night before, sitting on the floor, staring up at that little tree. I so wanted to take those Christmas lights with me. But Rutty wouldn't have wanted that. This was their tree, not ours. Rutty gave, he didn't take. If I had died instead of him, I don't think he would have even tried to pursue Ally, out of respect for me. There was no way I could take them and still do him proud. That would have been selfish and only helped *me*. Rutty died for *all* of us.

"We were in here last night, just the two of us, talking about Christmas. Did you know he was only nineteen?" I turned to her.

She shook her head.

"Yeah. Too young. Nineteen just isn't enough Christmases. I hadn't seen an actual tree forever. Neither had he," I told her. "Rutty said something about being in a world full of gorgons with no Christmas music. But," I lamented quietly, "we didn't sing. No songs."

Ally looked at me and she didn't smile. I could tell she was thinking. What was she thinking?

She looked away, her eyes moving around the room. A few precious minutes passed. Then she took a deep breath and drooped her head. I wondered again what was going through her head.

And there, in that darkened room, softly, reverently, with just the two of us, Ally began to sing.

Silent Night, Holy Night, all is calm, all is bright. Round yon' virgin, mother and child. Holy infant, so tender and mild. Sleep in heavenly peace, sleep in heavenly peace.

It was the last line that broke me.

Sleep in heavenly peace. That's what Rutty would have wanted. He loved God. He loved Jesus. And now he was sleeping. In peace. In heaven.

Sleep in heavenly peace.

I moaned, taking in the new meaning of that line.

The dam broke, and I shook and quaked as I hadn't before. Ally grabbed me as I sobbed, and held me as I bawled into her shoulder, quaking violently.

I must have gone a good ten minutes of violent shaking and wailing. The trauma of the sight of it all was still all too present in my mind, but that's what did it: that's what made the last line of that blessed song so impactful: this young soldier, so deprived of peace in life, now got to sleep forever in it. It seemed a horrible trade off if you only looked at this life.

Maybe Rutty was right after all about God. I don't know. All I knew now was that I wasn't done bawling.

Ally held me, and she too began to weep. I think she understood what sent in the floodwaters, and she shared my grief. There, in the *stille nacht* of that room, dimly lit by the light of that silent and holy tree, soundless, voiceless, I heard Rutty whisper "Merry Christmas, man" one more time.

I voiced it back. "Merry Christmas, bud."

Ally heard me and pulled me tight, the tears renewing in her eyes. "Merry Christmas, Wyatt," she said.

I laid there against her, our tears becoming rivers of grief and labored joy at his deliverance: he no longer had to fight a war. He got to be with his God. He was sleeping in heavenly peace.

Goodbye, Rutty. Not for the last time, I'm sure. Goodbye, my beloved bro.

•   •   •   •   •

It was nearing 1200. Ally and I stayed there in 302. Eventually Bassett found us. He opened the door to the hall, and white light came streaming in. He didn't turn on the light in 302, but he saw us there, bathed in the soft light of the tree.

He did that stupid clenched-lip *I feel your pain* thing that we all do. "Just about time to go," he started, preceding an incredibly long pause in which none of us spoke.

Slowly, eventually, he made his way over to us. He noticed the Christmas tree in the corner.

"Jet, I'm not really good with words in situations like this. But I want you to know that Command has a commendation. And," he said, coming a bit closer, "I know Rutty was a man of faith. If there's one thing I remember from my time in Sunday School, it's John 15:13: *Greater love has no man than this, that a man lay down his life for his friends.* I promise to honor him as long as I live."

I nodded and took a deep breath. Ally looked at Joe, and I could feel her nodding too.

"Rutty laid down his life for his friends. I'll never forget that. I owe him," he stopped. "*We* owe him," he corrected himself. "We just got word from Command that they've got a position on that gorg." My guts roiled.

"It looks like it's with a group of them because the signal keeps getting shrouded, and they appear to be clustering back at the Cumberland for now. My guess is that they're feeding off the dead gorgons that that DTF hit. So, if they don't move, then a choice lies before us. We have to find a different way back, and that means either the Cunningham bridge, which will take us about two and a half miles south of here, which is a lot of walking. Or…some other way."

"What other way?" Ally asked.

"Well, I don't know, but I do know that none of us want to try the train trestle way again, I'm sure. No swimming, and no heading that way. Too many gorgs."

Ally looked down, thinking. "Aren't we supposed to hit any of the other buildings on campus while we're here? For supplies, I mean?" she asked. "That was the mission of course."

He shook his head. "No, not anymore. Command sent word that the Alpha team made it back in one piece, and they were able to bring in some fresh supply and ag for the hydroponics. There are a few farms south of the Blockade that helped with that: they still grow naturally." I nodded. I knew that. "Our original mission was usurped when we got the order to lojack that thing. There will be other missions."

"Has the Beast said anything?" I asked.

"Beast?" Bassett tilted his head.

"Yeah, it's our supercomputer in the data room back at the Blockade. I don't know how long it's been running. Long time. They feed it data all the time: various intel, probable locations, thermals, infrared, etc. It's basically trying to figure a way out."

He shook his head. "Oh, that. Yeah, I saw it. I haven't heard anything on it. We don't have one of those in Alpharetta. Glad you guys do."

Thinking, and listening to the two of them, a third option presented itself to me. "Well, why don't we all just heavily arm ourselves and bring these refugees back to the Blockade with us?"

Bassett heaved a big breath and half shook his head. "There's no way we can house all these civies, Jet. We're pushed to the max as it is in each Blockade, and we barely have the resources to sustain the current population. These guys have survived here in various demographics for a decade and a half. I mean, if a few of them wanted to enlist with us, they wouldn't be turned down of course, but we can't overwhelm this Blockade by taking in stragglers.

"Also," he voiced, "that's a lot of people to herd back home. The thought of losing even one of them on the return journey chills me to my core."

I hardly thought these guys were stragglers. But he was right. And there were doubtless more. There were so many buildings on this campus. And there were a hundred businesses within a square mile of here, all with varying resources and equipment to sustain life, or at least to create a makeshift refuge that could mount a reasonable defense.

They would have to stay put.

"Command wants us to leave a headset with Preston to communicate with him as needed, and vice versa. We can definitely do that."

I nodded. That would be Rutty's.

Bassett knelt down in front of me. "You ready to do this, soldier?"

I nodded. He was right: we couldn't help everyone. And we needed to get back. I honestly now just wanted to get back to the Blockade and back to my bunk. I wanted to attend that memorial.

He looked at Ally, and she nodded too.

"Alright. Let's get a move on then. It's noon. We have an hour. Let's prep for evac, and gather our things."

He put his hand on my shoulder and squeezed, and did that clenched-lip thing again, but I appreciated it. He was only trying to help. At that moment I remembered him knocking out the gorgon with the fire hydrant, and my hope in him was renewed. He knew what he had to do, and rose to the occasion to do it.

There was just one more thing to address.

"Bassett," I said. "No more secrets this time. I mean it. No secrets."

He nodded. "You have my word. I'm actually stepping down now. You're back in charge. Command sent that through as well."

Just then I wondered how I would have fared being in command of the lojack mission. I couldn't blame him. It was actually planned and executed decently, and I confess I was moderately impressed with his strategizing.

He squeezed my shoulder again, arose, and walked out. There we were, alone again.

I turned to Ally. "Did we ever have a prayer on this outing?" I asked her.

She stopped, thinking, and she nodded. "Oh yeah, Cam. I mean, the whole thing sucks, but we did what we needed to do. If Bassett's right, if everyone is right, then we now have the opportunity to see where exactly they go and what they might be doing, now that we can track that gorg. As long as it doesn't get killed by us or them, we can follow its movements, and that's pretty valuable intel."

I looked at her. "I'm so glad I have you. I don't know where I'd be right now if I didn't."

Ally smiled. "Probably back at the Blockade in those nice boxers you had on."

I found myself laughing. It was an odd sound and just kind of escaped me, but it was certainly welcome right now. Ally laughed alongside me, there in the dark. I took her head and touched mine to hers.

If everyone is right, I thought.

Everyone had better be right.

We got up and walked out, hand in hand, back to the bunk, to gather our things and prepare for the return trip home.

It would be a long, solemn one.

•   •   •   •   •

It was almost 1300. Our belongings were assembled, and we were down in the tiny kitchen again. I was actually famished at this point, and wolfed down an egg sandwich, some stale Saltine crackers, and dried fruit. Jesse was there.

As it turns out, he told me that the Morgan University Center was loaded with food and supplies, plenty of which had enough preservatives to sustain life until Jesus returned. A lot of stuff went bad, but you gotta love those tightly sealed packages. They even had stale frozen bagels there that, once warmed up a little, went down properly, as long as you cut out the mold. Canned fruits, vegetables and beans, dark chocolate, dried fruits and pasta, Jell-O powder, honey, popcorn (you just couldn't pop it), grains, molasses, powdered milk, and even some pickles and canned tuna that were still good.

This was encouraging, because it meant that if the refugees needed to branch out, they certainly could. They could move as needed. They'd just need to employ the same clandestine operations and utter secrecy that they must have needed to in their initial reinforcement and shoring up of Harvill Hall.

A few others eventually came in. Ally had gone to the restroom, and now it was just myself, Fox, Vera and MeeMaw. The first thing they did when they saw me was do that lame lip-clench thing as well. That was getting old.

I greeted them, and they feebly offered various incantations of "sorry about Rutty." I thanked them, and quickly moved on to other matters, like the food, which I was now devouring. Vera had quickly mustered up some food and whipped me up that sandwich.

"You guys about to head out then?" Fox asked. He had a bit of a stern, resolute look on his face.

"Yeah. 1300," I mumbled through sandwich bites.

He paused. "You taking any of us with you?"

"Hadn't planned on it. Not unless they enlist."

I looked over at Fox. His stern expression didn't change at all; just stared at me intently.

"You're enlisting?" I asked him. "After what you just saw?"

"Yeah," answered Vera.

I turned to her. Fox had nodded, but Vera had answered. "You wanna join up too, Vera?"

She nodded as well, valiantly.

I was enheartened by their valor and bravery. I just didn't know if they had fully seen what the gorgon did. I stared at them, looking them up and down. Fox stood up a little taller when he noticed what I was doing, as if he were trying to score more height points on a chart, or was asked to suck in that gut by a drill sergeant.

"Let me see what I can do. I'll ask Command. You guys armed? We don't have armor for you guys, and we only have two masks for the way back."

"We know," Fox said, looking over at Vera. "It's all good. We're doing it for Rutty."

I practically choked on my egg sandwich. I clenched my jaw, nodded to them and gave them a light half-assed attempt at a salute. They saluted back. Seemed way too formal and dramatic, but whatever.

"Don't go anywhere. Be back in a bit," I said. I looked down at my watch. It was already 1240. "Second thought, you better get ready just in case."

They went to a corner under the table that was there, quickly extracting two backpacks.

I actually laughed. If Rutty could see this, he would have smiled too. Down one, and up two, just like that.

"How old are you, Fox?"

"Nineteen. Twenty in May."

Rutty's age. I bowed my head. He must have found that out somehow. I put my plate down and walked over to face him. It was all I could do to hold it together. He was only three, like Rutty, when the gorgons arrived. I wondered if Fox was at home, shielded by a stay-at-home mama, when his older brother or sister burst through the doors and told them they were under attack, scooping into their arms and finding shelter to hide out for the next sixteen years.

I looked at Vera. "And you?"

"Twenty-seven. I had an older brother at Richview. Lost him a few years ago." She lost an older brother like Ally had.

"Do either of you know how to handle a rifle? Shooter? Grenades?" I looked down at their shoes. "Looks like you got good travel boots at least."

"Yes sir," Vera asserted. "Good as anybody else."

"Definitely," Fox replied.

"What's your name, Fox?" I asked.

"Liam," he answered.

"Well, okay then. Liam, Vera, I'm Cameron. You can call me Jet if you want, that's my nickname, but I'm Cameron. And you're Vera, and you're Liam," I said to Fox. "And you'd be welcome in my unit." I smiled at them. "You guys are alright."

"Thanks. I'll stick with Fox," he said.

"OK Foxy," I laughed back. "No problem." He smiled. I think he liked *Foxy*.

The two recruits smiled back. I couldn't help but be drawn to Fox: the same age as Rutty, the same youthful swell of bravado, the same eyes.

I turned to Vera. "Rutty really liked you."

She blushed.

"Come with me, you two."

We headed out of the small kitchen, MeeMaw clapped the shoulders of each of them as they came out behind me, in support of them. We walked down the hall to the main entrance, and held there.

"Hang tight here, I need to round up the rest of us."

Just then, Ally was walking down the hall with one in tow. It was Jesse. "This one wants to joi-" she stopped short, seeing Vera and Fox with me, their backpacks slung over their shoulders. She pointed at them and looked at me.

"These ones joined up too," I said. "Hey Jesse."

Jesse nodded and smiled.

Joe rounded the corner just then as well, his pack over his shoulders and his hat on. He looked at all of us. "Well, I'll be," he voiced. He walked closer, looking us all up and down. "And then there were six."

The six of us turned and looked at ourselves, as if to verify the count.

"Motleyest crew of fuzzy patches I've ever seen," Joe said to the three newcomers. "You guys sure you're up to the challenge?"

"Yes, sir," they replied. I just looked at him with a half-hearted smile. I could tell he was looking at Fox and thinking of Rutty too. I admit I was as well. I couldn't help but mirror that. They looked nothing alike, but there was a similarity there: young, cocky, ready to go. I just hoped that we'd be able to protect this one. That was gnawing at my conscience: for *all* of them.

It was time to go.

We were at a seminal moment, a liminal phase, and things would never be the same.

10 | NEVAEH

We were now on our way home. 1300 hours. Our bellies full, Preston kept the headset and waved us off. Ally and I would wear the other two. Bassett graciously went without. Preston hugged me, which was awkward. I never really was much of a hugger. Except with Ally and Runo…no…what was I thinking. Just Ally now.

Foxy had Rutty's RPG launcher.

The three fuzzy patches said their goodbyes to the other refugees. We found out then that MeeMaw was Jesse's mom. That was a bitter parting. In a world where children were a danger to birth, this poor woman was losing her only one who had far outstayed living under the same roof with her. MeeMaw wept terribly. We also learned her real name: Rebecca.

I checked the weather, and informed our group that this wasn't going to be easy. Temperatures were down today. High thirties. It was overcast. All prime conditions for gorgons. I wondered briefly if we should be waiting to return on another day with more ideal conditions. But we had accomplished our mission and had been ordered back. Our own team could go, but we had no supplies or equipment for the new recruits other than their own weapons and their own meager packs: for them to make the journey, later, alone, would be asking too much of them.

Vera herself had never been out of Harvill. I was so stunned I had to verify that with her. She confirmed it: not once. She was admittedly an inside girl, and mainly helped with food prep. But, like Ally, she also had weapons training with her dad as a kid. The truth of the matter was that she stayed inside out of fear. Couldn't blame her one bit.

I informed Command we were inbound. "Copy," came the confirmation. Joe switched on his m-deck. No signals. Unceremoniously, we exited: surreptitiously, slowly, out the south door again, as we had done less than six hours earlier on that accursed mission. I could instantly feel my cheeks turning red with the cold through the mask I was wearing. Ally had donned the other one.

I wanted to pass that library as quickly as possible. I didn't even look at it.

Ally and Joe went first, though she looked back at me and smiled before heading out. Jesse and Vera went next, and Fox and I took up the rear. All of us crept silently out. We could see the spot where the grass was smashed down in front of Woodward where the heavy berserker lay.

I slowed, and then stopped. Fox passed me and turned around. He was masked over his mouth, and wearing an APU hat. He looked at me curiously, and I could see his eyes firing off the query, "What's up?"

I didn't want to turn back, but I did anyway. The trees called my name. I could barely make out the small hump of newly dug earth piled in brown, protective reverence over my little brother. Over Rutty. I kissed two fingers on my left hand, pounded my fist on my chest and made a "V" for victory towards him. I wouldn't let him down again. I wouldn't let any of us down.

I turned back to the group, and they had all stopped and turned as well. "Had to say goodbye," I puffed.

Joe answered. "All good, kid. We all did."

I joined them and we went up the slope, each in turn slowly turning away from Rutty. From Harvill. From the Woodward library. From the horrors that Joe, Ally and I had known for just a day, and the comfort our new enlistees had known, some for sixteen years.

Jesse was the last to turn. His mom had come down to the south entrance, and brought him a wallet picture of their family that she had treasured. No words were exchanged. She slipped it in his hand and fled tearfully back to the cover of Harvill.

•　　•　　•　　•　　•

Our plan was to make for the Cunningham bridge this time. It was a much longer trip southwest, but there would be plenty of shielding in alleyways between buildings, rather than open forest and open sky. It was a double-edged sword however: if they were *inside* any of those buildings, they would surely see us passing by. But we didn't have any better option. We needed to get home.

We would pass to the east of the train trestle, where the berserker and the other signals were, so that was taking a risk, but we were far enough removed from it for it to be a firm threat.

Command would update me every hour, par for the course, on the location of that berserker. It was still holed up by the Cumberland with the other signals, they said. It must have been a feast for them, I'm sure. *Disgusting.* I shook my head.

I was now leading our platoon, threading a path between buildings, and holding to as much cover as I could keep the six of us to, to avoid detection. We weren't in the thick of the commercial district yet, so it would be a bit before we really had substantial cover.

After thirty minutes of scurrying and weaving between buildings, we had just crossed over Main Street when Command radioed that they had a signal. I motioned for the group to hold. "Contact, thirty meters, bearing 65," they said.

Thirty meters. *Too close,* I thought.

Ally and I heard that and scrambled between two buildings between Main and Grant, looking up.

We all held still and studied the skies. I looked back at Ally, who was staring up. Joe was at the rear, surveying the way we had just come. Vera was closest to me at that point, and I could see the fear in her eyes. I reached back, and took her by the hand. Her eyes darted over to me at the touch, and I squeezed her hand. I could hear her swallow to compose herself. "Hold absolutely still," I breathed to the newcomers. I put my finger to my mouth.

"Ten meters, bearing 30. Incoming. Six meters, bearing 18. Caution, inbound."

My fingers tightened around the grip of my rifle.

We all froze, at least those of us who had headsets.

Horrifyingly, a gorgon whizzed over our heads, making a low humming sound. We all waited with sledgehammers pounding in our chest, drumming out the terror beats of our primal fear.

Another passed by close behind it. And then another. And then three more. It was too much for Vera, who let out a bit of a squeak in her angst. The others heard it and looked over anxiously. I whirled towards her and held up my finger to my mouth, while gripping her by the shoulder. It was practically vibrating with terror.

I slowly shook my head, and then lifted my hand in front of her, up, and down, up and down, simulating calm breathing. She blinked with an effort, and then mimicked me. I could feel her trembling slowly, and finally normalize.

I looked back up. I had counted six. There may have been more while I calmed Vera. She shut her eyes. Fox was nervously alternating between us and the skies overhead.

We wouldn't go out until she knew the sky was clear.

The horror of the gorgon was all too present in a few of our minds, even immobilized and unconscious on the grass outside the library. Nearly everyone had seen it.

We let a good five minutes pass until Command gave us the all-clear. Due southeast of us was nothing but vast parking lots for a smattering of churches clustered closely together, the lot of which provided us no cover. We stuck to Grant Avenue and took cover close behind some smaller outbuildings, eventually finding ourselves in an alleyway with a rusty overhang heading west. In another ten minutes of duck and cover, we were crossing North Fourth Street, and a host of businesses, churches, banks, law offices, and more, before we would reach Franklin Street south of it.

I looked at our coordinates and felt this was a bit off course, drifting too close to the trestle and the last known sightings of the gorgons: presumably where the others were headed who had just whisked by overhead.

It felt suddenly like it had dropped in temperature as well. I glanced at my watch. 1348 hours. Thirty-seven degrees. I looked up at the skies, which were threatening. Low hanging grey clouds thick with rain were drifting in, borne on a southern wind up towards us. It just might snow, which would provide excellent sound cover for us. I crossed the fingers of my mind.

After connecting with the team and ensuring that everyone was okay and had their wits about them, we set out once more.

Our team was heading due south at that point, and eventually reached Franklin. There was nothing for it. The cover wasn't ideal, but what thin alleyways we could find, we made for. We found one next to more than a few law offices and proceeded south again toward Commerce Street.

Rats in a maze: all of us…and for all we knew, gorgons were clustered en masse to our west, only a few streets over. We were getting dangerously close to the train trestle, with still some way to go to reach the Cunningham Bridge. Up ahead, off Commerce and Hiter I saw a parking lot with some tree cover, and an expansive building loom up with two large spires on the far side of it, close to the street. They looked to be modern-day bell towers. But they looked bent and crumpled inwards at the top, as if they had survived some kind of barrage. I couldn't see over the top of the building clearly, but it was obviously a church of some description. That would be a good spot to take some cover in, and break for some food. It had been almost an hour since we set out, with a few to go still.

Strangely, all this time, I hadn't thought of Harvill, and had thought little of our time there. I discovered a strange and newfound sense of purpose escorting these refugees, these new grunts, with us. They had the bravery to enlist, but did they really know what they were getting into? I didn't think so.

For me, it was my mission to protect them, and ensure the safe return of my team *and* theirs. Especially, for whatever reason, Fox. Whether it was the fact that he was the same age as Rutty or not, I missed my little brother, and perhaps Rutty had put in a good word for me to the Big Man to provide someone similar to comfort me in my loss. Or maybe that was just wishful thinking.

I was getting thirsty. I figured we all were.

In another ten minutes, we had crossed over Commerce and into the parking lot of the church. I could see the sign: *Madison Street United Methodist.* Any time we were almost to our destination, I was afraid of running into trouble right there. A cruel fate would throw a curveball at us right before the finish line, I anticipated. And the naked trees, devoid of cover, offered us little screen to hide under.

Fortunately, no such last-minute curveball.

The back door was locked. Looked like a handicap entrance. We had to go around. All of us slunk cautiously around the corner of the building, checking back the way we came, and looking up and down Hiter Street as we rounded the corner of the building, traveling up a slight incline parallel to Hiter, which sloped downwards going the opposite direction.

The building was vast, but a minute or two later we were at the front steps of the church.

We ascended the front steps past an entrance patio, and didn't have to check the doors for locks; they were actually ajar. I wondered what that meant. No one in their right mind would keep their doors unlocked, much less opened. Was this an invitation, or a trap? Gorgons weren't that smart: they don't set traps. At least, they never had to date. No: this was probably the hubris of some stranded yet purpose-filled holdout priest telling the world, with fine priestly sanctimonious oration, that all were welcome inside his doors.

We would soon see.

•　　•　　•　　•　　•

We were all in. Out of habit, I shut the doors. A blast of chill air pushed inwards at us, the last grip of lowering temperatures clawing at us one last time. It was definitely dropping out there.

I went over to Vera and whispered, "Are you okay?"

Vera nodded, and I could see the visceral relief on her face that we were now out of the open. Ally had also come up beside her and patted her on the arm in reassurance. Ally was an only child now, and never had a younger sister; now there were two women in our group. And though Vera was three years Ally's senior, she was inexperienced and afraid, which gave Ally an unexpected opportunity to come alongside her in sisterhood. I put my arm around Ally when she had finished with Vera, and hugged her tight, finishing it off with a kiss, and a look of understanding that we were okay for now. I looked at the front doors: glass, and frail, but some kind of barrier at least.

As I turned back to head farther inside, there, lingering in the corner of the narthex, I spied a twenty-foot anaconda slowly slithering across the floor. I was taken aback, but such sightings were not unusual. Snakes were one of the few species slow and imperceptible enough to survive the yearslong onslaught. Thankfully, it looked elderly. *Must be a zoo escapee,* I thought. I walked over toward it. It was beautiful, and natural, and I couldn't bring myself to kill it.

As I watched it, for a flash I had an unwanted cartoonish thought of gorgons swarming the church and being deflected at this holy portal: foiled by the doctrine of neutral "holy ground" preventing them from entering. They would have to snap their fingers in defeat, and move on to the next targets. If only it was that elementary and cutesy. And if a twenty-foot anaconda could make its way in here…

I looked around. Ally, Jesse, Vera, Fox. Wait –
where was Joe? Where the heck was Joe Bassett? I looked
around at the others and they held their hands up. No one
had seen him since before Franklin and Commerce. My eyes
widened in alarm. We branched out across the open floor of
the narthex and into the sanctuary. No Joe. Nowhere. "Joe,"
I whispered. "Bassett?" I heard the others whisper.

No answer.

Now I was getting worried. There was no way in hell
he would have just run off and disappeared. I tried him on
the headset. "Bassett, come in. Come in, Bassett." Ally
looked at me confused from the other side of the sanctuary.
She pointed at her headset and then shook her head. With a
shock I realized it. Of course. He didn't even have a
headset; he had left his with Preston.

I radioed to Command an absent-unknown code for
Bassett. "Sergeant Bassett is AUN, repeat, AUN. Location
undetermined. Searching."

"Copy, keep us posted," came the reply. I never
knew who that was on the receiving end of communications,
but the voice sounded familiar this time.

There was only one place he could be, and that was
still outside somewhere. Had he taken a wrong turn, or taken
a spill and couldn't let us know by crying out and thus
risking attracting gorgons? We had to be sure.

"Ally, take over. I'm going to look for Joe. Fox,
you're with me. Jesse, Vera, you're with Ally. Keep
searching inside and have Ally report back if you find him.
And watch out: there's a giant snake in the lobby here.
Anaconda. Don't give it any ideas."

Ally did not look pleased.

My watch said 1407 hours. But even more
astonishing than that, the temperature now read thirty-five
degrees. By all rights it should be holding at where it was
earlier. A cold front was obviously moving in fast.

I shuddered at the notion of having to go back out and search for Joe in the cold, and if it were snowing, we wouldn't even be able to track a gorgon on the m-deck. There would be too much movement and too much air to contend with, and it would be utterly unreliable.

"Command, what's the last known position of the gorgon you're tracking?" I inquired.

"Stand by," they replied. A moment later, "No change in position at this time."

"Roger that."

I went to the door, and turned back to Ally. She was watching me from the other side of the narthex, and she looked concerned. I know I did too. I checked my mag and made sure I had extras. Grabbed my water bottle and took a big heavy tug on it. Looked at the snake, looked back at her, back at the snake, and back at her. Shook my head.

"Vera, close this behind me after I'm gone, please." Vera nodded. Fox came in close behind me and followed me. He didn't look afraid. He had his mouth covered in that mask, so I wouldn't have been able to see it anyway.

I posted up at the door. "Command, I need your eyes please. Limited visibility." I sent my coordinates. They confirmed. Fortunately, or unfortunately, as we were pretty visible standing there, I could see out *and* above into the open sky. No sign of movement. Slowly and cautiously, I slid one of them open, and we both stepped out and down the steps. In a moment we were posted up at the corner of the building. I wasn't going to stay on this corner long; we were uniquely visible and all too naked and exposed there.

The door had closed behind us. Good girl, Vera.

The temperature was truly dropping, and I wasn't sure why. If we didn't find Joe, we were all going to spend a cold snowy night in some strange, apparently unoccupied Methodist church dang near gorgon central, and we would miss the memorial and have to spend another night away from the shelter of the gun towers. Man, we could use those guns right now. And I would love to have the m-deck with us right about now. But perhaps Joe needed it more.

Command radioed no movement, so we hugged the external wall of the church, parallel to Hiter, scanning the area. Fox looked up. From that point we could see far off in the distance black dots against the darkening sky. There were a few shapes shooting across the horizon, like bugs to a bonfire. They were going west, like the rest. *Dangit, Command. You have to be quicker than that.* They radioed two seconds later, "Contact, bearing 050, range 550 meters."

"Yeah, thanks Command, we already saw them."

"Roger," came the unapologetic reply.

If I didn't know any better, they were roughly over Harvill and the university logo dell. I watched them pass by over the horizon of the nearest buildings to our west, and lowered my eyes back to ground level. Thankfully, they left Harvill alone.

The best option would be to retrace our steps. I could only hope that maybe Joe had passed out somewhere or sprained his ankle or something, and just couldn't cry out. But that would create another problem: a sprained ankle or injury to any of our feet would seriously slow us down. And the gorgons wouldn't politely slow down to match. As predator to prey, they would seize and pounce mercilessly. I'd already seen it. My thoughts went to Rutty, and how fast that gorgon smashed into him in the library. I shook away the memory and moved on.

We threaded our way under the parking lot trees, crossed back over Commerce, and headed back into the alley next to the law offices. My eyes darted all over. I know Fox was doing the same.

It was pretty remarkable how he already seemed to have some military-grade posture, and the way he held his weapon was formation-ready. I had been teamed up with a competent recruit who seemed like he would be able to hold his own. For that, I was grateful.

We proceeded up the alley, flanking each other on either side. Fox started to get ahead of me, when I heard a faint tap-tap. It startled me. "Fox! Hold up," I instructed. We stopped. Tap-tap.

We looked around. To our right was an architectural office. A side door had been pried open.

And there, in one of the windows, looking out at us, was Joe Bassett.

He waved us in.

•   •   •   •   •

He was wounded, as I suspected. Taking up the rear, he thought he had spotted something behind us, and whirled around with the m-deck to verify. But a nefarious pothole had his number, and he stepped in it and sprained his ankle. *How do you like this new hand you were dealt, Joe?*

"Hey. Sprained my ankle. It's not bad," he said, but his winces belied the truth. It looked a bit swollen already. He had wrapped it with a brace and bandage from his pack.

I glanced down at my watch. "Well, we've gotta get you back. It's 1430 and we have a ways to go yet. Glad we found you. Do you think you can walk?"

"I'll bloody well walk out of here," he drawled. "It'll get stronger after some rest, but I've gotta join you in the church. I saw you guys made it inside okay. I could see you coming back for me. Thanks Jet."

"Yeah, yeah, no worries, Joe," I smiled at him. I was firming up his bandage for him, and looking up I offered a bit of a reassuring smile. Fox was keeping watch outside the windows.

"Fox, you take the m-deck in your left hand, and you can hold Joe up on your right…I'll take him in my left. Can you carry a handgun, Joe?"

"Yep."

Fox came over and took Joe's left arm over his shoulder. I took his right. We propped him up and made for the door, which was slightly ajar: that's how we were able to see the slight shadow moving beyond it. And suddenly we heard the sniffing. Fox's m-deck started blipping dead ahead.

Instinctively, we froze. I quickly appraised our surroundings. Not a lot to hide behind but a few desks. If we were lucky, it would only be one of them. We held still, and restrained our breath.

The door creaked open.

And in poked a little head, shortly followed by a little African American girl. She was in pig-tails, and I was swiftly reminded of Ally when we first met her, bobbing along at the Blockade. The little girl had colorful elastic beads in her hair, and she looked to be about ten. She was sniffing from a cold.

We quickly dropped our weapons and holstered them. I held my hands up as the little girl looked over at us in panic and alarm, breathing rapidly. She clutched a little pink knapsack in one hand and a ratty teddy bear in the other. Looked like she had been out foraging for leftovers, but couldn't leave her bear behind of course. She dropped the bag on the floor and clutched her teddy to her chin.

"Shhhh," I said, "it's okay. We're here to help. Are you lost, honey?"

She shook her head.

"Where are your parents, huh? Are they around here too? Are they in here?"

She shook her head again.

"It's okay, you can trust us: we're part of the military and we're heading back to our Blockade. We were just up at the college. Do you know the college?"

The little girl nodded.

I put my gun down on the floor, and slowly went over to her and knelt down. Joe steadied himself on the desk we were sheltering behind.

She sneezed and wiped her nose. I smiled.

"What's your name, honey?" I asked her. She didn't answer. "Look, it's okay, I know you're scared. We're not gonna hurt you. What's your name?"

She paused. "Nevaeh," she breathed out into the fur of her bear so quietly I had to ask her to repeat it.

"'Nevaeh?' That's pretty! I like that," I assured her, putting my hand on her shoulder. The slightest trace of a flinch. "Do you have family around here, Nevaeh?" She shook her head slowly. "Where are they?" Again, no answer.

I looked her up and down. She looked to be doing ok, not malnourished or in poor health. She was a bit cold but had on a dark red coat. I looked around the room. That's when I noticed the stash this little girl had going. This is where she had chosen to hide out. She definitely wasn't around when the gorgons first attacked; I guessed that she was here with one or both of her parents, and had since lost them. I stood up, keeping a hand on her shoulder.

"Well, you've managed to survive here for a while, Nevaeh. We've got soldiers with us. This is Joe and that's Fox. We're with the army, and if you want to come back with us, we can protect you."

She looked over at Joe, who was clearly favoring his injured ankle.

"Oh that?" I laughed. She got me. "OK, touché. Well, Joe, he stumbled into a pothole, but he'll be okay, I promise. He's just clumsy." Joe grunted. "We were just about to take him back with us and get him some help, and then get back on our way south. Do you know the Cumberland River?"

She stiffened. That meant yes.

"Don't worry, sweetheart," Joe said. "We're not going that way. At least, not to the trestle, and not for a while. We know that's where they like to hang out and drink. We can keep you safe."

Nevaeh looked back at Joe's ankle, then up at him, then over to me. Then she looked back at his ankle and began to retreat backwards from us, farther into the office. Nevaeh shook her head.

I had to ask. "Honey, where are your parents, do you know?" Nevaeh's eyes dropped. That told me all I needed to know. I sighed, and looked at her. "Sweetheart, we can't make you come with us. But if you want to, I can promise you you'll be safer with us. We live under these big gun towers that keep us safe. We have food, clothes, drink, warmth, shelter, guns, and military guys to keep you safe. Or…safer. And there are other children there too."

I could feel the impasse rising up. She didn't budge, and I didn't think she was going to. I didn't know how long she had been holed up in here, but she certainly didn't want to leave her sanctuary. Out there meant *out there¸* and *out there* meant *them*. We had over three miles to go southwest to get back to the Blockade: that was a lot of land to traverse, and it would mean shepherding one more human, and an unwilling one at that. We certainly couldn't take her against her will: who's to say she would respond calmly? I thought of the other little girl back at Harvill, humming noiselessly to herself. Nevaeh too had learned to adapt and survive in total silence, and that silence became her blanky.

I turned back to Joe and Fox. Fox was helping Joe reinforce his makeshift splint. I raised my hands up in futility and said "We can't *make* her come with us. We've got to leave her behind. We can let Command know she's here, and maybe send another recon team later." They both nodded.

"She's survived this long," Joe said. "We'll have to pray her luck will hold, and hope we see her again. You can't force her," he finished.

Fox nodded in agreement. He had lowered his mask and said, "Breaks my heart, but yeah, you can't force her to come if she feels safer here. She might break away and just head right back here. And if her parents *are* still out there somewhere, maybe this is where they would look. That could be catastrophic."

I turned back toward Nevaeh. "Ally," I radioed. "Come in."

"I read you, go ahead," she said.

"We found Joe. Sprained ankle but he's okay. We're gonna head back. We found a child here, unaccompanied. Little girl, about ten years old."

"Eleven!" Nevaeh burst out, but then she gasped, and her eyes widened, clutching the bear over her mouth to stifle her own sound. She looked to the windows.

I had to chuckle. "OK, uh, make that eleven, and she feels *very* strongly about it," I said to Ally. "She doesn't want to come, and we can't make her. Sending you the coordinates now. We're incoming with Joe."

"Roger that, standing by."

"Command, did you read that?"

"Affirmative."

"Relay the coordinates to Captain Stone please – if there's a recon team up here again, we wanna check on this little girl whose name is Nevaeh. What's your last name, sweetheart?"

Nevaeh looked around. Either she wouldn't tell or didn't remember.

"No last name for now. Just Nevaeh."

"Copy."

Fox had helped Joe shore up his splint and bandage with supplies in the office, a few rulers and notepads and some packing tape. It was rough fitting his feet back into his boots, but he did it.

I looked the two of them over, and resolved to get going, leaving Nevaeh behind. I didn't like it.

"Nevaeh, we're gonna get going now," I whispered to her, walking towards her and kneeling down again. "There's a big church south of here, the Madison Street United Methodist church, do you know it?" She nodded, but she looked concerned. "That's where we'll be for a little bit, but then we need to continue south. If you change your mind, you keep quiet, hug the sides of the buildings, keep looking up, and make sure the coast is clear before you come, okay? We'll take you with us and keep you safe. But if you decide to stay, keep this handy." I placed my Beretta on a desk near her piled-up belongings. "The safety is on. You slide this back if you need to shoot. The magazine inside is full of bullets, and here are some extra ones." I laid these out too for her. "Just in case," I said. "Don't use it unless you have no way out."

She nodded again and lightly breathed out, "Okay." Her eyes darted to the windows again.

"Alright, let's move," I said.

We collected our things, and resumed the position we had attempted before we met the little girl, and moved for the door. Nevaeh went over and opened it for us, holding it open all the way. The cold draft came in and nipped at us. I swear it was a few degrees lower than it had been just a bit before, but I couldn't see my watch as it was around Joe's waist.

"Thank you, my friend," Joe said to her. "Be safe. Stay here as much as you can." Nevaeh nodded. "I hope you find your parents."

I hoped that too, but couldn't be sure of it.

The three of us hobbled outside, looking up and surveying the area. This was going to be difficult. It had to be some three hundred feet back to the church, and it would be slow going with Joe in the shape he was in, but he was able to walk with a limp and a wince. Fox held the m-deck for him in his left hand. I carried his rifle between us, hugging mine, with Rutty's Glock 19 in my right hand.

We stepped out into the alleyway and started our slow, arduous walk back. That's when we all saw it: snowflakes. Tiny snowflakes, scant; but definitely coming down now. It was a welcome sight for many reasons. For Joe and Fox, I'm sure it meant obscuring our passage a bit more. For me, it meant a white Christmas. I thought of Rutty. *Fa la lalla la, buddy,* I wished him, looking up.

We had gone halfway down the alley toward Commerce, when we heard a sound behind us that sounded like a light clearing of the throat to get our attention. In the middle of the alleyway stood little Nevaeh, and she was waving her little bear toward us. We turned around as best as we could, seeing her standing there.

At that moment, I wasn't sure if we were doing the right thing, and I shook my head. I swore to Rutty not to let the guys under my charge down. She wasn't part of that oath, though. I wished silently that she wanted to come with us, but, as Joe would say, "that wasn't in the cards."

We waved back to her solemnly. She was too young to know the receiving hands gesture, so we didn't do it. But I wished it to her in my mind.

The snow continued to fall.

•　　•　　•　　•　　•

We made our way across the street. The snow was getting thicker now. I radioed to Ally to meet us at the back entrance at the handicap ramp. Somehow that made even more sense what with Joe injured. Mercifully, there was not a gorgon in sight: Ally met us at the back and let us in. The door was open by the time we returned, and she and Vera received Joe. By the time we were inside the doors, the snow was falling much thicker.

I took a long look back up the alley toward Franklin, wishing that I could do more, but vowing not to forget Nevaeh. Or to pray, as Rutty would have, for her safety.

At least we were back on our way home.

11 | HOLY GROUND

I didn't know how much more I could take.

The back door closed, and the ladies took Joe inside and to the left, past a row of classrooms, heading into the sanctuary. They laid him down gently on one of the pews in the massive room.

I was sweating, but the cold snow blunted it. Nonetheless, I was a bit panicked and frustrated that we had to go back for him. But at least we got him back inside in one piece, us included.

Jesse came running up in his socks so as to minimize the noise. "While you guys were gone, we found a kitchen off the hall downstairs that has food in it – real food!" he exclaimed loudly. We shushed him, but he kept on. "There's food cooking on the stove; someone's in here with us for sure!"

I instantly thought of Nevaeh, and I think Fox and Joe did as well. We weren't ready to mention her just yet. There might be blowback in that we chose not to bring her with us. In any event, it wasn't her: if she had made the food, surely she would have remained here to eat it.

My watch called me to its face. We had to get on the move soon. 1512. If we were going to make it back for that memorial, we couldn't stay here long. But I was obliged to check out the food situation. And we needed ice for Joe's leg. "Ally, can you help Joe? I'm going for ice, and to look for friendlies."

I didn't know who was here, and frankly, I didn't care all that much. Our bellies were still fine from eating right before we left, but that didn't mean I would turn down real cooked food if I had the chance.

As a species, we had really learned to work wonders with food, and to make it special. *If* we could keep that smell from the gorgons, that is. If it meant a choice between eating and dying, we were all too ready to starve. But that just meant that our bellies would rejoice all the more when we set our taste buds on what the cooks, in particular back at our Blockade, had whipped up. The stuff they provided at Harvill was far superior, however, and their ingenuity at masking the smell was brilliant.

I wondered where that snake was, and if they had killed it, trapped it, or set it free. Hoped there weren't any more of them slithering around in here.

We went downstairs below the sanctuary and found a bunch of classrooms and offices clustered close together before proceeding up a staircase into a fellowship hall. At the back, as Jesse had reported, there was a small kitchen. His nose had served him well. There was coffee brewing in there, along with a pack of cigarettes on the counter next to a lighter. On the stove there were hot vegetables in a pot that had been left simmering on a burner. I could smell the delicious salty seasoning. Next to it was a big pan of Spanish rice, and on the back burner was a huge stew full of meat bubbling in a savory sauce. It smelled divine. I was hungry, and everything else looked fine, but I confess I eyed the stew suspiciously. If that was some poor stray dog, or deer – or *gorgon* even, no thank you. We were all hungry, but not so hungry as to eat boiled gorgon. Needed to know what animal it was first.

My primary concern with all this was that we were very close to Commerce Street, and any exhaust fan would certainly send that scent outdoors. But perhaps the gorgons would be foiled by the construction of the building and the multiple floors. For now, I let the intoxicating scent of the delectable stew, rice and veggies fill my nose.

Before long, we returned with ice cubes in a few hand-towels we had located in the kitchen drawers, along with the vegetables and rice, poured out into separate containers for our platoon. Left the stew on the kitchen stove. I couldn't find any utensils, so we'd have to rough it. My thoughts went back to the coffee and smokes. That was next.

Joe was exceedingly grateful for the ice. At most, we could spare about a half hour in this church, and then we'd have to get on the move again. None of us fancied another night out here, especially so much closer to what appeared to be gorgon central. And how we were to get across the Cumberland now, with the snow falling and temperature dropping so rapidly, short of crossing the bridge itself, I had no clue. We'd have to cross that bridge when we got there, quite literally.

When Joe had been tended to, I brought some of the food to Ally in a separate container and told her quietly about Nevaeh. She understood the dilemma and said we did the right thing. Ally wolfed down the food, making yummy noises in plenty. That warmed my heart. "Good, huh?"

"Oh yeah. Spanish rice, wow…but who made it? That's the question."

We were all spread out across the pews now, legs outstretched and boots off. That was heaven on earth.

"Yeah, I don't know," I said, looking around at the vast arches of the sanctuary ceiling. The choir loft was at the far end of the sanctuary, and I could see the big organ pipes running up to the ceiling. "Somebody's running around here, or they're out on errand somewhere else. It wasn't Nevaeh, she was pretty insistent that she stay where she was."

"Such a pretty name, *Nevaeh?*" Ally asked. "Are you sure she was all alone?"

"Yeah."

"How horrible. Ten, no, wait; eleven years old?" she asked, remembering our conversation. "To be so young and so alone out here. I can't imagine why she didn't want to come with you guys."

"Me neither. I told her we had plenty of fruitcake to share," I jested, remembering our previous convo.

"Stop it," Ally barked.

I smiled at her, dimming into a look of calm understanding. "A lot has happened since this morning. I never got the chance to tell you I'm so glad you're okay." I cupped the side of her face in my hand and stroked her hair with my other.

"Yeah, that was something. I'm glad, too. Had you told me five years ago when I enlisted that I would be pulling a stunt like that, I'm not sure I'd be here right now."

"Oh, come on, where's your sense of adventure?"

She sneered. "Adventure. Yeah."

We both looked around at the others. It seemed we were all recharging our batteries well. "How you doing, Broseph?" I asked him. "Got any prognostications on that ankle of yours? You gonna make it?"

Joe sat up slowly. "Yeah, I'll be fine. The ice is really helping. It wasn't a bad sprain to begin with, but…well, a bad sprain for you at twenty-three can be a life-altering sprain for me at fifty-two."

I laughed with him.

"Who made the food, I wonder, and where did they go?" he asked.

"Beats me," I answered. "But if it were me, I probably wouldn't leave this place either. It's a freaking castle."

"Just shy of a castle, but nice in the summers!" said a cheerful, scratchy voice, projecting outward from up in the choir loft.

We all turned and looked up in alarm. Someone was standing up there, hands on the railing, studying us, and leaning out towards us with a curious smile.

●　　　●　　　●　　　●　　　●

"Name's Amos! I'm the janitor here."

The old man had retreated, descended the steps behind the choir loft, and now was approaching down the center aisle towards us. For whatever reason, I felt a strange foreboding as he approached. His voice carried, and it was reverberating up into the ceiling of the church, resonant and bouncing off the walls. That wasn't good in terms of attracting gorgons, and he needed to keep it down.

He had on a thick, plaid, flannel shirt and brown pants. Big mutton chops lined his face, which was wrinkled beyond repair. But his eyes were kind. At least, one of them was: his right lens was obscured with fog-glass, and the right side of his face drooped. That eye must not work anymore. Probably had a stroke, poor fella.

I stood up to shake hands with him and made sure he noticed that I was whispering, to give him the hint. "Nice to meet you, Amos. We're with a local Blockade, a few miles southwest of here, over on the teardrop by the zinc plant. I'm Shipley," I greeted him. "This is my team."

"Blockade? What in tarnation is that?" He shook my hand in both of his. Up close, he reeked of cigarette smoke.

My eyebrows went up. "Well, we're with the army, sir, all of us, and we're out on a recon patrol, returning back to base. The Blockades are where the brains are at in fighting back against the gorgons."

"Brains and gorgons! Lord almighty, isn't that something? You guys are all Army, in my home? What an honor! Welcome to Madison Street United Methodist!" he exclaimed a little too loudly, holding his arms out wide in salutation. We did the same, but mine felt a little half-hearted. I wished he would keep it down. "I keep this place clean. Seems like it's a bit futile nowadays but back then, whoo my! This place was bustlin.' I had my hands full then, with a bit more staff of course, but still. Now I just try to keep it neat and tidy for the Lord." He smiled. A tooth was missing.

"How long you been here, Amos? I take it that's your cooking down below, or do you have someone else here with you?"

"Nope, just me. Well, it was me and the missus. She died a few years back. Yep, she's gone now," he lamented, and looked up to the ceiling, signing the cross. He coughed quietly.

"I'm sorry for your loss."

"Yeah, me too. She sure was a good cook, lemme tell you!" Amos gave out a wicked and quick cackle. My lips reflexively smiled. "Been here since they first came, in, oh what was that, let's see…"

"'26," Joe said, helping him out.

"That's it! Yessir," Amos shot back, and he mock-saluted Joe. I wasn't sure what to make of that. "My oh my, but that's sixteen years ago, for goodness' sake. I'm eighty-two now. We were married for sixty-one years; would you believe it? I see you guys are all enjoying my cooking?" He pointed a knotted finger around at all of us with a silly, juvenile smile. "Good food?"

"Uh, yes, yeah, thanks a lot man," said Fox. "We were hungry."

"Really, very kind of you. I hope we're not imposing. We're on our way back and really need to get going," I said. I could feel Ally nodding in agreement beside me. The clock on the back wall of the sanctuary was an analog one, but it was still running: 3:27pm.

"What? So soon? You just got here! Oh, I wouldn't head out now, it's getting pretty nasty out there. I made dinner to warm things up in light of the snow. I don't eat that late anymore, and I retire early, heh heh heh!" His old cackle sounded like a wet rumble of age-old fluid in his lungs. Probably emphysema from the smoking. I didn't know if this man had excellent luck or if gorgons just plain avoided churches, but he was awfully loud in the face of such terror.

"Really, thank you so much for allowing us to take a bit of shelter in here," Joe insisted, rising. "We really need to get going. I was just needing to rest my leg." Amos stared at him in awe; for the first time he noticed he had a match in the southern drawl.

"You're from Georgia, ain'tcha?" he asked Joe.

Joe nodded. "Alpharetta."

"Ah, a little slice of home!" More cackling. "Welcome, brother!" He went over and hugged Joe. Joe received it sheepishly and not too certainly. "I'm from Atlanta. Moved over here in 2023. Right during the Israel Gaza war. Just celebrated nineteen years here last week!

Got some harassment where we lived. Seems people started to not take too kindly to us Jews since Netan-'yahoo' kept bombing Gaza and flooding out them tunnels and killin' hostages. I agree with what he did! But they didn't agree with me agreein' with him, so it seems."

"Well, I'm real sorry about that," Joe said. "Nice to meet someone from back home."

Amos nodded, and smiled, turning to all of us and smiling in turn.

Awkward pause. "Well, that's that," I said. "We really must be going now, Amos, but we want to thank you for your kindness."

If I hadn't known any better, I swear he frowned then.

"Ah well," he said. "No problem. Don't get many visitors in town here, and don't know when I last ran into so many, ha! But if you must be on your way, y'all take care now." We could all hear the note of sadness in his voice. It sounded like the old guy genuinely wanted some company, and we couldn't blame him, frankly. We all did. Ours felt like a luxury: the six of us traveling in a pack, assured of mutual company, at least for the time being, able to bounce conversation off of one another. Good banter, friendly exchanges, that's all he wanted.

Amos looked at the clock, and then his eyebrows went up. He waved suddenly. "Oh my! Better get back to work then," he said, and actually turned to leave. I felt bad, because he seemed like a sweet, lonely old man who genuinely hated goodbyes. But take our goodbye we must, and it was high time we hit the road again. We watched him disappear into the narthex and off to the side somewhere. He seemed to have a hustle about him, like he was keeping an appointment.

"Uh, careful, there's a big snake in the foyer," Ally called after him. Maybe it was his pet.

"You OK to go, Joe?" I asked Bassett.

"Oh yeah, I'll be fine now. Thanks, Jet." We grabbed our things. Joe was removing the ice and, with the help of Fox seated nearby, re-splinting his leg. The others were slipping on their shoes.

Jesse was taking a big all-out stretch when all of our hearts stopped. From high above, the deafening sound of multiple church bells sounded. *Clang-clang, clang-clang, clang-clang* they sounded. They were somewhat muted from here inside the building, but someone was ringing them with vigor.

"No, no, no, no!" I whispered, running toward the narthex. "What is that old fool *doing?*" I grabbed my rifle and scanned the area, but I couldn't find Amos. The snake was still there. I ran to the front door. Ally was on my tail. I peered through the glass outside, and up into the gray afternoon sky. The snow was falling heavier now. It was amazing to behold, as if the pent-up clouds were suddenly hellbent on unleashing their snow drifts down upon us in vengeance for being somehow sentenced to restraint. It was a flurry outside.

Nonetheless, I heard it loud and clear from the front doors. The toll of the bells was ringing off the adjoining buildings and reverberating back to us loud and clear. In my mind's eye I could envision little Nevaeh emerging from her shelter, staring down the alleyway at the giant spires in the distance from her, wondering what all the commotion was about. I hoped to God she was still inside her shelter.

That's when they came. Command echoed it in a scratchy transmission a few times: bogeys were inbound from multiple directions.

Like a swarm of honeybees desperate to evict a murder hornet, they converged from all points of the sky onto the church spires above us, slamming violently into them. Ally and I looked up with horror as gorgons from every angle were drawn as with a summons to the bell towers. It was then that I remembered from our initial approach that they looked misshapen and bent inwards. And suddenly the thought occurred to me: *Amos has done this before.*

That punk. I was going to find him. Ally and I retreated from the doors, farther back into the church towards the sanctuary. The bells were once again muted as they receded into the distance. I checked my watch. 1338. I hoped against hope that this wouldn't last, and that they would slowly peel off and abandon their pursuit. And that Amos would stop ringing those accursed bells!

"We gotta move," I instructed the team as Ally and I reached them. "It's not safe here. I don't know where that old man is, but this was his doing. Move. Let's find somewhere safer farther in, and below." The team nodded and we retreated farther into the belly of the sanctuary, out through a side corridor into what appeared to be classrooms. Thankfully, Jesse had put his shoes back on, and Fox had grabbed the rocket launcher as he passed by it. "Command, we are pinned down in an old church. Madison Street United Methodist."

High-pitched sound of glass shattering behind us, and a shrieking wind. *Oh, crap.* And why not? There were so many windows in that building, and Amos had sounded the dinner bell. Was it to keep us here? If so, why? He seemed genuinely disappointed that we were leaving. But this seemed like suicide, and I had had enough of suicide missions to last a lifetime.

Just then the power went out. All went dark, and I immediately suspected Amos of cutting it. What was the old man up to? I gripped my rifle tightly with one hand and with the other I fished out a chemlight from one of my side pouches. The green glow burst forth and gave us something to steer by. Shadows jumped up and fled around us as we softly made our way through.

The bells had stopped.

At that point, our fast pace became a clip now that we could partially see, and we ran, retreating down a corridor with a row of classrooms toward a stairwell. This was insane. We were only supposed to be sheltering here for a half-hour. Now we were at the mercy of multiple gorgons *and* an old madman. What had I ushered Fox, Vera and Jesse into? And was Joe keeping pace with us?

I looked back. We still only had two masks. I had one, and Ally had the other. Ally was donning hers. Good idea. I reached into my pack and pulled mine out and put it on. Fox was right behind me, and Vera behind Ally. Jesse was in the rear, helping Joe get more speed. Thankfully, we were all armed, but this place was an echo chamber: if not any longer for the reverberations of prayers and petitions, then certainly for gunfire and smoke.

We descended the stairwell, feeling blindly in the dark, retreating deep into the belly of the church. The green glow doubled as Joe pulled out a chemlight of his own. Ally couldn't as she had given Vera her jacket.

We came out in the corridor, and I looked around. Our hearts stopped cold. All of us listened. Horrible screeches emanating from somewhere above us, ricocheting throughout the church with spine-chilling echoes. *They were inside. A lot of them were inside.* The sounds were impossible to pinpoint. I looked back and everyone was still with us. There were a few restrooms to our left, and a library in front of us. No way in hell I was going into another library with these things flying around.

I recognized the corridor as one leading into the fellowship hall with the kitchen we had been in before, to our right. I made for it, and I heard the team following me. The kitchen would be a good place to make a last stand perhaps: there was only one entrance in and out of it. We could put our backs to the wall and fire away, sound be damned.

But why on earth would Amos ring those bells? I don't know where the old lunatic was in all of this, but he had to be sheltering in place as well. It sounded like there were a lot of them swarming above us on the upper floors, judging by the scattered pitch of multiple shrieks overlapping together into a cacophony.

I heard a shriek. It was closer than the others. We had just gone up the stairs, entering the fellowship hall, and were heading left toward the kitchen when I turned around. Jesse had thought we were going right! "Jesse, not that way! In here!" I cried, holding up my chemlight and waving him toward us. In the confusion and darkness, he whirled around trying to pinpoint where we were.

With terrifying speed, a gorgon swooped out of the darkness of the hallway just behind him and then stood up to full height to face him. He stupidly turned to face it, and was enveloped in mist as he fired off two shots, but that was it. My heart sank. Not again. Jesse froze. Vera screamed at the gunshots, which sounded a clear and deafening report in the hall. Ally screamed as well. I don't remember if I yelled in the horror.

I turned my face away and we all ran towards the back kitchen. The gorgon began to feed. As I ran to block us all in, I turned again and saw two more slowly float out of the corridor behind where Jesse had stood. One took a bite out of his frozen legs, and he snapped in two and crumpled over. Grisly. I covered my ears, as I didn't want to hear that again. But not enough to screen out Foxy calling "Jet, move!" behind me. I whirled back around. He was holding up the launcher. In a second, he fired, and for the second time in three days, a torpedo sailed right past me.

A wild explosion sounded behind me, and I was thrown forward toward the kitchen. The sound of deafening shrieks behind me erupted into a howling wail of pain in unison. Flames everywhere. Gorgons burning in an inferno. No sense keeping quiet now. I got up, turned around and mowed down two more gorgons who had been drawn to the noise, beyond the fire, and then bolted into the kitchen. My rifle rang out proudly, sending a hail of bullets, cutting them down. They each splattered into chunks at the south entrance to the fellowship hall. I could hear more of them converging on us, doubtless drawn in by the salvo of sound we had just launched at their comrades.

I turned around and ran just as the automatic fire extinguishers kicked on, and the ceiling started to rain down everywhere. A dim staccato blip began to sound out through the building, accompanied by a periodic flash from wall alarms.

To my right I noticed an exit, and I briefly considered it, but then we'd be out in the open, and there was a horde of them still around here. Maybe it was a stairwell to the other floors above. It would have to wait.

I retreated into the kitchen, slammed the door and locked it, sealing us in. "Good job, Foxy. Thanks, man," I said. They were all dripping wet from the fire extinguishers.

My team wheeled some large gray, plastic serving carts into place behind the door, as if those would really slow them down. We retreated. I was breathing hard, trying to slow my chest and quiet down. I turned and was greeted by a screen of guns pointed my way while I scanned all of the faces around me. Foxy, Ally, Vera, Joe. Good. Everyone was here except Jesse. *Poor Jesse.* MeeMaw would be crushed. I wondered briefly if out there amidst the blackened rubble a family picture was crumpling up in fire and smoke.

Dammit, I wasn't going to let anyone else die. Everyone's breathing was up, but they were quiet. My mask was getting a little foggy inside. I put my finger to my lips and showed them a tightened fist. *We got this.* I don't think it conveyed much confidence to them.

I joined them against the back wall of the kitchen, turning to face the door. The rain pattered and ricocheted off of our gun metal. We couldn't hear anything through the water falling, except the muted shrieks from inside the cathedral above, and the flickering flames of the fire at the far end of the hall. That was going to be a concern if the fire extinguishers didn't put it out completely. At one point there was the sound of a rushing wind outside the door, and some blue-green mist began to filter under the door, but it dissipated, and the gorgons moved on. Good thing they didn't know how to open doors.

All we could do now was wait. I looked at the dimly lit clock on the wall. Four PM.

Short of a miracle from heaven, there was no way in hell we were going to make it back for the memorial now. Not by sheltering in place with a murder of gorgons floating around, a madman on the loose, and a fire breaking out.

I hoped they had eaten Amos. And I hoped he had felt every single bite.

• • • • •

We waited a good five minutes, without saying a word, crouched there in the dark of that kitchen. I could hear the occasional creaking of the floorboards and the shifting of weight as we occasionally repositioned and tended aching and tight muscles.

The bells had stopped, the shrieks had vanished, and all was quieting down. There was little sound beyond that door. The fire had slowly been put out, but we could smell the smoke out there.

"Are they gone?" Vera whispered.

I couldn't be certain. In our haste, we had left a few packs and the m-deck up on the pews above us. We needed that m-deck. And we needed to put out that fire, or what was left of it.

In the dim green glow, I could see that Vera was quaking. Ally had taken off her jacket and put it around her earlier, and now I could feel Ally trembling a bit too. I don't know how well Vera knew Jesse, or how long they had known each other, but there was another loss of human life to one of these things. I looked over at Foxy. He looked at me. I gave him a thumbs-up signal and tilted my head. He gave one back, assuring me he was fine. I did the same with Joe, who was against the far wall.

I took a deep breath as the extinguishers stopped. The flashing continued.

As I did so, Vera mumbled, "Why would he do that? Why the hell would he do that?" I looked back at her.

"Don't know, Vera," Ally answered. "People do crazy things when they're alone for a long time. Sounds like his wife was the last thing he had, and all he knows now is cooking, cleaning and cigarettes."

I crept up silently toward the door. Not a sound on the other side. I carefully slid one of the gray carts out of the way, slowly, noiselessly, and crept up all the way to the door. There was no sound outside. The flames had warmed things up, and it must have been stuffy out there, but our door wasn't hot.

I tried to think where we were in the building: directly outside the kitchen was a sort of bar where they probably served coffee. Yes: I had seen a few beverage dispensers on the back wall out there when I first came down and noticed the food. Beyond that was probably that stairwell on the exterior of the building. I remembered seeing one when we came up the outside of the building on initial approach, looking in through the windows. After that it was just a maze of classrooms, restrooms, offices, the library, and then outside. I think there was a closet right outside the kitchen. There was also an elevator in the corridor just outside the fellowship hall. I didn't know how many floors that accessed, however. I could hear my own heartbeat continue its dull thud as I searched in my memory for another place to hide that might be more fortified than this. It was hard to think.

No, we'd probably have to sit this one out.

At least we had vegetables, rice and stew on the stove. I went back and checked the fridge. Bottled water only. But that would be enough.

I really had to pee.

"I say we wait it out here. If that old man made it, he's gotta come back here sometime for his food, right? Anyone else gotta pee?"

Everyone raised their hand.

"Right. I say we give it ten more minutes. Gotta hold it. The good news is that the bathrooms aren't far. Just outside this hall and down the corridor on the left. We'll go in pairs, armed, and then get back here as soon as possible to ride this out. We all need to make sure that fire is out. But it sounds like it's died down.

"That's the good news. The bad news is that I don't think there's any way in hell we're going to make it back to the Blockade tonight."

•　　•　　•　　•　　•

That was the slowest ten minutes of my life. Time crept by ever so slowly, while we just sat there, listening and watching the clock, the loud ticks of which could be heard annoyingly clear. We searched in the kitchen and were able to locate some fire blankets, thank God. Those would come in handy. The sound of fire extinguisher canisters going off would be too much noise. I counted it our good fortune that, mercifully, the building still had fire extinguishers.

Occasionally there came a muted noise from above, a dull thud or other, or the distant sound of rushing wind accompanied by a faint shriek. There were no windows down here, as we were below ground. We had no way of determining where they were at, if they had all gone, or what the weather was like out there now. At least it felt somewhat warm in here: the stove had been on fairly recently for Amos to cook his food. Though the power was out, the residual warmth was encouraging.

During that time, we each had a bit of the stew and the vegetables: too tired to care, and too hungry to starve. We didn't leave any for Amos. I fetched bottled water from the fridge and passed them out. What I wouldn't give for a soda right now, a thick, syrupy Dr. Pepper; but can or bottle, it would have made a sharp noise, and that would be most unwise. We ate everything up and drank it all down ravenously, leaving nothing for Amos but the washing up.

Ten minutes had elapsed. I took a deep breath and went to the door again. There was no sound on the other side, and it felt less cold now. I turned around and pointed to Ally and Vera. Ladies first, although I was cognizant that that might be misperceived. We certainly weren't throwing them to the wolves, just trying to be chivalrous.

I hugged Ally tightly and gave her a kiss. "Come back," I said.

"I will," she promised, and smiled.

"When you're outside, shine your chemlight through the door sweep. We'll see the glow."

She nodded.

They were both armed, and the two of them slowly crept down the hall and to the corner where the hall met the corridor, lingering there and peering around. I peeked outside the door, and, despite the incendiary damage of that RPG, it looked like the fire extinguishers had taken care of putting it all out.

Ally gave an all-clear signal and began to move. Vera followed her. We shut the kitchen door after them and locked it. Only a few minutes had passed before we could see a faint green glow coming from the other side of the door.

I opened it briskly and they ran inside on their tiptoes. "Fastest pee of my life," Ally breathed.

Vera laughed nervously under her breath. "Me too."

Next up, Foxy and Joe. I'd stay here with the ladies and go last.

Same as before, they went out. Joe led Foxy as he had seniority, and Foxy stayed close behind him. I hoped Joe could protect Foxy. What was his name again? I couldn't remember. He had told me, but then insisted that we still call him Foxy. I was still thinking about it when after a few moments came the same familiar glow signifying their presence on the other side.

"I trust you flushed and washed your hands, fellas?"

They chuckled and didn't answer as they came back in. It wouldn't be long before the bottled water we had just downed would require another visit.

Joe locked the door behind me and sat down. Then it was my turn. I brought a new chemlight with me. In its faint radiance I could barely make out the exact point where Jesse fell, there in a concave hole on the floor, in a fruit salad mix of tile, concrete, and chunks of flesh of I dared not guess what species. I couldn't be certain if that was Jesse or not, and I wasn't about to go check it out. No trace of his body was found anywhere. *Disgusting.*

That poor guy didn't last more than three hours with us. A pang of guilt washed over me. We were down to five, and I hoped to God that we would all make it back in one piece.

My chemlight emitted an eerie luminosity that made everything appear sickly and livid around me. These unholy walls all appeared to be wickedly unwell.

I rounded the corner into the corridor, and made it into the bathroom. It was clear where Joe and Foxy had peed. Mercifully, these weren't auto-flush toilets and had doubtless been installed before that became a thing. *Old churches,* I thought, with indictment. Had those suckers gone off, that could have been a death sentence.

I finished up and opened the bathroom door, then stopped dead in my tracks.

•   •   •   •   •

It was Amos.

He was sweating like a pig, and covered in it, all the way down his flannel shirt and pants. At least I think that was sweat. He was carrying a butcher knife.

I recoiled from him, raising my gun. My shoes made an irritating squeak on the floor as I jumped back.

"Wait, wait just a minute!" he pleaded under his breath, looking around. "There might be more of them!"

"What did you do, Amos? Why did you ring that bell?" I growled at him.

"I didn't ring the bell! Let me explain! But first can we please get somewhere safe?"

I looked him over. What was he dripping with? Was that blood? I couldn't tell in the darkened corridor.

"Oh yeah, then who cut the power, huh, Amos? I suppose that was a gorgon? Gorgons mess with breaker boxes now?"

"No, no, no," he said, waving his hands at me. The knife was glimmering green in the dark. "You've got it all wrong, let me come back with you and explain!"

I looked at him. I didn't want to. And he had a lot of explaining to do.

"Put down the knife, Amos," I ordered him. He complied immediately, placing it in the middle of the corridor, and lifting his hands up in surrender. "Command, come in," I transmitted. Static.

"Command, Shipley, over?" I repeated.

Still nothing. Probably too deep in the belly of the church.

"Let's go," I said to him. "You in front. Head to the kitchen. Keep your hands where I can see them."

He took the lead and kept his hands up, as I had ordered. We rounded the corridor back into the hall. He seemed to notice the area where Jesse had died, but then looked back and scurried toward the kitchen, throwing a nervous glance back at me.

"Step aside."

I shined the light under the door, and they opened it. I went in first, keeping my gun trained on Amos, and then beckoned him inside.

The team gasped when they saw that I had someone with me. They gasped again when they realized who it was.

"You murderous punk!" Joe nearly yelled, lunging toward him.

"Wait!" I said. "Hold up. He says he has an explanation. So? Let's hear it, Amos. Explain yourself."

The door was locked once again, and Amos nervously backed away from us. They slid the carts quietly in front of it once more while looking at him most accusingly, and I kept my gun trained on him. We must have looked like death warmed over, underlit by the pale neon green of the chemlights, our features darkened.

"Speak."

Amos sighed. "I don't blame y'all for thinking it was me. The bells go off at the wrong time now. They were supposed to go off at sunset, but what with clocks being off, and the weather of the world, why, they go off earlier now. I had only just remembered and was heading off to make sure that I could get somewhere safe before they did. I wanted to tell you, but, well, it appeared so much like you all were heading off anyway.

"And," he admitted, "yes, I cut the power…that's the only way I can prevent them from going off. They're on an automated chain system now; we installed that a few years back for the reverend. But I don't know how to disable it, and I gotta do it every single day: turn the power on to *have* power, turn it *off* before those dumb bells go off, then turn it back *on* again afterwards."

I remembered how he had fled somewhat urgently from the sanctuary, disappearing into the narthex, so this made sense. But it didn't help with the appearance of impropriety.

"Where'd you go after that? Did you hear or see the gorgons? Where did you hide?" Ally chirped at him suspiciously.

"There's an area that I call the belfry. It's not really a belfry, but close enough to it, and there's a small brick room in there that I hid in. Any time there's a swarm of the God-forsaken things, why, I run there. It's the one place I can stay in and feel safe."

The poor old man looked like he was trembling. I didn't like this; it felt like an inquisition, and perhaps we should have been more trusting of him.

"What's that all over your shirt and your pants?" I asked him.

He looked down, sullen. Amos sighed in embarrassment. "Well, I don't like to say it but as you get older you start to lose control of some of your bodily functions. I must admit I got a bit scared."

The old dude had wet himself. Now I recognized the scent. It had smelled like coffee. Which reminded me, I still hadn't had any. I glanced over at the coffee maker, and it had shut off by now.

I looked at the team. Joe raised an eyebrow but shrugged his shoulders. Ally looked over at me, and I could see shades of sympathy.

"I see you all helped yourself to my dinner. Did you like it?" Amos asked kindly.

"It was fine, Amos. It was fine. I'm-" I caught myself, not ready to break the questioning yet, "I'm sorry about… about everything. Just…sit down. Relax."

Amos slowly hopped up on the counter by the sink, a remarkably spry move for an eighty-two-year-old. He reached over and pawed some of the veggie entrails out of the pan in the stove, and began to run his fingers inside the pot and lick them.

"You must be hungry," I said, with a sigh and a furrowed brow. "Sorry we ate all your food."

"No, no, it's ok, be my guest. Anything I can do to take care of such fine Army folk in my castle!"

I didn't like that he kept calling it that.

"Well, we're going to have to stay here, Amos. It's nearly 1700 hours. Uh, 5pm," I clarified for him, "and that means its getting dark outside. We should have been long-gone by now, but we're not, so we're gonna have to camp out here for the night. Dang," I said, wanting so badly to get home. I could see on the others' faces that they were none too glad at this news as well.

"Are there any places in here that have more comfortable accommodations than a hard kitchen floor and countertops, Amos?" Joe asked him.

"Oh, for sure, for sure!" he chirped. "Most times I sleep on the pews, or up in the choir loft up there, there's a couch off to the side. But the staff offices are much closer, we just passed 'em coming back in here, after the lavatories. The dear reverend had a big one that belonged to him in his office, and there are a few couches and loveseats that belonged to the others as well. They're all unlocked, I made sure to do that so I wouldn't never have to find my keys again." He chuckled.

Good thinking, ya old bat.

I observed that he was talking past-tense about these people. I wondered where they were. I wondered if we would be awoken in the middle of the night by flashlights in our face, and a white-frocked priest demanding his couch back, Amos by his side with his butcher knife.

"Alright. Well, we've got some staples, and we've all eaten. I need to get somewhere to send a clear signal to Command and update on our progress. I'll be back in a few minutes. Vera, why don't you come with me this time." I grabbed my mask.

Vera looked up at me, nervously. "Uh, okay," she reluctantly agreed.

"I'll need your help. If we can make it back up to the sanctuary, we can fetch the rest of our bags and the m-deck."

"M-deck?" she asked, puzzled and nervous.

"That's the device that Joe was carrying: it measures movement and can let us know if we have incoming."

She nodded in comprehension. Her eyebrows went up. By all appearances she'd like to have it with us as well.

I didn't want to take Ally, as I didn't want to lose two team members if we were beset, and I couldn't take Joe in his condition. Besides, this would be good training for her. "Ally, can Vera borrow your mask?"

"Yeah, definitely." She adjusted it and put it on Vera's head. I put mine on as well.

I gave her a chemlight to hold in one hand, and she had a rifle in the other. "Might wanna check your chamber," I said, looking down at it. There was nothing in the chamber. In her haste, she had never cocked her weapon. *New recruits. Fresh meat,* I laughed to myself, shaking my head. "It's alright, ya fuzzy patch; here, go like this." I showed her how to chamber a round, and smiled at her. She nervously smiled back. I placed my hand on her shoulder, reassuring her. At least she wasn't trembling yet.

Amos watched us as we walked to the door.

"Be right back," I said to Ally, Fox and Joe. "Stay with them, Amos, for your own protection." He looked at me but didn't say anything. He was still licking his fingers from the stew. He nodded and waved.

Unlocking the door and looking out, we stopped to listen. Nothing. We proceeded out into the hall and back to the corridor. They again locked the door behind us. My heart was beating, but it wasn't full of terror this time. It felt good to have a new trainee under my wing that really needed some guidance. Foxy seemed pretty secure in and of himself, although he had said very little on our mission.

Vera needed some work.

She took up the rear, and we entered the corridor. I quickly peered inside some of the offices, and, as Amos had mentioned, there were definitely some places to lie down in comfort, if even without a blanket. And the offices seemed warm enough. Amos had kept this place, his castle as he called it, squeaky clean and operational.

In the middle of the corridor, I noticed Amos' knife where he had left it on the floor. We passed it by and continued on, back to the stairwell we had come down earlier. I opened the door and peered in. There was no sign of any movement up top.

We slowly ascended the staircase. The green glow of the chemlight helped us watch our footfalls.

We made it to the second floor and peered through the windowed door. Nothing. I could just make out the end of the corridor beyond, looking north, out into open sky. The sun was definitely setting, and in the half-light illumination of the street I could see the heavy falling snow. It was coming down thickly now.

"Command," I said, as we stepped out, not daring to raise my voice above a whisper. "Command, Shipley, DN436, do you read?"

It took a second, but there was a staticky rumble that finally materialized into a human voice.

"Yes, Shipley, go ahead, we read you. What's your status?"

"Unsure of hostiles. Pinned down in the church and unadvisable to resume journey tonight. One human survivor, janitor of the church. And one man down," I said, looking at Vera sadly.

"Staff Sergeant Bassett?"

"Negative," I said, but then I stopped. What was that? I swore I heard something down the hall.

"Sergeant Shipley, come in?" questioned Command.

It wasn't just me. Vera had heard it too. Down the corridor towards the sanctuary. I raised my weapon, and so did she. I turned and told her to wait there.

"Come in, Sergeant Shipley?"

"Command, unfriendlies. Hold transmission," I instructed them.

Curiosity moved my feet forward. What if it was Nevaeh? Would she have changed her mind and followed us here? I would soon have the answer.

I clung to the wall and did that thing where you listen with your eyes. I couldn't see anything that far ahead with the chemlight, but I didn't need it. The last light of the setting sun was shining brightly through the windows of the church ahead. I handed Vera my chemlight and put two hands on my gun, proceeding down the hall toward the sanctuary. Turning around I could see Vera posted up with nearly her whole body around the corner.

I turned back toward the sanctuary. A sudden unreasoning feeling of dread fell upon me. I don't know what told me to run, but it was compellingly strong. I stopped in my tracks and backed up. I waved behind me for Vera to get back in the stairwell, and continued to back up.

At that moment, many things happened. Vera's shoes squeaked on the floor as she was crossing. I looked back at her in dismay, and then whipped my head back toward the sanctuary again. A bluish-green mist began to float down from the top of the doorway. And then, there it was, silently floating down over the threshold, and looking right at me. I fired instinctively. One, two, three shots. I didn't miss. The thing recoiled and hissed sharply. I saw it fall back. But the mist was still there.

Vera was safely in the stairwell.

In a heartbeat, more shapes. More gorgons drifting down from below, and from the sides. They had somehow gotten into the sanctuary. Then I realized we had left our food containers up there, and a few of our packs with our scent all over them. I fired again, and a few bullets found their mark. I couldn't see super clearly, but I did see one of them open its maw and hiss at me, hurling all its venom my way. That's when it launched. I will never pretend to know how they do that: how they pick up such horrifying speed.

Intuitively I dove toward the floor and felt a rush of wind pass over me. My mask got momentarily dislodged from my face, but I watched it try to track me as it flew over. A cold mist enveloped me and chilled my bones. I restored my mask and got to my feet, Glock in my left hand and rifle in my right. All I could do was spray a cover fire down the corridor back toward the sanctuary. With my left hand I released round after round of hate into the body of that beast that skidded to a halt and turned to growl at me. The bullets punctured its chest and it fell backward with a cry. Anything coming in the opposite direction was pretty much toast before it left the threshold of the doorway, as I continued to spray a volley of bullets toward it.

I jumped into the stairwell. Vera was inside, covering her ears. She started to descend, and I was right on her six, when we both looked below us. There was a gorgon down at the bottom flight of stairs, looking this way and that, uncertain of where to go.

We wasted no time and went up the stairs instead. Now we were cut off from our group. There were gorgons in between us and them, across multiple floors. "Ally, Ally, come in!" I said at normal volume. No use trying to mask it anymore; the jig was up. "Multiple bogeys. Stay put and do *not* engage, do you read me?" No answer came through, or at least I didn't hear it.

We were flying in a frenzy up to the third floor instead, and out into the next corridor. A silent shape hovered down the hall by the windows, and whirled to meet us. These things must have fanned out in their search. Before I could raise my weapon, Vera was facing it and raised hers. *Pop-pop-pop-pop-pop…*she squeezed her trigger and sent it careening backward, flying into the wall next to a restroom door. It fell to the ground and left a concave indentation in the wall. *Good girl, Vera!* I thought again. But we weren't out of this yet.

Something scrambled came through faintly on my headset, but I was distracted. Yet another gorgon was rounding the corner at the opposite end of the corridor, coming from the sanctuary. The shriek raised the hairs on my neck and arms. We did not want to go that way! That seemed to be where they were all clustered and were fanning out from, as if from a nest. I unloaded on the gorgon and dropped its sorry ass.

We ran down the corridor, and I could dimly make out the opening to another stairwell. We could make for that – maybe – if there were no gorgons headed our way. I could hear noises behind us and beyond the stairwell door that we had just come through: virulent hissing and shrieks.

But going for the stairwell would take us right past the sanctuary entrance from the third floor, and we might be walking right into a trap. Alternatively, if we decided to descend the staircase, we would undoubtedly run into trouble back on the second floor. I never got a good count of how many I saw slam into the building when those bells sounded, but it was more than twenty to be sure.

In a reflex, I whirled us back around and made for the bathroom. We jumped over the corpse of the fallen gorgon Vera had taken out, and, as quietly as possible, entered the restroom and closed the door. There was only one stall with wooden walls, and we entered it, closing the door and locking it behind us.

Muted sounds out in the corridor. Sounds of thudding and shrieking: some passing by; some lingering.

We waited. I looked at my watch. 1722. My heart was thudding within me, and I could hear the thunderous passage of adrenaline shooting through my veins. My throat caught and I swallowed. Vera was next to me in the stall.

The bathroom door burst open. Hissing. Something was skulking around in here. *It was inside.* It was just beyond the stall door.

Suddenly, and with horrible speed and noise, it slammed into us, and the wooden door burst asunder: the gorgon was upon us, inside the stall, rending the wood and splintering it to our left, sending sawdust and fragments in every direction. It was disturbingly reminiscent of the library…of Rutty. Our guns, our packs, our green chem lights went flying and landed somewhere nearby. The back of the door slammed into my face and knocked my rifle from my grasp. My mouth tasted like iron, and I could feel the hot blood running down from my forehead. Something hard smacked into the bone of my left hand.

Green shadows barely revealed an alien monster crawling up and settling onto each of us, digging its claws into our shoulders and pinning us. It froze there, locking eyes with Vera and then me. I don't think it expected two of us together. It began to hum eerily.

The cold mist was everywhere and was filling our nostrils and icing our bones. Vera let out a terrified shriek followed by a despondent moan. One of its meaty paws had claws right through her left shoulder, impaling her. One was into my right shoulder. We were sandwiched together, and I couldn't reach Rutty's Glock, which was holstered, or my rifle, which was thrown from my grip and on the floor beside me. All I could do was try to push the gorgon away from me; Vera did the same. My pack with my sippy had been pushed behind me and was trapped under me. The thing was horribly strong and heavy.

Whether it couldn't decide which one of us it wanted more, or whether it was entirely foiled by the masks we were both wearing, it wasn't getting what it wanted, and it growled and hissed vaporously.

I had never been so close to one of these vile things, and the smell was revolting. It had lifeless pale slits for eyes, and a long, narrow inset mouth that leered with row upon row of teeth. I was reminded of the Great White Shark again. On each side of its head were several long, parallel flaps.

I felt sick to my stomach. I couldn't even radio to the team, as my headset had fallen off behind me. My head began to swim, and I realized that was the deadly telepathy beginning to have an effect on me. It was marginal at best, but I felt it. The mask didn't render their power completely impotent, but it reduced it to such an extent that I was still able to move; but I was swooning. If that thing had the smarts to rip off my mask, it would have been all over.

Just then, the bathroom door opened up slowly, quietly, behind the gorgon…I could see it swing wide. The gorgon was so intent on us that it didn't see or hear it. Someone was approaching stealthily behind our enemy. *Please let it be Joe and not Ally,* I thought, summarily assigning expendability to him instead of her, as if that was even remotely fair.

Vera vomited. She was feeling it too. The gorgon let out a gasp that sounded like delight, and it sniffed and feverishly lapped up her vomit.

Just then, in a flash of green and silver, a twelve-inch butcher knife whistled through the air repeatedly down into the gorgon's head, and it was cloven in two. I heard a breathy gasp as it retched and gagged and flailed about miserably, pulsating with mist that swirled into the air, directionless.

The gorgon lay still. In all the commotion, its claws had dug in and swirled around inside our shoulders. I almost passed out from the pain: thankfully, just this side of it.

It was Amos. His fury and speed were astonishing. He had saved us, whipping that knife down and shredding the gorgon right through its cranial cavity. I don't even want to mention what I saw in there. Its dead head was resting on my chest, leeching fluid all over me. Row upon row of fibrous tissue ran along its skull. The stench was overpowering. I gagged and looked up at Amos as he wrenched the knife out of its head.

"Amos, my God…thank you!"

He stood there, staring at us, between heaving breaths. Amos turned around and looked at the door, perhaps to make sure there weren't more of them coming.

"Yes, Amos, thank you, oh thank you!" exclaimed Vera, ripping off her mask as if deprived of oxygen, and dropping it to the floor beside her. "Oh, thank God - please get this thing off of us!" She struggled and pushed.

Amos looked at her with a blank expression on his face. And then, swiftly, he struck.

Wordlessly, his big butcher knife came straight down upon Vera and split her head in two with a sickening crack. She screamed in terror and put her hands out and up in defense. I was spattered with her blood, and all I could hear was bubbling and gurgling, and myself trying to scream over it in turn.

Something splashed from her head and sprayed me.

"Stop, Amos! What are you- stop! *AMOS!*" I couldn't form an intelligible sentence; I was stuck between trying to move out of the way and attempting to possibly deflect his blows upon Vera. He was doing it all as silently as possible too: disquieting and eerie.

The dead gorgon was sliding off of me while this madman continued to hack away at her. He was saying something, what was that? *Food! Food! Got to have food!* Amos was viciously bringing the knife down again and again upon her head as her arms senselessly flailed in front of her, only to receive more cuts and injuries.

What deranged psychopathic evil was this? I was next, I was sure of it.

The gorgon had nearly slid off of me as Amos attacked. I looked down at the floor. Lying there, still out of my reach, was my rifle. But now, easily accessible at my side, was Rutty's Glock 19.

Amos started to turn his attention away from her, and toward me. He was breathing hard now. He raised his knife, but it never fell. Without thinking twice, I whipped out Rutty's Glock and fired five shots instantaneously into his chest. Amos blinked stupidly in confusion, and I heard him gasp as he slammed backward into the bathroom tiled wall, still holding the knife. The air was knocked out of him. His left side now looked as stroke-stricken as his right.

Vera was dead. She lay quietly next to me, gently slipping down onto the floor, her jugular shooting out recurring jets of crimson that painted the supposedly holy walls of that church.

"I," Amos breathed, "I just needed some more meat. Just some protein," he muttered blankly, and then he sank to the floor, a long trail of red clumps sliding down the wall behind him. His head drooped.

More meat? What did he mean? *Did he kill her for food?* Is that what he was saying?

It was then that I remembered the stew that we had all eaten. Stew that Amos had made.

Stew from *humans*.

My stomach revolted, violently churning, and I leaned forward and projectile vomited all over him, making sure to spray the lunatic in the face. I think I passed out shortly right after that, because I slipped on the floor and hit my head.

I couldn't shake the feeling that I should have grabbed that knife when we passed it. But then, Amos wouldn't have saved us from the gorgon. I wondered if Vera would have preferred death-by-gorgon to death-by-butcher-knife. I would never know the answer. And Amos would have found a way to kill her anyway.

There were a ton of churches up and down Commerce. Why on God's green earth did we have to pick *this* one? A vision of that anaconda came to my mind, and I shook my head angrily. There had been *two* snakes slithering around in here. *Den of vipers.*

I should have seen it coming.

And I really didn't know how much more of this I could take.

12 | SOJOURNERS

Things are never what they seem to be.

The flickering fluorescent lights of the bathroom buzzed fitfully overhead, mesmerizing me and sending me into a swampy deluge of cerebral reflection.

Somehow, the power had been restored. I didn't know how or when, but it was back on.

The crazy old man *had* rung those bells. He *had* attracted the gorgons to us to keep us here. He *did* cut the power, so that we wouldn't be able to escape. He *did* try to kill us. And all of that…for food. He was trying to survive, at the cost of human souls.

I lay there in the bathroom, floating seemingly in a pool of blood and vomit, and my mask was hard to see through. I didn't care anymore about any gorgons. I didn't care about getting home. I just wanted to lie down and die.

In the midst of all that we had suffered as a civilization, that one man could so heartlessly resort to cannibalism was absolutely beyond me, flummoxing me to my core. We were supposed to be man against gorgon, not man against man.

There was nothing to grasp or to hold onto, but somehow, I found myself climbing out from underneath three carcasses piled on top of each other there in that bloodied restroom. I don't know why I did it, but I felt I had to wash my hands. I also wanted these stinking fatigues off of me. I was sweating through them, and they were damp with Vera's blood and vomit, the creature's entrails, and my tears: I realized I had been crying. *I lost another one* was all I could say to myself. I wondered how and when Ruby would find out about her sister. And as I pulled off my vest, I found myself missing Rutty incredibly.

Then, suddenly, I thought of the others…

The others! How were they faring? Where were they? *Ally! Where was Ally?*

I had to move past the carnage. I had to get out of there and find Ally. I reached back into the putrid mess of flesh and retrieved my rifle from the floor, fetching Vera's as well.

The stench was overpowering, and I wanted out of there. Even if I had to trudge and stumble my way down the hall, I was going to go out in a blaze of glory and give 'em both barrels. I would see Rutty again soon, I thought.

I shook the blood off of both of them and stood there for a moment, breathing hard, steeling myself with fiery resolve: a machine of unstoppable iron will with a deep-seated thirst for stern revenge. The creatures that hovered out there somewhere beyond those doors weren't the enemy; they were nothing but meat, and I would reduce them to such *meaty nothingness.* I had seen them up close: felt their scaly biceps; been enveloped in their mist and yet I emerged breathing once more; experienced their fierce jaws, their heavy weight and their stench.

But now I had seen the *real* enemy: the depravity of man pitted against man, even as our species was in the very throes of a death spiral. Even there, on the brink of extinction, the savagery of man lived on and prevailed. Had we learned nothing all this time?

Somehow Amos had gotten loose, and I had to make sure the others were still alive.

Especially Ally.

I slung Vera's rifle over my back and grabbed her mask off the floor, shaking it out as well, and rinsing it in the sink. I stuffed it in my pack and reloaded all guns with fresh mags. And it was finally time to make use of something absolutely unthinkable: grenades. I had three. Just pull and pitch, that's it. I put them in my pack.

I was about to leave, but stopped, looking down at Vera with pity. She was unrecognizable. *Thanks for the bacon and eggs, Vera.* It wasn't so long ago that I had met her and Ruby in that small kitchen not so far north, but it seemed like an age ago.

I was filled with purpose, and now I had light too. The gorgons couldn't see well; now I could see them perfectly. I knew what they looked like up-close. I had stared one down. I didn't care how fast they were, how remorseless they were, how gruesome they were. I had guns and was going to make them feel pain. I was no longer afraid. They were flesh and blood, and could be killed like any other predator.

That's just what *I* was now: *a predator.* I would hunt them down, one by one, and destroy them. They would feel my wrath. They would grapple with my fury, and they would know that they messed with the wrong species.

For Dupre and Hickey.

For Vera. For Jesse.

For Rutty.

I smeared my blood off my face, and Vera's as well. Donning my headset, I filled my lungs with air, pulled my mask down over my face, and stepped out into the hallway.

There was one floating there motionless at the end of the hall, staring blankly into the stairwell. It turned to face me and never got in a single hiss. The corridor lit up as with firecrackers. One down. The glorious recoil was like a warm blanket. Another one was triggered by that sound and came flying out of the stairwell cavity, whipping to face me. It didn't even stop; it hurtled straight toward me with venom, mouth elongated. I raised my Glock 19 and shot it in the head less than five feet away from me, firing two shots. The gorgon fell to the ground and twitched. My chamber smoked. I wasn't done.

I hovered silently over my victim, sending two more shells straight through its cranium, as any good alien executioner would. I felt nothing. I couldn't even feel my heart beating.

More flew down the hallway at me without warning. I whirled toward them, firing rapidly. I found myself shouting "Wyatt! Vera! Jesse!"

Crack. Crack. Crack.

I doubled back, peering into the stairwell, and checked up. Checked down. Nothing. Stairs lightly danced beneath my feet as I made my way down to the second floor. One floated there at the end of the hall, coming my way. Boom. Boom. Boom. Down. I grabbed a grenade and pulled the pin.

About six or seven were alerted to the sound and converged upon the corridor entrance from the sanctuary, hissing wildly. Several high-pitched shrieks went up. They had spotted me. But they were distracted by the small thing that I had spun down the corridor at them.

I retreated back into the stairwell as the grenade hit the bottom step where they lurked. A burst of flame and destiny incinerated most of them. The fire was roaring at the end of the hall, and I could see a few of them on the other side of it, whirring away from the flame and heat, seeking a different vantage point to attack from. I had a few marks. Fired five shots. They fled. *They're heading toward the front, and perhaps downstairs to the fellowship hall from there.* I had to beat them.

My eyes went wide, and I dashed back down the stairwell, down to the first floor. I ejected my spent mag and slapped another one in hard, then readied another grenade. Emerging from the stairwell I could just make out a few of them up ahead, buzzing through the hall and attacking the door of the kitchen. I hurled another grenade in their direction. The stairs to the fellowship hall exploded. I wasn't sure if I had hit anything. My feet stopped in their tracks, and I posted up, summoning up all the breath and volume I could.

"Ally!" I cried. "Joe! Stay there! I'm coming!"

I was probably a little too loud, and something else easily heard me. It whisked around the corner of the fellowship hall entrance and hovered there for a moment, hissing at me.

Standoff. The last lap before the flame. I wouldn't get through without a fight.

This one was a berserker.

I couldn't see any bandage on its arm, thank goodness. This wasn't the one that got Rutty. That meant I could kill this one with utter abandon. And delight.

"Get away from them," I hissed at it.

It hissed back, and then put its long spiny arms behind itself, and launched at me.

But I launched too. I had holstered Rutty's Glock, firing a few rounds from my XM5, hoping against hope that my mask would stay on. It was coming right at me, and I ducked and turned my right shoulder into it as it barreled into me. We crashed together, and I'm not sure who tackled whom. Something cracked lightly in my right shoulder.

The gorgon was on top of me, humming. I swung wildly, hitting it in the head, the face, the stomach, or whatever raunchy tissue it was that these things were made of. The mist encircled both of us, and I shivered. It held still; but was frustrated: this berserker wasn't getting what it wanted either, and began to hiss and jerk violently, twisting its head this way and that. It didn't understand why its prey wasn't stationary. I could see it growing angry and it opened its mouth to take a bite anyway.

I went for my Glock.

In that moment, I remembered Rutty, and I wasn't going to end up like him. I was going to honor him.

The bullet found its mark, straight through the gorgon's core. It reeled backward and clutched its chest, and as it did so, I sat up and shot right through the vile flaps on the side of the berserker's head. It screamed a shriek I had never heard one of them shriek before: the sound of a thousand wallows of pain-laced suffering: a hideous cacophony of multi-noted misery, like the sound was emanating from those flaps. It fell sideways and tried to steady itself, holding its ear and looking up to the ceiling, as if to stare into the heavens and question *why?*

No answer for you today.

I drove my foot into the ground, pushed off and threw myself on top of the berserker, piling my left elbow into its throat, pinning it. It scratched my leg as it flailed. My Glock was against its temple, if you can call it that; and I sent a final emissary of death through this abhorrent creature's brain. Gunsmoke mixed with blue-green mist in an eerie toxic plume, filling the corridor. *Boom.* Remember Rutty. *Boom.* You're done. *Boom.* Payback.

The berserker lay still, lifeless.

I got up, grabbed my rifle and rounded the corner into the kitchen, painting fiercely, leaping through the flames that had engulfed the hall entrance. "Everyone! Get back!" I yelled, and mowed down two gorgons that were repeatedly ramming the kitchen door. They never heard the gunfire, and fell dead. My twenty rounds were expended, and I slapped in a new magazine as I raced back to the kitchen. My leg and my shoulder were burning.

•   •   •   •   •

"It's Shipley, open up," I whispered. I heard a gasp inside, and footsteps. The door was unlocked. They opened it, and it shuddered on its hinges as it opened. I looked up and could see the framing around it was beginning to crack from the gorgon assault. They definitely had wanted in.

We slammed it shut and locked it.

"We have to leave."

"Where's Vera?" Ally asked, and then she stopped, staring at me. They all did.

I shook my head, as I went for some bottled water. There was none. "We have to get out of here. This place has become their nest. Everybody ok-" I stopped. "What?"

They were studying me up and down, with mouths agape. I realized then that I was covered in human blood, vomit, and gorgon brains. I was missing my jacket, and the skin-tight tan T-shirt I had was disfigured, ripped, multicolored and laden with chunks and ooze. I now felt cold and wet.

I heard Foxy moan. He was over in the corner, on the floor. His arm was wrapped up with paper towels. He was missing his hat, and his blonde locks were darkened and plastered to his head from the extinguishers.

I ran to him and enveloped the little guy in a huge bear hug. I wasn't letting go. This poor kid was all we had left of Harvill. I knew he didn't understand my embrace, but I would tell him in time. I was shivering and spent. Just needed some water and a second wind. I continued to feel the burning of my scratched leg, and some slight pain in my impaled shoulder. It could wait though. He moaned again, and I let go. "Sorry. What happened?" I asked.

"Amos," Ally said.

I shook my head. "I'm sorry, Foxy. He got Vera too."

"What? How?" Foxy asked.

"No time. And I wouldn't even want to tell you if there was."

I bent down to him, examining his arm.

"Amos came up behind him and held a knife to his throat," Ally said. "He was going to kill him unless we let him go." I could see a pink scratch around his larynx.

"We didn't understand. There was all kinds of gunfire and commotion happening up there; we didn't know what your status was or where you were. I was just trying to radio you when Amos grabbed him. I think he sounded those bells, Jet…I think he killed the power too."

I nodded. "Yeah."

"Anyway, he ran out. He actually tried to slash Liam's neck in the process! But he wriggled out and I guess his arm took the brunt of it instead. We locked the door behind him. He probably figured he'd be better off being eaten by a gorgon than us having at him," Ally finished.

If only that were the truth, I thought.

"We were all listening and heard a few blasts coming from above. Then you showed up."

Foxy's arm looked bad, but not fatal. He had definitely received a sizeable gash across his bicep, right through the meat. "Did you treat this with anything?" I smelled alcohol.

"Yeah, we had some hydrogen peroxide, but that's all. That stuff works though. We just had to wrap it up with paper towels: that's all we could do. But he needs that wound closed, or he'll keep losing blood."

Indeed, the paper towels were soaking through. It looked like they had used the entire roll. I looked over at Joe.

"You ok? Can you walk?" Joe nodded.

Ally walked over to me, lightly took me by the arms and stared into my eyes. She flinched for a minute. I was covered in blood, and it wasn't all mine. Not hardly any of it. "Cam, what happened to you up there?" I looked at her, coldly, emotionless. For a flicker, I remembered that she still hadn't told me why she had to volunteer back there on the lojack mission, so it was probably fair if I didn't have to tell her this yet either.

"Look at you," she said. "You've changed. You're…so cold. What happened?"

I wasn't ready. I looked over at the pot on the stove that Amos had been licking out of with his fingers. They weren't ready for that news. "I'll tell you later, I promise. We need to move. Out of here, back up the hallway, and across the hall from the elevator: there's stairs out to an open area that leads back to the handicap entrance we brought Joe through."

She nodded sadly and hugged me tightly. I winced. "Oh, sorry, what did I-?"

"It's ok," I reflexively shot my arm to my shoulder. "I'll be fine." I moved my arm in a circle at the shoulder. *Wow that hurt*, I thought. I remember hearing a slight pop when I collided with that berserker. "We can see to it later. I can move. Foxy, you gonna be okay?"

He nodded.

"Good. I have a medi-kit in my pack. We'll get it on you at our next junction. You good to hold a rifle?"

"Yeah."

Joe pulled him up and got him to his feet. I looked them over, pulling up my pantleg and pouring some of the Hydrogen Peroxide over it. I wrapped it with some of the paper towels as well.

Then I straightened up to them. "Don't be afraid," I said, steely. "They can be killed just like anything else. They'll hear you if you shoot. But they'll kill you if you don't," I breathed. "Do not be afraid."

I could see all of them looking back at me, and I looked each one over. "This may be our last stand, but I'm tired of hiding. We're going home. We *will* get home, all of us. I promise you."

They nodded and gripped their weapons. Moment of truth. "Foxy, you get a mask this time. Ally, you get the other. We're down to four again, people. But we're stronger. We can do this." I took Rutty's RPG launcher and slung it over my shoulder, putting the two torpedoes sticking out of the top of my pack.

And then, somberly, Bassett lifted his hands out. The others followed, and I echoed it. It was a moment of deep love that moved me beyond anything I had ever experienced. This was no formal ceremony; it wasn't required. We had done this a million times before. But now was different. We had faced tremendous loss and were potentially evacuating to perhaps even less shelter out there, to a fairly certain death beyond. But they were ready for it, and that made me all the more ready.

"Let's move," I said, and we turned toward the exit.

Everyone gathered their things, and we crept up to the door. Remaining quiet out of habit – no need to draw them to us until we were ready – I unlocked the door and swung it inward. All of us headed out single-file: guns forward. Two of us were wounded; one of us badly.

The lights were on now, and we could see clearly. The blackened hunk of debris from the blast at the end of the hall was now painfully visible. "Don't look at it," I urged the team, as there was no way to be certain who was what. At any rate, gorgons had been there, and they had partially consumed the rest.

We rounded the corner. Rifles at the ready, and one hand grenade to our name, we proceeded down the corridor. I stopped at the corner by the library, and peered around to the right. Glanced at my watch. It was now nearly 1800 hours. Hard to believe less than an hour had passed since I had left Amos alone with them in the kitchen.

All clear.

We rounded the corner and went down the corridor toward the back entrance, carefully passing over the fire there. There was a long, low freezer plugged into the wall in one of the last rooms there that I hadn't noticed when we came in with Joe earlier. If there was more bottled water in there, we needed to grab it. The team ambled past me and filtered outside, and I went in and checked the freezer. I only had it open for a moment, but then gasped and shut it quickly. Ally heard me. She turned and asked, "What is it?"

"Nothing. Just- let's go, quick," I replied. There was no way in hell I was going to let her, or anyone else, see what I had just discovered in there. I guess I'd been desensitized by this time, because I just switched to full-on cold robot machine mode. *Just move out,* I thought.

We headed out the back entrance and cautiously peered up. We could all hear the shrieks and hisses, but they were behind us, and above us, over the front of the church.

We were at the back. The gorgons were still hovering around the bell spires for whatever reason. I wasn't sure where to go, but going north would be the wrong direction. We needed to head south and west. Perhaps we could double-back toward the jail again: it was familiar territory, and it was only a few streets over. We made for it, heading out of the parking lot and once again onto Commerce, bearing west.

I kept shaking my head. Couldn't get that freezer out of my mind. I pressed onward.

The snow was falling thick, and thankfully, obscured the sound of our passage. "Command, Shipley, do you read, over?" I breathed quietly.

"Shipley, Command, we read you, go ahead," came the staticky response.

"We're on evac. Proceeding west towards Second Street, back toward county jail on Commerce and First. Human assailant down. One additional refugee down." I despised having to radio these types of updates.

"Roger, proceed with ca-"

"Roger," I interrupted them. *Give me a break.* That's all we did was proceed with caution. That's all *they* did, back in their cozy Blockade. All *anyone* could do anymore was proceed with caution. I sneered.

We looked back and for a moment could see the tall spires of the church retreating into the background. There was a horde of gorgons circling around them, repeatedly, like honeybees around a nest. It was obvious that a few dozen more had converged upon it since the attack. Maybe even at least thirty…or more. We'd never get past all of them.

And then I had an insane idea. "Wait here," I motioned to them. We were all perched in the shadows along the corner of Commerce and Third Street. I looked at them and surveyed the surroundings. It was cold, but not too cold, and the snow still fell.

I crept down Third Street, heading south, keeping watch on the sky above. On my left was an old building labeled *Weight Watchers*. I had to chuckle grimly. Like we all weren't thin and starving enough.

Madison Street drew near. I checked both ways and then looked back. Through the snowfall I could barely make out Ally watching me around the corner of the last building where they had taken shelter before Commerce. Looked like she was putting her hair in pigtails again.

I turned back and then slowly walked out onto Madison. I had a clear view of the spires. I kept walking. I was now in the middle of the intersection of Madison and Third. I looked up at that stupid church where more than alien enemies attacked us, and I wasn't done with payback.

I cautiously unslung Rutty's launcher and knelt to the ground, loading a torpedo into the shaft. And then I took aim. I looked through the scope and zeroed my target. The base of one of the bell tower spires, nearest me. That seemed to be where they were converging.

The torpedo went sailing out from my launcher at a delightful clip, skewering the snowy air at a hundred and twenty meters per second. It slammed into the bell tower with a horrifying explosion that engulfed the church in a deafening inferno and shower of iron, metal, brick and gorgons. I was thrown backward to the ground and hit my head.

What? Rutty's little rocket launcher couldn't have done that. They were incendiary, but not *that* much. I looked at it, confused. Shrapnel flew in all directions as what was left of the church rocketed skyward, and a monstrous fireball floated toward the heavens with a tremendous resonant boom and crackle.

It was as if someone had dropped a nuke.

I could barely make out what happened. My eyes flickered through snow and smoke and ash, trying to see through the dust and fume, shielding my eyes. Something heavy was noisily rolling up the alleyway between Union and Madison, and it was rolling fast. It looked like a dark shape with treads and a double turret.

Was that a tank? Where the hell did a tank come from? The smoke seemed to swirl around it as it rumbled across the ground in triumph, and then launched a second blast. What was left of the church was reduced to blackened ash, as fires leapt upward, and debris rained down. A giant beam and timbers landed nearby me.

I shielded my eyes again. It was definitely a tank.

"Command to all units in C-Range, Command to all units in C-Range, power down. This is Captain Stone. Kill power and stand by."

Kill power? What did that mean?

I didn't know what else to do; I powered down my headset and hoped that Ally had done the same. She would have heard the transmission. I looked back up the alley but couldn't see any of them.

Someone was then counting down from twenty in my headset earpiece.

In less than twenty seconds, I would know exactly what it meant. I heard a swelling noise emanating from the tank, a tone both steadily climbing in pitch and also reverberating in soundwaves through the air all around us. The power of it…it was like driving past someone playing urban hip-hop way too loudly. Or, at least that's how I remember it: more felt than heard. Its turret turned about sixty degrees vertically in the air as the remaining gorgons locked onto it and tried to smash into it in their fury.

Out of the smaller turret, it launched its last salvo.

The tiny projectile flew up about two hundred feet, silently. It reminded me of the fourth of July, and I beheld its diminutive light framed against the night sky as it lingered there, soundlessly. It was both beautiful and gentle.

The blackness exploded with light into a horrifying detonation that belied the miniscule size of the projectile. There was a momentary delay…and then sound came crashing into me. The same rolling thunder of sound from the previous one hit me like a rolling pin, flattening me as it cascaded outward from a central radius.

The gorgons were caught in the flash of high-pitched dissonant sound, and some of their heads exploded as they clutched their ears, being this close to the epicenter. They careened in every direction trying to escape from ground zero, but it was all in vain. Every single one of them fell to the ground dead, writhing and bleeding from the ears.

We were unaffected, all of us humans.

It was another DTF.

Such a little thing; but it wreaked immeasurable havoc and ruin on the remaining gorgons. Those on the far perimeter who were swooping in to investigate did so to their own demise. The rest fled shrieking.

I lay there, laughing. *Keep the change, ya filthy animals.* I remembered some Christmas movie from long ago with that line in it. "Gorgon-*zola!*" I cried in hysterical amusement.

But my laughter eventually died and turned to frosty sobriety: the coldness of my spirit blending with the frigid temperature of the pavement on which I lay.

Goodbye, Jesse. Goodbye, Vera. Curse you, Amos.

That sickening freezer again. Sometimes you wish you could unsee things. I never could.

The burning embers came floating down, mingling with the snow: drifting fireflies mingling with snowy will-o'-the-wisps, creating a breathtaking panorama of contrasting color as they all silently descended. I reached up my finger and let one of them alight on me. To this day I don't remember if it was snow or ice. But either would have felt fine.

I thought back to that tiny little DTF that had just been launched, hovering there in the sky. Those gorgons hover and bring destruction. But now we had something similar, and it would bring them destruction. Perhaps the tables were finally turning for good.

A miniscule missile like that, with a colossal punch that sent our enemies flying.

An old janitor who turned out to be a psychopathic, homicidal, knife-wielding cannibal.

A blonde kid who turned out to be a warrior.

Things are just never what they seem to be.

13 | HOMECOMING

My team followed me.

The coast was clear. There was Joe. And Foxy.

And there was Ally.

I rolled over to face them, and Ally came to my side, shoving off a hunk of flaming shrapnel that had landed near me. I was actually smoking from a bit of burning embers that had landed on my legs. Son of a gun. Didn't feel a thing.

She knelt down beside me and took my face in her hands. I could see her hair swirling in the snowy wind, through the plentiful flakes falling on my face. She cradled my head in her chest. No argument from me there.

Ally released me, and I could see Joe approaching behind her. He still had a slight limp, but he was ambulatory. Foxy was beside him. Still no hat, but he looked ok. He was gripping his arm. Something about the way he looked made me hasten. I sprung up as quickly as I could, though all my joints ached. I'd had enough of flying backward for one night. "Come on, Foxy," I said. "Let's get you to that tank and get a medi-kit on you. You need some fresh bandages and that needs to be sewn up."

I hugged him gently, then turned to Joe. "Nice shot, ace," he grinned toward me with that southern drawl. Another hug, but this one a little longer. I guess hugs are okay.

"Let's get outta here, yeah?" I said to him, but directed it to all of us as well. Ally helped gather my things, which had scattered in the blast. My backpack, Rutty's launcher, my rifle and sidearm: it was all gathered, and we slowly made our way over to the tank. It was a big beast. Both turrets were still smoking as we approached, and the top hatch opened.

"Welcome to MS 43, fellas! Oops, and lady!" greeted an infantryman with a camo helmet and goggles, and he gave a nod to Ally. She smiled. "Let me give you a hand inside."

I was utterly fascinated by the presence of this massive destroying machine as we all climbed up and crawled inside. And shocked as well. I had heard no word that our army, or *anyone's* army – had any tanks anymore. This one had some special equipment on the top of it that looked like a functional radar, and what resembled a giant black box with grills on the side for ventilation. Or…was it for sound? There was a low throbbing pulse coming from it, but I swear I could also hear a higher frequency as well, as we drew near to it. Some kind of harmonics? I wasn't sure. It was pulsating.

We climbed into the belly of the beast and shut the top hatch. It was entirely bathed in crimson inside. The thought occurred to me to pop open some more chemlights, and then we'd have red and green: a real Christmas. But it would just be all red, bathed in the glow of those interior lights.

I hadn't felt this safe in days. Kinda like being at home under the gun towers. We rolled out. All of us felt it turning south. I pulled my medi-kit out of my pack and began tending to Foxy. He groaned and winced as I pulled the bandage off of him. "Oh stop, ya big baby," I chided him. He mock-glared at me. I poured some of the hydrogen peroxide over the needle and began to sew him up. I gently pulled off the paper towel mass, and he bit his lip and stifled back a cry. It was just serum now. He gripped a side-handle of the tank, squirming and squealing.

Joe was across from me, massaging his own ankle. Ally was on the other side of me, stretching out her legs.

Then it was time for me. I peeled off my jacket and shirt, and poured hydrogen peroxide on my shoulder, sopped it up, and began to sew myself closed. That hurt like a bugger. Ally helped me. It was a deep wound, but not big.

I turned my attention to the gunner. "How did you guys get over here? Did you come from DN436?" I asked him. "I wouldn't think the Cunningham could hold you!"

"It can't! No way. This baby's forty tons of steel. No sir, we came up from Greenwood. There are thirty of us. But that's where we're going."

"Thirty *tanks?*" I asked him, incredulously. "Did you say thirty tanks?" The gunner nodded. "When did you…where did you… how long have you been around?"

"The past two weeks," he confirmed.

My mouth was agape. Right now, all kinds of questions were swirling around in my mind for Stone, and they were adding up. I was paying so much attention to the soldier, and the road was bumpy. I accidentally jabbed Foxy with the needle straight into his arm, and he cried out. "Sorry, man. I'm sorry." I swear Foxy was crying now.

I was grateful for the rescue, but where had these guys been when we could have used them up north? And why weren't we told anything about them? More surprises. This stunk.

"Hey, are you guys on rescue ops?" asked Joe.

"All the time, why?" said the soldier.

"There's a little girl about six hundred meters north of us that's all by herself. And there's about eighty refugees stuck up at Harvill Hall on the APU campus. That's where we stayed. They helped us lojack the gorgon."

The soldier whipped his head over to Joe. His eyebrows went way up. "You guys lojacked a *gorgon*? How the hell did you do *that*?"

"It wasn't easy, man," I said. "We got one, but it got us too." I didn't want to talk about it and detail how it all went down. "Anyway, those guys are stranded there, can you pick them up?"

"I'll call it in," the soldier called. "You said one and eighty?" he asked, indicating the quantity of survivors in the two locations. I nodded. He sent the update in to Command. I was amazed. Where did all these guys come from? Where had they been for all these years? Could it be that all those stragglers in Harvill…that Nevaeh… would finally be rescued?

I felt uneasy. These were a lot of increased surprises. Far more developments than I was aware of; than Bassett had been privy to; or than the Captain had seen fit to share with us. It all pointed to something more epic going on that we were never told about. I mean, I guess that's the way of things: the higher-ups call the shots, and us grunts down here get moved around like chess pieces in order to fulfill the great stratagems of war. And if they lost a few pawns in the process? No problem. There were more pawns to spare. I looked over at Foxy. Here I was, bringing them another pawn to move around. It made me mad.

It was all one giant setup for the chess queen to strike, and it was our part to play to advance the mission and keep taking ground. The bishops and rooks and knights could help until the queen was ready. I wondered what part the tanks played: were they bishops, rooks, or knights? And who the hell was the queen? I guessed that was Stone.

I finished up with Foxy, poured some more hydrogen peroxide on him and washed him up, then gently bandaged up his arm. I turned to say something to Ally, and noticed that she was asleep against the tank. Joe was nodding as well. I didn't blame them. By all rights I should be zonked and comatose too.

I turned back to Foxy. "There you go, Foxy. Good as new." And then I looked at him, and swear I saw Rutty. I don't know: something about the light across his face, it teased me with memories of my kid brother. This young man soldier, Rutty's age, wounded in battle, had saved me back there. He kept going. He was made of stern stuff. I was glad to have him. I patted him on the leg and turned back to the gunner.

"Nice shots back there. You really laid 'em out to dry."

"Thanks!" he enthusiastically accepted. "Yeah, we've been on patrol on the outskirts for a while. That's the call letters: *MS 43:* Mobile Scout Number 43. They rigged these up with some heavy-duty sonic equipment that you might have seen on your way in: those gorgons don't like the high-pitched stuff, so the military's been working on some tech that fuses ours and theirs, and lets us send out some pretty uncomfortable DTF signals that mess with their ears. I don't understand all of it, ha! Just glad it works!"

"Ours and theirs…you mean the amulets," I said.

"Oh, you know about those?"

"Oh yeah. Not until a few days ago, and only yesterday learned what they're really capable of, but yeah."

"Yeah, well, that DTF had one. And we're carrying one in the back. Gotta keep it in a stabilizer 'cause it gets hot." I remembered Dupre. "But it puts out a signal every three seconds in all directions, like a mini DTF without the explosive force, but enough to drive 'em away and keep 'em at bay. So, we don't get chased. We call it The Warhorse Morse." Morse Code. Warhorse. I get it.

"Amazing," I said, and shook my head. "How long you been working with this stuff?"

"Dunno. Seems like they've been working on it since they got here."

Sixteen years? This whole time? That seemed excessively long. I didn't ask any more questions. I'd save them for Stone.

There was a lull in the conversation.

"Anyway," the gunner began again, "Captain Stone sent a message. They've delayed the memorial by a few hours. 2100. He knew you'd want to be part of it. We're bringing you all in."

I looked at my watch. 1830 hours. The news made my heart glad, but I wouldn't call it rejoicing just yet. We had paid for this return with heavy losses. No one had heard from Preston yet, and the DTF could very well have utterly disabled all of their electronics, including his headset. Nevaeh was out there somewhere. We had lost Rutty, Jesse, and Vera, all for what…to track a gorgon that we could now seemingly annihilate with a DTF? It screamed futility.

Stone better have some answers, that's all I had to say about it.

•   •   •   •   •

My watch said 1915 by the time the tank came to a stop. By then everyone else was asleep, and I was lost in thought. Ally had been shaken by the sudden jerk of the tank coming to a stop. She awoke, looked over at me and smiled. Foxy had toppled over with his head on my shoulder, and I hadn't even noticed. Rutty used to do that at nights when we'd stay up for a movie. I looked down and saw his blonde locks over my shoulder; I tilted his head gently the other way against the wall. He stirred but remained dozing. "Stop drooling on me, Foxy," I chided him sarcastically, and looked back at Ally with a smile.

Joe was coming to, and turned toward the gunner.

"We're here," said the gunner. The driver undid his seat belt, got up and stretched his body. Then he moved to the back and threw open the hatch without even thinking twice. I remembered their Warhorse Morse. The abandon they each had was enviable to watch. Here we were: clinging to the shadows and threading the mazes of the city streets like mice, keeping absolutely quiet and still, and here they were brazenly out for pleasure cruises like drunken frat boys on a Friday night. If they didn't have that signal generator it would be another story entirely.

I heard a din of activity outside.

"We're to let you off here. Boat'll take you to the other side, and we'll have another MS over there to take you all the way back."

I checked the coordinates on my watch. Close to the Cunningham Bridge, which was just south of Liberty Park and the Clarksville Marina. I was a bit incredulous that we were going to ride a boat across the Cumberland, as noisy as boats were – until we hopped out and I saw the boat. I helped Ally out and then turned around. I couldn't believe it.

We weren't going to *ride* a boat; we were going to *cross over* a boat!

There it was. It was an LST Dodger-Class tank landing warship, moored near the dry flats south of the marina, bordering a park. Its ramp was down, and there were still tanks coming out of it. It was narrow enough to fit in the Cumberland, but how far had it traveled? The river started in Kentucky and ran seven hundred miles to the Ohio River! I wondered where the base was along there that had dispatched this sucker. Bizarre, but I was sure glad it was here. At some point the bow had been pointed west across the river, because there were tanks that awaited us on the west side as well. I briefly wondered if they encountered any gorgons face down in the river along their passage.

But the handsome truth of it stared us in the face. Here, in all its mustered glory, was the cavalry.

"How did you…?" I asked the gunner.

He laughed. "How did we get in the channel? Easy. We're blowing bridges along the river, the ones that we can't pass under, at least. We need tanks more than bridges now. No one's driving anyway. Bridges can be repaired. We need to get these things far inland. Army and Navy bases up and down Kentucky, Tennessee, Georgia, The Carolinas, Alabama, they're all sending these bad boys out. There's Destroyers and subs too. And Sabre Airfield northwest of here, up at Fort Campbell? They're about to get their remaining jets retrofit with these babies too. We should be able to mount an aerial defense coming up here soon as well."

Made sense to me, yet I felt conflicting emotions. The sight of that warship, and all of those glorious tanks rolling out and lining up, was immeasurably rewarding beyond belief. These things could actually contend with the gorgons and drive them off, even kill them at close range.

However, the government must have been preparing this and working on it, clandestinely, for years. All those ships, all those bases, all those tanks. I wondered how far back it went, but we've had sixteen years to figure it out. Still, a deep-seated feeling of discontent was growing. Embers of cynicism were continuing to stoke in my heart: where had these ships and these tanks been all this time? Surely, with how well-equipped everything at this makeshift base was, they would have been far more able to subdue and track a gorgon. Why send us all to our doom? We were now strolling along an island of impenetrability and bravado that was seemingly nowhere to be found on planet Earth just one day prior. And I wanted to know why.

We were all groggy, but we dismounted and said our goodbyes to the tank crew, boarded the ship, and began to cross over. There were gun towers all over it, and I thought I saw similar-looking devices such as the Warhorse they had on our little tank, which now seemed so dwarfish by comparison.

The place was abuzz with activity. There were floodlights erected on steel towers, the sound of construction machinery nearby laboring endlessly, vehicles going here and there with supplies and personnel, and more tanks rolling out across the flats. Many of them were wearing the same type of mask that we had, with the gorgon-reflecting tech.

Awestruck, we made our way through the mayhem, and onto the stern of the giant ship.

Ally came up to me and walked with me, her arm around my waist; mine around her shoulder. I kissed her.

We were greeted by an ensign that the tank must have radioed ahead to, because he greeted me by name. "Sergeant Shipley!" I nodded. "Ensign Matthews. I'm to escort you to the bow. We've got an ultralight that'll take you to the other side. Safari. Gotta make a few runs though."

That was news to me. I had never seen an LST before, but these ones must have a pretty long bow if it was to accommodate a helipad. "Why don't you have a chopper down here?" I asked him.

"Well, as much as we'd like to say we've won the war, it's not over yet. They're still out there and mad as hell. They see a chopper go up over a great distance, they wanna charge at it. Can't take that chance yet. And the rotors' audio patterns scatter and disrupt the soundwaves, so that doesn't help us. These are for short runs only. Don't worry. They won't come within a mile of here."

I nodded again. We ascended up the ramp and into the hull. In a few moments, and after a bit of claustrophobic and breathless stair work, we were nearly at the bridge. Mingling among the ensigns, we could now distinguish a few officers in tan, bustling about and giving orders. Mounted high atop the antenna array, there were several large boxes with similar flaps such as what we had seen on the back of the combat vehicles. It had to be more DTF-emitters. Only, these ones were mammoth. I guess you needed that in order to cover more area: forming more of a defensive perimeter required more juice, and more amplification. Basically, the difference between headphones and concert speakers.

We passed a few cargo hatches. The troop messing and berthing were below. The ensign led us around the flank of the gray steel walls. High atop that ship, I looked back north, and through the swirling snow I could dimly make out a mass of gorgons back north of where we came. There were a few dots scattered elsewhere on the horizon. They were definitely still out there. But for the first time, we all looked out and beheld an enemy full of fear, steering clear of us, knowing full well the agony they would encounter were they to descend within a few thousand feet of this invisible yet protective dome encircling us. The reverberating tones could be heard humming throughout, blending into a warm and felt rhythm, throbbing all around us. I had to manually pop my ears to adjust.

A fatigues-over-dress-uniform wearing Naval officer approached us, and we saluted each other simultaneously, and then chuckled. No idea who was who anymore: the military was one big happy family.

"You must be Sergeant Shipley! I'm Captain Benson," he said, shaking my hand. He was a husky man with a fierce, gritty southern twang. Reminded me of that *beef: it's what's for dinner* commercial guy. Sam something or other.

"Glad you made it! Let's get you guys home!" he growled, and I stifled a laugh at his overly-patriotic drawl. It was true after all: we were going home, and looking forward to it. All of us. I turned around and they were all still behind me: no lacerated arms, no twisted ankles. Ally, Foxy, and Joe. We were going to make it, *and* be in time for a much-needed remembrance.

•   •   •   •   •

Before too long we were aboard an old Safari ultralight chopper. We had to make four roundtrip runs to accommodate each of us with the pilot, and I'd never been more nervous than when it touched down for the last time and finally dropped off Joe. I think I actually cared about the guy. He'd gone from Bassett, to Sergeant in Charge, back to Bassett, to Joe, in a short while, but he'd done what was needed, and he could keep up with us young'uns. I admired him. I was grateful for him. He had played his hand well.

The Safari touched down in a small clearing on the west side of River Road, where another tank with a DTF-emitter was waiting to meet us. It took us out and down onto River Road, then swung a wide left onto Zinc Plant Road.

Soon, we were rumbling along the concrete thoroughfare, loudly, as if the gorgons had never known about Earth, and never descended here. Practically the only things we were missing were a song and a banjo.

But for whatever reason, I kept thinking back to Amos and that freezer…and Vera. I hadn't shaken that memory, and couldn't bring myself to tell Ally and the others that they had eaten human flesh. My stomach groaned a bit, and I needed fresh air. I tapped the gunner and asked if I could swap places with him and stand up top with the hatch open. He handed me his heavy-duty headphones which masked the sound of the Warhorse, and I stuck my head out. I probably looked like some dog on a summer road sneezing at the wind with my long ears flapping behind me. I probably looked like our old dog Jack before we came to the Blockade.

We passed by an old mini-mart and a country kitchen. Then a church. Then another church. I'd had enough of churches for now. In twenty minutes, we rolled off the road and were rumbling along the grass.

We passed a few barren trees, and then I saw them, twinkling in what little reflections of moonlight or far away lights glanced off of them through the snowing clouds.

The gun towers. I breathed contentedly at the sight of them. It was so good to be home after this one. Ally squeezed right up next to me through the manhole and out on top, putting her arm around me.

"Hey, you okay?"

I sniffed and wiped my eyes.

I wished that Rutty was here. He should have been here with us, coming home and being welcomed in as a hero. We did our mission, but hadn't heard jack about it. And as grateful as I was for this new technology to push back the gorgons and offer us some sanctuary, I couldn't help but feel that the whole thing to put the tracker on that gorgon was futile, and that we were set up to fail from the start.

It took me a while to answer, but I nodded, "Yeah. I'm good," I said, looking over at her. "Good to be home. With you."

She put her head on my shoulder, and we rolled up to the front entrance.

I hoped they had fixed those dang rusty doors, which only made me think of Rutty, and his WD-40, even more.

The doors split in the middle and slipped open both ways. There was the Launch. And there, standing out in the open, defenseless and brandishing no weapon and no military fatigues, only a simple tan shirt and jeans, was Stone.

He walked out and down the berm to greet us in the cold night air. The snow fell freely onto his fuzzy hair.

I stared at him for a moment, but then dismounted and walked up toward him. My heart began to pound.

He was the first to say anything.

"You'll have answers, I promise."

I gritted my teeth. "I better." And his clenched jaw softened into a smile, and he came over and hugged me. I didn't hug him back. It was cold, and I was trembling. He grabbed me by both of my shoulders and looked at me.

"Nice to see you again, Jet."

"You too, Captain Stone," I said coldly, and with that, he cocked his head to the side and gave me a pensive look. I smiled weakly and moved past him.

I felt him turn towards me as I passed by him. Ally came up next and walked by my side as we stepped onto the Launch.

"Jet!" Stone yelled. "I'm sorry about-"

"Don't!" I yelled, and surprised myself with my volume. "Don't you even say his name, Captain!" I pointed fiercely at him from up there on the Launch. My blood was pounding, my throat was dry, and I needed water. I took a deep breath as I looked at him square in the eyes. "Don't."

He waited and then nodded, looking down at his shoes and then back up at me.

I turned and went back in, dutifully placing my finger on the lick-n-prick as I returned into the shelter of our Blockade, and my team followed me.

14 | REMEMBERING

I can't even begin to describe it.

That shower felt *so* good.

I looked at the clock before stepping in. 2015 hours. The memorial was in 45 minutes.

I had parted with Ally in the corridor after passing the data room and the Beast. *The Beast.* It seemed so useless now. It's like we already knew everything we were going to know. Who cares what they were doing out there in the ocean? I knew everything about them I needed to know: they were animals, they had killed my little brother, and it was easy to drive a bullet through their temple. Right now, all I cared about was a shower, and attending that memorial.

•   •   •   •   •

I returned to my room. Block 237 opened up, and there were the empty bunks again. I saw them after I left Stone and Ally behind. I had speedwalked back to my room, unlocked it, and hurled my pack at the wall, throwing myself down on the bed. I wanted to stay there, but I didn't have long. We had a memorial to get to.

But there they were again, solemn, quiet: the only remnants of my family. Never again would Rutty fill one of those bunks on a sleepover. Never again would I lie on the floor, listening to him above me talking about all things book-related. This book, that book, this story, that novel. These characters and their journeys. That epic plot. Man, he loved books. He had loaned me some, and they were right there on the shelf opposite my bunk. Each one of them Rutty's; none of them mine.

And speaking of dead, I would soon need to talk with Ally…and the rest of them. They would want to know about the freezer…and the stew.

I didn't have any dress clothes. None of us did. I simply put on a pair of jeans and a standard issue tan t-shirt, combed my hair as nicely as I could, sprayed on some cheap cologne, and made a half-assed attempt to shave. I wasn't the focal point of this thing: the other three were. So, it really didn't matter.

Before long there was a knock on my door. It had better not be Stone.

I opened the door and Ally was standing outside. She was dressed just as informally as I was. But in here, stripping off the fatigues and remnants of war made for simple, purer and more innocent attire that was far more welcome for such events. And I thought she looked relaxed and beautiful. She had even put on some makeup.

"Hey," she breathed.

"Hey, come in," I said, taking her by the hand and sitting down on my bunk together. We looked at each other, and she clenched her lips together. This time I didn't mind the sympathy. She held her fingers up and counted one…two…three. At three, she took a deep breath, and I instinctively joined her. I pulled her against me, and we both sat back on the bunk against the wall. The door was still open.

"You okay?" she asked, tenderly.

I had to think about it this time. The shower had relaxed me, the books were a memorable testament to a solid brotherhood, the room was warm, and I felt refreshed. But something was missing. "Not really," I said.

"Yeah, me neither," she agreed. "Stone has some explaining to do."

"Yeah he does. They all do."

•   •   •   •   •

2058 hours. We headed down the corridor toward the center of the Blockade, hand in hand. In a vast, open meeting space in the middle, nearly a hundred feet across underground, with various vertical sections of each still left intact to support against a sagging roof, there we gathered. We just called this meeting space 'the pavilion.'

All the big, important meetings were held here. Clandestine councils were called as well, I'm sure: councils that I was becoming increasingly aware that I was not allowed to be a part of.

That was the west part of the pavilion. In the east, we had our hydroponics farm: lettuce, tomatoes, potatoes, etc, and they supplemented our grains and everything that we could occasionally harvest above ground, like natural fruits and other vegetables.

But now, on the west side, there were chairs. A huge mass of folding chairs had been set up, and a makeshift dais erected at the far end, with some copper vases filled with an assortment of echinacea, crested iris, purple coneflower, columbine and rudbeckia on either side of the stage. There were a dozen trees in planters that had also been unearthed with care above, and brought down into the depths of the earth to provide some cheer and joy, flanking the stage. Now they were adorned with white Christmas lights. Where they had acquired those, I didn't know. But the sight of them made my heart glad.

A humble wood lectern stood lonesome, in the middle of the stage.

Overall, it was barren and fairly cheerless. The fluorescent lights buzzed noticeably, and it reminded me of that haunted bathroom in the church after the murder of Vera. I guessed there would always be something here to remind me of something there: it was almost like a past life you couldn't just shake off like a bad habit. It stays with you. I think every mission was like that anyway. The one with Markus, who we'd still heard no word about. He was presumed dead. But protocol was to not hold a memorial for someone until it was clear beyond all doubt.

The mission where I distracted them from Rutty.

The one with the toy chest.

You take those memories with you.

Joe was already there, seated up front with Foxy. They had both cleaned up, and Foxy's wound had been redressed. Joe was now sporting a better splint around his ankle, and his weathered hair was neatly combed.

We rounded the front row of chairs in front of them, and they looked up at us and stood. Big hugs. These ones I was ready to hug, no problem. I thanked Joe for everything, and then tousled Foxy's hair and play-punched him in the shoulder. He complained, and then adjusted his hair to his liking again.

I asked him if he was okay. He was the only member of our team to lose more of his own people than we did. I would tell him about Vera in time.

People began to filter in. I had forgotten how many people took shelter in this Blockade. There were plenty of civilians: people I had never met and probably never would, always being out on missions.

But there were plenty of military personnel too. I saw Harrison enter from an entrance on the far side of the pavilion. He took a seat a few rows back from us. Ferro, Pettijohn and Wilkes ambled in from another side of the pavilion. I was glad to see them all in one piece, but I couldn't shake a feeling of inequity and unfairness. Must be nice to be a whole unit still. I thought back briefly to when Sarah and I had dated. She had moved on.

In a few minutes, it was standing room only. The only people seemingly not here were the Sentry at the Launch, and those manning the gun towers.

Then Stone came. He was not a religious man, and would not be officiating this memorial. We had Pastor Rosie for that. She was a sweet elderly Mexican woman who was simply in Tennessee visiting family when all hell broke loose. As luck would have it, she made her way to our Blockade and was welcomed by all…especially Rutty. Seemed fitting that she would be speaking today. She was wearing all black, with tiny loafers on her tiny feet, and a beautiful red rose in her black, wavy hair. It was impossible to look at Rosie and not smile, especially when she looked at you over the top rim of those tiny, black, librarian glasses. She had an air of matriarch about her that we all loved.

Stone sat down three seats away from me, by himself. I didn't look over at him.

Pastor Rosie ascended the dais and turned to face us. She had a few notes in her hand, and she placed them on the ground in front of her. I knew exactly what she would do next. In a gesture both gracious and graceful, she both beckoned us to stand *and* receive, as she lifted her diminutive arms palms outward and upward in token of that. We stood, and mirrored her. I could hear the steady beat of my heart as a full minute went by.

She turned to me, Foxy, and Stone, and then to members of Dupre's and Hickey's families who still lived here, and nodded. They were across from us in the left bank of chairs to Pastor Rosie's right.

"Friends, family, neighbors, human souls. We are gathered here today to remember," Rosie began. "Three days. Three deaths. And more beyond count that have and will forever go unsung." My thoughts immediately went to Vera and Jesse.

"It's been sixteen years since our world was forever changed by the arrival of the enemy. Sixteen years of toil, prayer, heartache, progress, setbacks, hopes, hopes dashed, life," she paused, "and loss.

"In those sixteen years, we've had many heroes. We've had many souls who have forsaken self, stepping up to serve humanity in the best way they know how, using the gifts that God above graciously gave them. I'm seventy-eight years old. And I remember each of the sixteen years since I was sixty-two, and the skies were filled with those things out there. They have been out there a long time, and they might still be.

"But there are less of them out there now. And more than that, the *fear* of them is lessened now, because of the bravery of those we celebrate and remember here today." She paused and collected her notes.

"William Francis Dupre was born on August 27th, 1973, and was admittedly a huge science nerd," -here the crowd laughed- "who loved to tinker." As she spoke, one of three slim projectors behind her, to her right, floated an opaque blue image of Dupre, wavering lightly in the heat of the room. It held steady, and those who never met him felt now like they could put a face with the name.

"William saw a need here to fill with tech support, research, and more. Those who knew him best will say that William didn't talk much. But when he did, it was always affirming, always encouraging. He had a sunny outlook and a sneaky personality." A few snickers from the crowd from those who he may have 'snuck' from. "He passed two days ago while helping to ascertain the potency of a new weapon we have against the enemy, and he will be sorely missed."

Rosie shifted her notes.

"Shannon Eleanor Grace Hickey was born February 12th, 2015, and always had a passion to join the army in the footsteps of her father, Gerald."

The next projector, directly behind Pastor Rosie, illuminated a beautiful image of Hickey from what must have been her early twenties. It flickered upward and held steady. It wasn't anything formal, but it was a close-up of her doing what she did best: painting. Like Hickey's, the image suspended there, lightly moving with momentary glimmering, as the projection reflected her beauty.

"Isn't she beautiful?" Rosie asked. Affirmative murmurs from the audience. "Private Hickey loved art, and was a tremendous painter." Rosie beckoned to the back, against one of the supporting columns. We all turned around. There, set on easels, were various works that Hickey had painted in her short tenure here. I never knew. You always learned more about people in death than you did in life. I was struck that she was the same age as Vera. She, and her paintings, were both beautiful and striking. Rosie continued.

"It was her deepest desire to serve in the infantry, and to strike a blow at the heart of our enemy. She studied ballistics and explosives intensely, and helped with the disarming of potentially lethal mines and tripwires that this Blockade had set in preparation for its further reinforcement in 2031. Shannon's contributions to our society, and to humanity, both in the areas of protection and the arts, will not be forgotten. We lost her three days ago while on mission." I was grateful that Rosie also didn't say how she died.

Rutty would have appreciated that tribute to Hickey. He knew her better than I did, and had spent time with her on patrol. Perhaps they shared the same faith and had discussed it. I would never know. My heart began to beat faster for some unknown reason. Then I realized that it was because I knew who was coming up next.

Again, the pastor shifted her notes. My heart began to thud.

And then the last projector fired up, washing the air with a beautiful image of my baby brother, Wyatt, from his high school graduation, with my arm around him. I choked and gulped hard. I had forgotten that moment: anytime there was a graduating class (always a small number, and shrinking each year, I grant you) they would bring out some of those academic trencher caps with the square tops, and the kids would don them. It was just me to celebrate it with him. I remember he was bummed because mom, dad and Sissy weren't there. Even through his disappointment, you could see his gregarious smile holding fast. Ally grabbed my hand as I clutched my knees and my body started to lightly tremble. Foxy put his arm around me. Pastor Rosie began.

"Wyatt Rutledge Shipley," she began, and then stopped, and turned to face me over her thin glasses. "*Rutty*," she said with a warm smile. I clenched my lip back at her. It was hard to watch her as I wanted to keep my eyes sealed on the projection. I had seen that picture several times before, but this time I wanted to cement it in my mind.

"Rutty was born on June 12th, 2023. He served in the infantry for nearly three years, and loved being the wingman of his brother, Sergeant Cameron Shipley. When he wasn't serving on reconnaissance missions, everyone knew what he was doing. And what was he doing?" she asked the crowd.

Books! Reading books! Reading! came the scattered replies amidst laughter. I had to smile.

"That's right!" she gleefully replied. "Rutty loved books. This young man was a scholar-in-the-making, a true heart, trusted friend, valiant warrior, and a reliable soul. He had a can-do attitude, was amazingly skilled at Scrabble, and loved kids." I thought of Nevaeh and the impression she would have made on him. "Rutty died in battle yesterday morning while on a special mission from Command, a mission wherein he fought bravely against our foe." Rosie choked up and had to compose herself briefly.

My eyes welled. *She didn't need to go to such detail.*

"And though he was lost at the young age of nineteen, his spirit lives on in the hearts of all of us who long to see that mission fulfilled: *learning.* His mission was one to enable us to learn more about our enemy, and ascertain why they are here." She paused, and smiled soberly. "He was a learner. He died during a mission *enabling* learning. And he died in a *place* of learning: a library."

This was too much. It was like I was back there yesterday in that stupid library, rooted to the ground with horror and crying out my baby brother's name. My body quaked, and I brushed away the tears.

"He will never be forgotten, nor will his bravery."

Rosie paused again. "There is an unfortunate cruelty at play here, and that is that of the three souls departed, we were allowed to only have one of them with us. William

Dupre's body was buried yesterday. Shannon Hickey's body was never found. Wyatt Shipley's body was committed to the earth yesterday as well, where he died. Though none of them are with us, they are heroes: one and all. We remember them today in the face of such cruelty, this seemingly never-ending war that has ravaged our planet, and we commit to them anew, that our plight will not last. Our suffering will one day end. We will one day be delivered, and we will all fly free once again, as these souls are doing now. Until that time, we also pray for Markus Jentzen to be returned to us."

I thought of that beautiful heron soaring along the Cumberland River, and how it had taken Rutty's breath away.

"And like the faith of Private Shipley, we serve a God who will one day emerge victorious and 'return to gather all those who are left up in the air with him, to be with Him forever,' as the scriptures tell us. Amen?"

I stared at his projection, my heart pounding. I couldn't respond, though the audience did, with a somber "Amen."

"Amen," Pastor Rosie echoed. "Let us never forget those who went before us to bring us peace, including our Lord and Savior Jesus Christ, to whom we commit their bodies, and their souls, for all eternity. Amen. Let us pray.

"Our Father who art in Heaven, hallowed by thy name."

Oh no…not that prayer…

"Thy kingdom come, thy will be done, on earth as it is in heaven."

Stop…just stop… My body was racked with tears.

"Give us this day our daily bread, and forgive us our debts, as we forgive our debtors."

I couldn't take this. *Stop.* That was my brother's last prayer. *Please don't say the last line. Please. I beg you.*

"And lead us not into temptation, but deliver us from evil," she enunciated clearly, as if she were there the morning of the raid and heard Rutty's solemn prayer.

Deliver us from evil.

"Enough! Stop!" I stood and cried out. "Just stop!" The focus was broken and there were scattered gasps. I could feel all eyes on me, back to Rosie, back to me, back to Rosie, wondering what she would do.

The slender, elderly Mexican woman looked over at me with understanding and pity, then unhurriedly descended the dais and came over and took my hands, standing directly in front of me as I looked down upon her. I couldn't stop the tears. One of them landed on her hand. She looked down and scooped it up and held it up to me. "There will one day be no more tears. For Dupre, and Hickey, and Rutty," she said, "that day is now."

We looked at each other, and there was a moment of understanding where it seemed the rest of the pavilion darkened, and only Rosie and I remained. She took my hands again. "I know this hurts, Cameron, and I know this pain all too well. I lost many to them as well, including my sister. I lost all of my children: all five of them. And I've had to ask myself for sixteen years now, *why?*"

My eyes were wet with tears, and I could see hers were as well. She loved Rutty so much. "I know the answer now." She smiled and squeezed my hands. "I *know* it now.

"The answer, Cameron, is that this all has a purpose, and I'm but a small part of it. Just like when you get a cold, it's to make you stronger. It's to build you up and strengthen you from within, so that when the *real* threat comes, you're ready for it. As the saying goes, 'prepare the child for the road; not the road for the child.' You are not a candle in a wind-free world." She winked at me.

The *real* threat? What did she mean by that? And what was this about candles? Was she speaking in some arcane code that the others weren't privy to? Some sort of a prophetess? What the hell was the threat that we had been fighting all this time then, if not gorgs? I tilted my head.

"The answer, Cameron, is so that you can be ready to weather it when it comes."

I took a deep breath and smiled at her faintly. She backed away from me, and lifted up her arms, palm upward.

She never dropped her arms; but instead kept them upright as she reascended the dais and walked back to the center, behind Shannon's projection, and just stood there with her palms up, receiving.

Slowly, the rest of us received as well. And then Pastor Rosie looked over at me and smiled warmly, the most tender smile of understanding that I think I've ever seen.

"Amen," she said again, and retreated once more from the dais. We all returned to our seats one by one.

There was a long reflection of silence as the three projections flickered in tribute for us to behold. I could feel the eyes of all of us on my brother and the others. It was a fitting tribute. I just wished it was over already.

•   •   •   •   •

Captain Stone took a deep breath after a few moments, and then solemnly rose and ascended the stage. I swallowed hard and braced myself, furrowing my brows. He and I hadn't spoken yet, and I wasn't ready to call him 'Dad' by any stretch of the imagination. That would take some time…if it was ever to be again.

"Thank you, Pastor Rosie," he began, looking over at her. "And thank all of you for being here to remember those lost. Mrs. Dupre, Mr. and Mrs. Hickey, and Sergeant Shipley, thank you for your sacrifice."

Sacrifice. I was not in a mood to receive this. Any of it. Nonetheless, he continued.

"You'll pardon me if we shift gears for a moment. This is, after all, a military outpost on the frontier of war. These are uncertain times. We never really know what the next day will hold. We have lived under the shadow of this alien threat for far too long, sheltering under a false sense of security that eight gun towers offer us above. We've had to live this way. It hasn't been easy, but many have made it possible to survive. The people we remember here today…made it possible to survive. We thank them."

Stone paused and looked down at the lectern, and his notes.

"Many of you have been made aware that the military has stepped up its presence in the region. We have a warship on the Cumberland now. More will come. I've personally been assured by The President of the United States, that in three months' time, we'll have a fleet of two hundred tanks here, and a battalion of armed forces at the ready, prepared to partner with the local Blockades. We're bringing in heavy firepower all over the country, and nearly all of it is being dispensed by the United States Navy. In three months, we'll have thirty warships nearby, up and down the Cumberland," he said lowly and gleefully.

Scattered murmuring and gasps. Some isolated applause.

"For too long these gorgons have taken our waterways and our oceans. For the survival of our species, we are inclined to take them back. Our payback is going to be underway in a week. They've taken the fight to us and driven us away from the water. And now, we're going to take the fight to them. You've all heard of the new technology that our scientists have been diligently focusing on: DTF's. Dissonant Tidal Floods. These are EMP's at powerful magnitudes with destructive force, using the enemies' own technology against them. More importantly, these DTF's do not affect humans, as far as we know. And more powerful ones are being built. The President is also prepared to exercise, at long last, a nuclear option: one which would greatly increase the blast radius of the DTF's, and disable or kill the gorgons on a mass, planetary scale."

I'd heard nearly all of this already. How disgraceful. Turning a memorial into a briefing. Where was the honor? Rutty's image seemed to flicker in disapproval behind the Captain. All of theirs did. But going nuclear? There would be tremendous fallout! Depending on the prevailing winds, we'd be forced to live underground for years, even *decades,* more! I looked over at Ally and Joe, who looked back at me incredulously. Foxy had put his head in his hands.

"Our civilization is preparing a massive counterattack that we've all patiently awaited sixteen hard years. That time has now come. You'll each be briefed on your respective assignments in two days. For now, we've been granted furlough, in tandem with a celebration to honor those lives lost, both here and abroad. Sergeant Shipley's command has received help from several refugees at Austin Peay University northeast of here; they'll be escorted down to more secure lodgings with more generous provisions, under the protection of the United States Armed Forces. Tanks and APCs are on their way there now, to rendezvous with survivors and bring them here. They've been on land east of us for six weeks now, readying, and similar missions are underway all over the states as the military gains an increased footing."

Wait - six weeks they've been here? Six weeks? The gunner had said two. What was going on here?

Stone paused, looking us all over intently. "This is the beginning. This is where the end of their road, and the beginning of ours, converge. And now? Operation Deliver Us From Evil starts…with DN436!"

Deliver us from evil.

The crowd cheered deafeningly and ceaselessly.

But nothing could assuage me: I couldn't take any more of it. Maybe I was a loose cannon after all.

I shook my head and ran out. Ally ran after me.

All this time they've been planning this assault. Those boats could have been sailing up the Cumberland and those tanks could have started their northward march at least a few weeks earlier or more. My brother would still be alive, sitting here right beside me, instead of flickering from the stage; full of life, not eulogies.

The blood was thundering through my veins, and my head was pounding with fury.

I can't even describe it.

15 | ANSWERS

The truth of the matter is that reality can be pretty painful.

Ally was right behind me, and we ran into my room. I said nothing. How many of these solemn, wordless exchanges would we have, I wondered. But I was hot for silence now.

"What was our mission even *for,* Ally? Out there desperately trying to scare up food, desperately trying to find survivors, losing our own flesh and blood in the process, huh? What was it all for? *Lies!*"

I slapped a bunch of personal memorabilia off of my wall shelf, narrowly missed hitting Rutty's books in the process. All those beloved books that he would never read, because he was sent out on some fool's errand.

"It was all lies," I moaned, plopping myself down on my bunk with my head in my hands.

"I know," she whispered to me, coming in, closing the door, and sitting opposite me on Sissy's bunk. "I know, Cam. I don't get it either."

I just shook my head. That's all I could keep doing right now: shake my head in disbelief. Ally finally breathed, quietly and gently: "What do you need from me right now?"

My head was spinning. "I need answers," I blurted out. "And I freaking deserve them, what's more. We all do."

Had I known that I would be walking into a trap, I wouldn't have said that. Unbeknownst to me, Ally *did* deserve an answer to a question she had asked me earlier, and she was unfortunately ready to ask it again.

"Cam," she whispered.

"What?" I lazily grunted back.

"Cam, look at me. Please."

I turned to her half-heartedly, not really wanting to dive deep into a sappy conversation. I'd had all the sap I could get from Pastor Rosie.

"What was in the freezer? That's the answer I need."

I recoiled with a deep breath, leaning away from her. All I could do was look down at my feet.

"Who was it?" she asked.

I jerked my face back to her. "*Who?* But I thought-"

"It's OK. I figured it out. The way you pulled away and just whisked us out of there, I put two and two together. Cam, it's a freezer all alone in a room by itself, in a crazy lonesome church with a crazy lonesome man who, by the looks of it, was hungry."

I exhaled in disgust. She had figured it out alright.

She paused and looked at me. "Was that what was in the stew as well?"

I thought about whether or not to bring this to her, but nodded slowly in admission, and then looked away.

This was painful.

She clenched her lips and bit them. Huge sigh. "Yeah, ya know, I didn't want to believe it myself, but all the signs kind of pointed to it."

"That's not all, Ally. He murdered Vera right next to me. He butchered her. She would've been in that freezer next. Amos came in and skewered this…gorgon…it was on top of us, trying to get at us…we both had masks… but then he just-"

"Shhh, it's okay, I can imagine. I don't need to hear it. How horrifying. I'm so sorry, Cam," she said. "Did you… did you get him?"

"Yeah," I muttered. "Shot him point blank. And about a dozen gorgons on the way back down. Rutty's gun and my rifle. And a few grenades, which it sounds like you heard from in there. I'm sorry for what you went through with him too." I looked off into a thousand-yard stare, past her. "I shoulda grabbed that knife." But I had already been over that in my mind, and that was futile to rehash.

She looked at me confused for a second.

"Amos' knife. I passed it in the hallway on the way up. When I finished up on our little potty break, I opened the door and – well, there he was. Waiting. If I hadn't made him put it down, I could have been next right there in that corridor, trusting this old man who seemed so sweet."

We both sat in silence for a moment.

"Ya know," she began. "People can put up a good front. You think you can trust them. They're sweet, they're mysterious, you're drawn to them," she said. "They're alluring. And you want to believe the best in people. You want to believe that people have the best intentions and that they would never hurt you. No one saw that coming from Amos. I think part of him was a sweet old man, but when all was said and done – it was just a dang good front, and the hunger won out in the end." She paused, thinking, and then let out the tiniest of somber giggles. "If you think about it, he was kind of like nothing more than a gorgon: alluring, mysterious, and we wanted to believe the best in him."

I turned to her. "But the hunger won out in the end, right?"

"Something like that. But I think time has shown all of us that they were never here with good intentions, and there was nothing positive to believe about them. They came, they saw, they conquered. I'm just sorry we got caught in the crossfire."

I looked sidelong at her, taking note, perhaps for the first time, that she had gorgeous sea-green eyes. I wondered if she had gotten them from her mother or father. "I'm sorry your brothers did too, sweetheart."

She nodded and attempted a smile. "Yeah."

"Tell me why you volunteered," I said, nearly instantly after that. "Tell me why I had to almost lose you."

Now she laughed. It was like the sound of falling rainwater on musical strings, clear and refreshing. I hadn't heard a good full-hearted laugh in a while. Hers was like a short, sweet song.

"Why did I volunteer...oh my. You sure you wanna hear this?"

'Yeah."

At that moment, my intercom buzzed. "Shipley, Sergeant Shipley, report to Captain Stone's office immediately please."

The wind was knocked out of my sails, and my head bowed. What irritating timing.

Ally shook her head and smiled. "Never a dull moment with you," she said. "Don't worry, this is now the second time it's been put off. Third time's a charm. I'll make it up to you. I promise."

"You promise?"

"I promise. Remember," she said, touching my face, "you promised me, and you kept it. So, I promise you right back."

I kissed her then and there, and took her in my arms.

Our time would come. That's what furloughs were for. That, and demanding answers.

· · · · ·

I had to walk past the data room on my way, and there were Joe and Foxy in there talking with a tech whose name I didn't know, in front of the Beast.

Joe saw me first. "Jet," he greeted me, walking right over. Seemed so very different now, greeting this salt-and-pepper-haired man that I utterly disdained early on. He had proved his worth. And so had the kid beside him.

Joe hugged me. "That was a bunch o' hogwash if I ever heard it, wasn't it, man?"

"Tell me about it."

"I, uh, I was touched," he changed his tone, "to learn a little more about Rutty. I like Scrabble myself," he snickered. "I thought Pastor Rosie did a good job commemorating him. I hope you were honored."

I nodded and swallowed.

"Anyway, I'm glad I caught you. I just heard that the Captain's looking for you, and you're on your way now. Listen, I been active military for a long time. I know you want answers, and you're entitled to them. Just be careful not to bite off more than you can chew. Don't carve him a new one."

"Meaning?" I asked rather briskly.

"He takes his orders from people just like you and me. The man's been like a father to you and Rutty, like you said. I'm not a fan of all of the behind-the-scenes goings-on either, but I know he's gotta fall in line like the rest of us. Just take that into your meeting with you. That's my two cents."

I nodded again. "Seems more like ten cents to me," I jabbed. "What, no card game metaphor this time to send me on my way with your blessing?"

Joe laughed. Another deep, hearty laugh that sounded like music. In here we could finally laugh. There were gun towers, warships, and tanks nearby. We could actually laugh.

"Nope, no metaphors for you. Consider yourself graduated, kid. Oh! Sorry. I mean-"

I put up my hand. "It's all good, Gramps. You're fine."

He gave me an understanding smile of respect, and we did a high shake, clasping hands.

"Thank you for what you did after my brother, uh…" I couldn't finish the sentence. "You know. That fire extinguisher move. Pretty spry for an old guy."

"Spry enough to kick your ass," he joked back, still eyeing me respectfully.

"Place and time, baby," I joked.

He laughed again. "I'll see ya. Trying to figure out some of this fancy tech with Halcyon," he said, retreating back toward the Beast. Foxy turned to go with him.

"Foxy!" I spoke. "Wait. Come here for a minute."

He came over, shyly. He had a new hat on…a teal one that said *Seattle Mariners*. I had no idea where he had gotten it. His wavy blonde mop poked out from underneath it. He smiled. "I like that, man. *Foxy*. Has a nice ring to it."

"Ha! I hoped it would." And then I looked at him. "Hey, did you know Vera?"

"Not really well. She was great at meals though. And super-hot," he added that last part with a wink.

I laughed with him. "Yeah, Rutty thought so too. You remind me of him in a few ways, bud. Don't change. I want to say thank you for all you did out there. You saved me in that church hall. I won't forget that. Ever. Thank you for everything. And I'm sorry about your arm."

"Oh that! No worries. Thanks for tending to it. I almost have feeling in it again!"

"Oh cool, lemme jab it with another needle and make sure, cool?"

"Don't push your luck, man."

I laughed it off. "Glad you're with us, buddy. See ya around here. Don't learn too many bad habits from Bassett."

"I heard that!" Joe yelled over his shoulder without turning around.

Foxy fist-bumped me and strode off.

•　　•　　•　　•　　•

At 2230 hours I strode into Stone's office. It was close to Command, in a tight array of hastily erected plywood structures with actual working doors. Not too soundproof though.

My gait slowed as I approached. This was not a conversation I was looking forward to. In many ways, Bassett actually felt more like a father figure to me now than Stone did. Joe and I had faced the heat of battle together, surviving gorgons, explosions, raving lunatics, starvation, DTF's, bad bunks, stale coffee, and finally, some good eggs from Ruby and Vera.

Vera. I wondered if Stone even knew or cared about Vera, Jesse, or if he would even fully appreciate what Foxy had done for me and us.

I approached his office. There was a sentry outside standing guard, and a dim lamp on inside. I could see his bald head and light reflecting off of his underlit glasses as he was writing on some papers on his desk. He heard my approach, and waved me in.

The sentry opened the door for me, and I solemnly strode in, without a salute, without greeting him, warmly or coldly.

•　　　•　　　•　　　•　　　•

We sat in cold silence. It was annoying. Finally, he spoke.

"Jet, I know how you must feel right now."

I was ready to let him have it.

"And how do I feel right now?" I asked Stone, stonily. "How exactly do I feel right now, Captain? You sent us out on a mission without any intel. You supplanted me less than a day into the mission with someone, who, as fond as I am of him now, is not even from around here and doesn't know the lay of the land a tenth as well as I do. You gave us a mission that required at least three times as many soldiers as we had. All along, you've been sitting cushy on a mound of warships and tanks at your disposal. And we bust our asses to get back here on time for a memorial to honor my brother and others who gave their lives to further the cause, and you turn it into some kind of chest-thumping pomp and circumstance.

"So, please tell me, how *exactly* do I feel right now?" I delivered to him dryly; but I could feel the heat in my face.

"Well, I'd say first and foremost that you're out of line, soldier. You ought to stow that post-haste," he said, with a dead-set grim expression. And then, softening, he said, "However, I understand how you feel." He sighed.

I rolled my eyes and looked at the ceiling, beyond him.

"Believe it or not, Jet, I have been there myself."

He had long been removed from the battlefield, pushing pencils and armchair-quarterbacking operations from the comfort of his office while we put our lives on the line out there. Fine. He may have been there himself, but I doubted it was anything of consequence. Anyway, it had been a long time since that was the case.

"Jet, I grieve with you. I loved your brother too. Please believe me when I say that. And I know that losing him…you're thirsty for blood. I get it. I truly do. So, if you feel like you need to let me have it, then let me have it. Give me both barrels, because I can take it."

I looked back at him, and we just stared at each other for a moment. It was a visual standoff of high caliber.

"Captain, I lost my brother. My best friend, and the last part of my family. Rutty was *all I had left*. You weren't there when he died. You didn't see it. He went out fighting, slamming his fists into that thing with all he had, and there was nothing…we…could…do. *Nothing*," I said, leaning forward into him. "We should have had more masks. Then we get back tonight and nearly *all* of those soldiers out there on the landing across the river have masks. Sitting atop their precious little tanks and amped-up LST, they could have won this war six weeks ago. And Rutty would still be alive. But he's not, Captain! He's not, because *you* sent us out there, and *you* took me out, and *you gave the order!* And I wanna know *why*."

I was thundering now, and I didn't care.

Mercifully, Stone allowed the air to clear momentarily, to allow the return of some calm. I finally looked away around his office, shaking my head again.

"We couldn't even give him a proper burial. They had to bring him back in *sections*, Captain. They had to bury *both* parts of my brother. No coffin, no real grave, no headstone, buried out there under loose earth, as loose as the missions we've been fed over the past few months, while this whole time, to our eyes, it looks pretty well like we've had the grunts and muster to take care of them for good. So, I ask you *why? Why us? Why?*"

Stone had put both hands up and clasped his fingers together, and he was looking at me over his knuckles, as if he was weighing something heavy.

At last, he spoke.

"Jet-" he began.

"Sergeant Shipley, if you please," I retorted, frosty and aloof.

Pause. "Fine. Sergeant Shipley, I've known you a long time. I've always counted you as one of my own, one of the finest soldiers in this battalion. Indeed, one of the finest in all of our Blockades. You're unpredictable, you run your own drills sometimes, and you run with your gut, even if it's counter to orders given. You're capable of switching things up and rolling with the punches, sometimes even going your own way. But you always seem to end up on the right side. For that, I commend you.

"But, as it happens," here he stood up and started to walk around the desk, "forces have been moving beyond my control and above my paygrade for a while now. We've had sixteen long years to get the wheels in motion, and finally, they're turning. They're finally turning, Sergeant! But sometimes," he said, planting one cheek on his desk and looking down at me, "people get crushed under those wheels. It's not intended, it's not ideal, and it's not what anyone planned. You're old enough to understand that sometimes ops go sideways. That's the cost of doing the job, soldier. I can never place one soldier's life over another's, and neither can you. In the end, we suffered minimal loss of life, and I'm just relieved we got at least three of you back. Bringing Joe and Ally – but also that civie back – is *beyond* commendable."

That civie. Good grief. Foxy is more than a civie.

"And you are to be commended," he leaned toward me when he said that. "Your entire team is going to be awarded Silver Stars. And as for Rutty – I pushed for this – he's going to be awarded the Service Cross, posthumously. But that's not all, Sergeant.

"When I informed the President about your entire mission: what you did with those gorgons on the Cumberland, the tracker, taking out thirty-three gorgons at that church – that's right, the tanks are there and they were able to count the bodies because the DTF drove off the rest – she put you in for a commendation. You're going to be a Lieutenant. You've earned it."

I didn't know what to say. I was honored, sure, but the thirst for power, for climbing the ranks, didn't have a home in me. With the new title would come dignity and maybe some recognition, but little else. And frankly, I just didn't care about any of that right now. None of it.

"Look, Captain," I shook my head, "that's all well and good, but, I…" I trailed off lamely. I wasn't in the mood for a promotion, earned or not. "All I wanted was answers."

"Well, I hope you got some, and more," he answered. "I didn't bring you here for a lecture. I wanted to give you answers, because I know you wanted them. So, I'm going to answer with three things, and be honest with you," he said, walking back around and sitting back down behind his desk.

"One, I wanted to tell you welcome back. Your dad brought you here when you were only seven. Your dad was one of the best officers this Blockade had ever seen. And you boys," he chuckled, "you sure gave us all a run for our money!"

I looked at him sidelong. I wondered if he was enjoying his little stroll down memory lane.

"I was with you when we lost your dad. When your mom died from cancer. And I'm with you now in the loss of Rutty. I'm glad you're back, Shipley. Jet. Cameron. Whatever you want to be called now, I'm glad you're back."

He took a deep breath. "And secondly, I wanted to tell you about this promotion because you've earned it. You'll be commanding up to four squads. President thought you should skip a rank, and I did too, because your meritorious performance out there is exactly what we need in the next stage of the war against the gorgs. It's precisely the right diehard boldness and determination, service, and commitment that the Armed Forces need, because we need it, Jet. You're the kind of soldier that can be a model, an example, and a leader for the rest of us. You're cunning, you have instinct, and you know what to do in a pinch. I don't know what all happened to you out there because I wasn't there, but you're different. Changed. You've got steely resolve in you now; I can see it. You're a man of character and drive, Shipley, and I'm proud to serve with you."

This was going on too long, and it sincerely felt like buttering me up for something. Did he even have a point in all this? I fidgeted, breathing out of my nose like an ox.

"Now, thirdly, I brought you here because you deserve to know what went on behind the scenes. You're not going to like it, but I think you can handle it."

I turned back to him, confused. "What are you talking about?"

He took a long hard look at me, as if he was measuring up my fortitude to handle whatever news he was prepared to deliver.

Stone sat back and crossed his arms, staring hard. "We have news on that berserker you guys caught."

I was not prepared for that.

"Your tracker worked, Sergeant. We tracked that thing all the way to the Cumberland: erratic movements in all directions, sometimes remaining immobile for hours on end, doing probably what the rest of them have been doing out there during the day. Who knows. What we *do* know is that it was just one of several identical operations to find and track a gorgon, and you were a big part of that."

Several identical operations? Did he say 'several'?

"Wait – what? What do you mean, *'identical operations'?*"

"What I mean is that several units were assigned the same thing: find and lojack a gorgon. That's the order that came down. Get the tracker in it, and we'll follow it. For as long as we need to of course. Which," he paused, "in most cases only needed to be a day or so."

My heart skipped a beat, tremoring at this. "A *day?* That's all you wanted it for?" My voice rose, and I nearly did as well.

"I didn't say you were going to like it, Jet. But yes. See, we had the teams, we had the manpower, and we have all these warships and battalions coming our way, but ultimately, where the real battle happens is in the face to face on the battlefield. Could our men dependably face off against an arguably superior species, hold their own, and take it down without getting subdued? Could we actually pull it off? That's the question the President was asking. When all the bombs have been dropped and all the missiles have been fired and we're walking into the smoke to root out the last of them and drive them from here, would our men be able to hunt them down and drive them out? Or would they cower in fear and run?

"And so, the orders came down. We were to see if it was really possible to do. We dispatched the orders to both of our recon teams the second day of your missions. Simultaneously, similar orders were issued at other blockades, and we all had to do the same thing. The op was, for lack of a better word," he paused so long I swear I went to sleep, "just a test. To see if we could actually do it."

I rose from my chair. "You have got to be *kidding* me. *What???* This is bull!" I screamed at him. "Are you telling me that that's all we were: guinea pigs? This was just some…some *experiment?* You lied! Bassett told us that you gave the order and that it was for reconnaissance, to see what they were doing out over the oceans! That's what we did, because that's what we were told! If you would have told us the truth, we would have told you to shove that mission right down your throat!" Now I was pacing back and forth like a tiger, and I could feel the veins popping out in my neck. In the corner of my eye, I saw Stone's Guard turn and look inward at us. "Lies! All of them!" I shouted at him.

"I understand you're upset," he said, holding up his hands at me, warding me off. "Yes, it was not the whole truth – but I was following orders too. You have to believe me. Truth is, we already know why they're out over the ocean. They're draining the planet dry, Jet. They're taking our water. We can't allow that to happen. And once we got the minimal intel we needed, we terminated the mission."

"And just how exactly did you terminate that mission?" I didn't care about the oceans just yet.

"We shot it down. Surface to air, locked on to its tracker. Somewhere north of the Red River basin, north of the quarry. Yesterday morning at 0900 hours."

I did the math. That didn't add up. But then, it hit me. I was sickened, and felt myself turning ashen. I turned to Stone in horror. "That was the explosion they saw. I- I forgot to ask Command about it. That was you? Stone - you shot that thing down after only an *hour* of life, after my brother gave his own life to get your tracker implanted? Is that what you're saying?" Stone didn't answer, and that was his answer. I felt a thrill run through me: a thrill of rage and disbelief embroiled acidly together. "This whole… thing… was an absolute lie!" I hissed at him, stoically. "We were updated every single hour by command on its location; they told us that it was at the Cumberland, and that it hadn't moved! And you! You *just* sat there just now and told me that you had tracked it for *hours:* those were your words! My little brother died for a lie, Stone!" I couldn't hold back the tears anymore.

He held his hands up defensively. "It was all part of a plan we had to do, Jet," he exhaled. "The President ordered it, and I green-lit it. There's something else you don't know, and I couldn't tell you: those berserkers…they aren't totally gorgons; they're genetically engineered, and they were an attempt to eradicate the enemy from within…which, unfortunately and spectacularly failed. But the President had to try! Don't you see? We've all – *all* of us – always had to try, and that unfortunately involved breaking some eggs in the process, Jet, don't you see?" he clamored at me. Stone eventually calmed, and then the punk showed signs of a cheap, smug smile. "It was all part of The President's greater mission, what your brother prayed: *deliver us from evil.*"

I couldn't restrain myself. Loose cannon or no, and whether he intended to be smug or not, how dare he. How *dare* he invoke Rutty's words in this second pompous, self-rousing speech of the night, in the face of such lies and deceit.

"You miserable piece of-" I screamed as I lunged toward the Captain, and swung hard. All I remember next was him dodging, the Guard flying into the room, and the butt of a rifle into the side of my head, then blackness.

•　　•　　•　　•　　•

I awoke in the brig – if you can call it that. More cheap plywood hastily assembled, with a guard stationed nearby. Bright light overhead. I turned on my bunk and looked at my watch. 0130 hours the next morning.

My right temple ached and throbbed. That Guard got me good. Someone had had the kindness to provide me with an ice pack and a bandage to hold it in place while I slept. But no one really sleeps on these cheap bunks.

My thoughts went back to Nevaeh, wondering if she was still okay, and if she had been picked up. Even if they had told me she had, I wouldn't believe it until I saw her. No one was ever really safe until they were inside here with us, but the harsh reality was that inside here was now unsafe as well.

I heard a bit of commotion outside. A guard called out "He's awake." Then a familiar voice.

Before long, Bassett's face appeared at the makeshift window of the door. He looked sleepy. "Hey Cam," he said. "Heard about your short-lived promotion. I warned you not to bite off more than you could chew, man."

"What do you want, Joe?" I whined.

Joe sighed. "I'm sorry about all of this. I want you to know I knew as much as I told you. I'm not the Captain, and it was never mine to keep anything from you, so I won't keep this from you now either." I turned to face him.

"Graham's been on the move, as you know. Well," he paused, "she's coming here. To this Blockade. In two days' time. Among other things, she wants to see you, Cam."

President Jean Graham was coming here.

Pastor Rosie's words came back to me. *The real enemy.* I was not a candle in a wind-free world. No: I was a torch, burning bright, and getting hotter by the minute. Now I knew who the pawns were, and I knew with dangerous clarity who the Queen was.

President Graham was about to feel my reality. And the truth of the matter?

Reality can be pretty dang painful.

TO BE CONTINUED...

The war for the planet is not over yet.
Visit dissonancetheseries.com for news and updates.

Read all the books in the series, in chronological order:

Dissonance Volume Zero: Revelation
Dissonance Volume Up: Rising
Dissonance Volume I: Reality
Dissonance Volume II: Reckoning
Dissonance Volume III: Renegade
Dissonance Volume IV: Relentless

I AFTERWORD

I need to create. I've authored ten books so far in my lifetime, under various stage and real names. Only one other has been fictional in nature, and it was not under a pen name.

I began sculpting a science fiction novel when I was in my early twenties, and I had actually reached about two hundred fifty pages. At the time, it didn't represent where I wanted to go in my life with Christ, and I wasn't dead-set on pursuing a vocation as an author. It was called "The Omega Room," and I ended up showing it the "omega" by intentionally hitting the delete button on my old word processor machine somewhere around 1996 or 1997. I daresay that a geek squad somewhere would have been able to undelete it and rescue it from oblivion. But that wasn't my interest at the time. The amusing thing is that I had accidentally deleted it once before that as well. I was using the same computer, and

I don't know what I did. But when the file was nowhere to be found, I remember sitting, frozen, at that computer screen for ten minutes. I finally did the only thing I could do: press on and start all over. But it ultimately didn't last. I'm beyond thankful I didn't accidentally or intentionally delete this one.

In my life, I've pursued varying interests, all of them thoroughly satisfying: music, acting, voice acting, performing, poetry, graphic design, commemorative productions, videography, and other multimedia pursuits. After the death of a dream of mine to return to music in 2023, I was contemplating where I should go and what I should do.

I knew it had to be something creative, as that's the only way I would really thrive, be intrinsically satisfied and fundamentally fulfilled. As God's creations, I firmly believe we were created to, in turn, create. It's one of the ways that we mirror his mighty ability.

I set out to tell a story in November of 2023: one that represents two genres that I love: science fiction/fantasy, and dystopian novels. That was, after all, the direction of my ill-fated first attempt. I wanted to incorporate everything, or at least, as much as I could, about everything I had ever loved from novels or cinema. Things that inspired me. Things that terrified me to my core. Things that moved me deeply. There have been several passages in this novel that have fulfilled those in various capacities, and I'm grateful for that. In turn, it is my deepest hope that this novel inspired you. Terrified you. Moved you deeply.

I love the writing process, and have a great respect for it. This book evolved organically, through several iterations and plot corrections, and more than a few alpha readers. Thank you, to all of you, for your help. Thank you so much to Michael Babski and Walker Armstrong for the invaluable Army insight and terminology. To Roland Kouhsen for your knowledge of ecology and nature. I have thoroughly enjoyed writing and editing this, through and through. In addition, the lengthy research I've needed to conduct on all things military, Tennessee, weather and political have greatly helped. Thank you, Google. I certainly hope no one checks my Internet search history; I'll probably look very much like a terrorist with all the things I've had to research for this book. But it has shaped me into either a bona fide detective or a scholar, and I thoroughly approve of the process.

Like the protagonist in any good story, I also must proceed on a journey of awareness and change. I trust that you have seen that process unfold as you have read *Dissonance*.

I wrote the first draft of this story beginning on November 21st, 2023, and was finished with it on December 16th. In less than a month, I had come up with the basis for a new series of stories that I felt needed to be told.

Thank you from the bottom of my heart for partaking of this story I've sought to tell, and for celebrating with me the fact that this novel has been adapted for the screen and is currently being pitched to streaming networks. I am incredibly optimistic and await good things to come!

With love,

Aaron Ryan

I ABOUT THE AUTHOR

Award-winning and bestselling Christian author, speaker, panelist, workshop presenter and voice actor Aaron Ryan lives in Washington with his wife and two sons, along with Macy the dog, Winston and Tibbles the cats, and the finch named Fry.

He is the prolific author of the bestselling *Dissonance* 6-book alien invasion saga, the Christian dystopian fiction trilogies *The End* and *Carbon*, the *Talisman* trilogy, the sci-fi thrillers *Forecast, The Slide, The Phoenix Experiment, Blood Echoes* and *The Darkness Within,* the nonfiction book *God Is Not Santa,* six children's picture books, the business reference books *How to Successfully Self-Publish & Promote Your Self-Published Book* and *The Superhero Anomaly,* 6 business books on voiceovers penned under his former stage name (Joshua Alexander), as well as a previous fictional novel, *The Omega Room.*

When he was in second grade, he was tasked with writing a creative assignment: a fictional book. And thus, *The Electric Boy* was born: a simple novella full of intrigue, fantasy, and 7-year-old wits that electrified Aaron's desire to write. From that point forward, Aaron evolved into a creative soul that desired to create.

He enjoys the arts, media, music, performing, poetry, and being a daddy. In his lifetime he has been an author, voiceover artist, wedding videographer, stage performer, musician, producer, rock/pop artist, executive assistant, service manager, paperboy, CSR, poet, tech support, worship leader, and more. The diversity of his life experiences gives him a unique approach to business, life, ministry, faith, and entertainment.

Aaron's favorite author by far is J.R.R. Tolkien, but he also enjoys Suzanne Collins, James S.A. Corey, Michael Crichton, Marie Lu, Madeleine L'Engle, John Grisham, Tom

Clancy, Tim Lebbon, Christopher Golden, C.S. Lewis, Stephen King and Dave Barry.

Aaron has always had a passion for storytelling. Visit his website at https://www.authoraaronryan.com, join his exclusive Facebook group at https://www.authoraaronryangroup.com, or check out his store at https://authoraaronryanstore.com.

Visit the Dissonance website for the full story at www.dissonancetheseries.com.

I ALSO BY THE AUTHOR

As Aaron Ryan:

Dissonance Volume II: Reckoning
Dissonance Volume III: Renegade
Dissonance Volume IV: Relentless
Dissonance Volume Zero: Revelation
Dissonance Volume Up: Rising
The Complete Dissonance Sci-Fi Alien Invasion Saga
The End: Alpha
The End: Omicron
The End: Omega
The Complete THE END Christian Dystopian Saga
Carbon Volume I: Programming
Carbon Volume II: Reformatting
Carbon Volume III: Rebooting
The Complete Carbon Trilogy
Forecast
The Slide
The Phoenix Experiment
Blood Echoes

The Darkness Within
Talisman: Subterfuge
Talisman: Nexus
Talisman: Halcyon
The Complete Talisman Series
God is not Santa
You are my whole Earth: A Daddy's love for his Sons
You're Going Straight To Helen (In A Handbasket
The Ring of Truth
The Sword of Joy
The Ring of Truth
The Sword of Joy
The Ring of Truth
The Super Ordinary Heroes: Empathy
The Super Ordinary Heroes: The Invisibility Cape
The Super Ordinary Heroes: The Time-stopping Hug
The Superhero Anomaly
How to Successfully Self-Publish & Promote Your Independent Book
Reflections: A compilation of journals and poetry by Aaron Ryan
The Omega Room
Glimmerings

As former stage name Josh Alexander:

Voiceovers: A Super Business, A Super Life
Voiceovers: A Super Fun Pursuit
Voiceovers: A Super Responsibility
Running a Successful Voiceover Business
How do I get started in Voiceovers?
Five T's to Triumph: The Secrets to Getting Cast in Voiceovers

If you liked Aaron's book, please visit the Amazon and Goodreads pages for this book and leave a positive review. Once it shows up, please email the screenshot of it to aaron@authoraaronryan.com for a discount on your next book purchase from him! Thank you so much! Reviews really do help a ton!

Visit the Dissonance Website and enlist at the Blog:

Subscribe to Author Aaron Ryan

Follow Aaron and connect on Social Media: